D0898549

Dusk *on* Route 1

CYNTHIA FRASER GRAVES

To Linda –

my friend!

Love

Cynthia Fraser Graves

2019

ANDROSCOGGIN PRESS

Androscoggin Press, West Kennebunk, ME
© 2019 Cynthia Fraser Graves
Graves, Cynthia, 1944 —
Dusk on Route 1 / Cynthia Fraser Graves

ISBN: 978-1-7329471-0-8
Library of Congress Control Number: 2018914868

All rights reserved. No part of this book may be reproduced, displayed, modified, or distributed by any means (electronic, mechanical, photocopying, recording, or otherwise) without the express prior written permission of the copyright holder, with the exception of brief quotations included in reviews.

For further information and permissions approval or to order copies of this book, go to www.cynthiafrasergraves.com.

Revised Edition, First Androscoggin Press Printing, 2019
1 2 3 4 5 6 7 8 9 10

Printed in the United States of America

PUBLISHER'S NOTE
This is a work of fiction. Names, characters, businesses, places, events, locales, and incidents are either the products of the author's imagination or used in a fictitious manner. Any resemblance to actual persons, living or dead, or actual events is purely coincidental.

DRAKES ISLAND

Seeds of summer scatter.
Burning monarchs lift
To gray skies.
September's Sunday floats free.

Map, light, direction each to each,
They fly for home
With winter dreams,
Goldenrod swirling on cool winds,
Riding crystal air,
Space filled with color of sun and frost,
Fading too soon from sight.

And all around
And in between,
The blue Atlantic walks a moored beach.

—CFG

DEDICATION

In memory of Edward J. Fraser, my beloved Uncle Ed

ACKNOWLEDGEMENTS

This work of fiction has taken many years to coalesce into the book you hold in your hands. There is the energy and support of many, many people within. In this second edition, the names that come to the forefront are Sue Morin, Eileen Stearns, Lorraine Johnson, Joy Poulter and Stephanie Kurkjian. Certainly, there are many more who have been instrumental in encouraging this author in her endeavors and I thank them all from the bottom of my heart.

Contents

Prologue   3

PART ONE: 1.   Requiem   9
    2.   Eastside Market   15
    3.   Ed LaCasse   29
    4.   Chick's Crossing   35

PART TWO: 5.   Missing Person   45
    6.   Shelter   53
    7.   Wells Police Department   63

PART THREE: 8.   The Maine Diner   75
    9.   Homeward Bound   89
    10.   The Subaru   95
    11.   Darnice   101
    12.   Something Extraordinary   107
    13.   Light   111
    14.   Colliding   115
    15.   Blueberry Lane   119

PART FOUR: 16.   Town Boys   125
    17.   Discovery   131
    18.   Morse Code   137
    19.   SOS   145
    20.   A Close Quiet   151
    21.   Among the Living   161
    22.   Traveling Mercies   169

PART FIVE: 23. Spreading Joy   177
              24. Christmas on Stephen Eaton   183
              25. Morning Light   189
              26. The View from Here   197
              27. The Day After   207
              28. 9:13 Exactly   213
              29. New Year's Moon   221
              30. On the Beach   225

Epilogue   231

Afterword   235

Dusk *on* Route 1

"Love must be as much a light as it is a flame."
—Henry David Thoreau (1817–1862),
Letters to Various Persons

PROLOGUE

Drakes Island
September 1988

Stepping out onto the parking lot, she is momentarily dizzied by the depth of a cloudless autumn sky, a tent of cobalt pitched above the sea, with no horizon visible. No one is on the beach; that's unusual for Drakes Island. Most weekends, even fair winter ones, families tug children and hold kites and dogs into the always-blowing wind. Today, the landscape is empty.

Taking off her jacket and tying it around her waist, she moves into her warm-up, a few lunges and stretches. The contrast of warm sun on her face in the cool September breeze feels delightful. Running shoes slap softly on weathered wood as she jogs the boardwalk. Securing her headset, she jumps off the solid footing of wood to the give of sand. A small surge of white ruffles at the waterline; when she pushes the switch, music spills into her ears. The Bee Gees ask, "How Deep Is Your Love?" A smile breaks her focus for a moment. The lyrics of this song are a secret code between Andrew and her, a shortcut into the heart of their love. Wherever and whenever she hears it, it is as if he were with her, beside her.

Forcing concentration back, Pamela settles into the easy push of her body. She has run this beach hundreds of times and can visualize herself up beach by the tidal river that separates Drakes Island from the mainland in Kennebunk. Here, surging tides crumble layers of marsh soil, peel it from banks, and push it into the wires of inlets on strong rifts, changing the actual topography after storms.

Twenty minutes into the run, her push pays off. Her pulse is up, a sheen of sweat glistening on her temples, and she breaths even and deep. She knows she can easily make it to the river.

But a bloom of color beside her takes her off stride. She turns her head, expecting someone to run past, but there is no one, only an empty beach.

Off balance now, she slows, turns, runs backward looking for what disturbed her focus. Again, no one—nothing. The abrupt sound of waves and bird cries doubles as she takes off her headset. Bending, hands on her knees to breathe, she feels her heart pounding in her ears as the unwelcome decline of runner's high gathers speed. Pamela circles, walks it out until her breath is normal. That's when she sees them in front of her, fluttering, unrolling; scarves of color undulating midair, trailing down the beach.

As they approach, Pamela braces herself, unsure of what will happen. Monarchs, now hundreds of them, roll and lift around her. At first, she gives herself up in delight. These harbingers are a familiar sight during summer months in Maine; their migrations launch from beaches like this one. To be present on the day they depart for their mysterious journey seems like the luckiest thing in the world. But delight soon turns to amazement—and then to disbelief—as more and more arrive to join the undulating cloud around her. Acrobats, they float, leap, tumble over and around each other until a new idea spreads and they become a pyramid, then a billow, then a cocoon which shape-shifts around her. She holds her breath in a mixture of wonder and unease.

Now at the center of the kaleidoscope of moving wings, Pamela enters the dance of startling beauty. Thoughts travel, moving on intimate highways; she understands they are meant for her. Motionless in this adagio, Pamela floats, no direction perceptible; all she knows disappears. Strong, dark tides lap shadowed banks, the sound of water purling in strong tides rises, and rowing oars, curling water around their tips dip and rest, dip and rest in a rhythmic dirge. In the ephemeral embrace of the beautiful messengers, she is not at peace.

As plovers flash in murmuration, a signal is given. The chimera of wings lifts; monarchs rise, and then leave her alone on the once familiar beach. She watches the tornado of orange and black spin up into the blue tent, gone away in seconds. Out to sea now, they embark on the blue highway, each following each, going home.

Pamela doesn't know how to come back from this; she has fallen out of time. Sitting by the dunes in the fast-cooling fall air, she struggles to understand what has happened. Some natural law did not hold. Had they come to be with her? Were the huge wheels of their cycles pausing on this island for her? Why?

As shadows shift on sands, the thoughts of her children and husband return to her. Anxiety pushes; she will be late for the Sunday they have planned. They are waiting for her.

She retraces her footsteps to the parking lot, opens the door of her car to return home. Catching a glimpse of herself in the car mirror as she backs away, she sees she is not the same woman who arrived this morning.

Part One

CHAPTER 1

REQUIEM

Kennebunk, Maine
1994

The hum of voices fills the hot room, is oppressive, and holds her down. How many funerals has this old house seen? How much grief has spilled on these floors? Her guess is plenty. As she looks, the patina of wood shines, forming a path down the length of the rooms to the windows. *These floors polished by sadness*, she thinks. Joy is hard to imagine ever again right now.

Pamela argued vehemently with Andy when he insisted on living in this old house. He never wished to leave, and denied her wish to move nearer to a city. He trumped her dissatisfaction with a sacred vow to be carried out of here "feet first." She wants to tease him about having gotten his wish, but teasing is an ordinary thing; nothing ordinary is left for them.

Pamela stands and walks to the bay windows, her sharp focus fixed out of here. The room behind her disappears. She is in a boat, alone, rushing with the rough water out onto Route 1. The boat is jumping, cresting waves that are the seconds and minutes of this day, and many more days to come, she guesses.

Waking from this ellipsis of reality, she startles as she realizes people look toward her, smiling; they seem to know her. Yet in this moment, they are unfamiliar. Each guest looks like someone she knows, but she can't say exactly who.

Eucalyptus from unmerciful bouquets seeps like fog along the floor, rising in small gusts with any movement in the room. The resinous scent chokes her. In years to come, she will make rash excuses, hurry to exit florist shops, gift shops, funerals, waiting rooms, anywhere this cloying smell rises. She will never be in a room with this hated scent without being back here on this hot, sad day.

The present moment continues to unfold in an advancing tableau. Pamela longs to move to the future, to be in secret, although she knows she can't do that now. Tonight she will be alone; alone in a new world—a world where nothing is the same.

Again, the ritual in progress snaps her out of her musings. She returns to herself and moves among the mourners. People repeat sentiments and cast timid glances toward her; she is someone as new to them as she is to herself. She feels their discomfort emanating; discomfort that he died so suddenly, so young, so like them, so careful with his living. How has this happened in their guarded world?

Pamela cannot respond to the kindly meant words; there is a delay in understanding, an inability to grasp meaning that keeps her silent. Her discomfort grows, and gathers around her in hot layers. She stops trying to respond and just looks back at their earnest faces, wondering how she can help them when she cannot even help herself.

The children are out on the deck with their friends. They are all grown now; a parallel ritual to hers plays out for them. The fact of their father's death will achieve its weight and shape in days to come. For now, they have a small sanctuary in the illusion that things will be the same. This morning in early intense July heat, Pamela was mowing the lawn in preparation for the day to come when her daughter called out of her bedroom window to stop making so much noise. It was too early, she was told. She stopped, of course, stunned that Leslie didn't seem to comprehend the dark gathering ahead of them. Her daughter, recently graduated from Brown and teaching at the university in Portland, and her son, returning to the University of Maine in September, are in their own lives, too far from the every days of this house to come home now. She will have to go it alone, will have to keep moving; the waves cresting at her back are rising with each minute.

Words flutter, rustle around her, hang for a moment in air, and then fade to silence. She is so distant from what they mean: Rotary Club meeting tomorrow, summer party at the lake next weekend, school beginning soon, someone's grandchild graduating next year; there is no possible connection between these events and her life now. She cannot respond, or even smile.

A deep need to vanish ignites with a surge of heat rising through her body. Pamela excuses herself, aiming for the kitchen while picking up an empty serving dish. She intersects the small islands of those present knowing they will not follow. This isolation is hers now, a neighborhood she has moved into.

Once out on the front porch, a circle of chimes in the hot breeze chants, "Nothing is left. Nothing is left." Was it just a week ago that these chimes were given to her for her birthday? Did she love the sound then? She reaches up to take them down, their sound unbearable this afternoon.

Here, on this empty street, on this hot porch, this new person needs a cigarette. Pamela needs this sting within her, needs the arrow of intimate smoke piercing her; she needs pain to cover pain. Something mighty is forming, moving, just out of sight now, but preparing a full assault for tonight when the ceremony is really over and everyone leaves. She is not afraid of the pain rolling in her, only curious; she knows there is always pain with birth. She is to live in a world of shadows.

Again, a deep need for the hot scrape of smoke urges her on. She wants to fill herself, to dull the razor thoughts spinning in her head. She pins her hopes of getting through this afternoon on imagining going to the store at the bottom of this once-sweet street as soon as everyone leaves; she will buy a pack of cigarettes. Tonight out in the backyard, alone, in the dark, she will smoke. The thought exhilarates her, confirms and baptizes her; she is living in secret now.

When she and Andy moved into the house more than twenty years ago, he insisted on planting vines by the porch where she sits. He said the day would come when they would be old and would sit together in the shade of the vine. Now, full grown, the vines provide a deep shade for her. She closes her eyes, remembering the ordinary day when they dug the deep, brown earth to plant the roots. But she cannot bear this thought for long; the brown earth of this memory is too fresh a wound to abide.

Shade from the heart-shaped leaves of his vine, Andrew's vine, rides her face, casting quivering shadows within the small touch of breeze. Pamela imagines the illusory cigarette in her hand, the smoke entering her lungs. She blows it out, and watches as shapeless, colorless smoke drifts away, bearing the past with it. When she opens her eyes, the air around her opens and deepens in hue.

Into her sanctuary of pretense, a single monarch butterfly flutters, embossing its color onto the air. Pamela focuses on the singular dancer, and feels a chill of recognition: that day on the beach springs to life from where it has been waiting. The fluttering Pied Piper of memory leads her, and she goes back to the island and to that afternoon years ago. While the clink of dishes and conversation flow in her living room, Pamela Iverson is with the monarchs again, held in their embrace. She sees them, feels them, and hears them speak to her again.

In the same flash as the rising of the kaleidoscope on the beach, she understands. Andrew's death began then. Her daily life—cloaked in minutes and hours, divided into duties and responsibilities—had forged ahead, anesthetizing her into forgetting. But it started that day. She had been warned.

It is a hot, quiet dawn. The breeze from the small stream at the edge of the meadow lifts the curtain in the room, blowing inward, stirring the air. Consciousness rises with light as if connected to it, and indeed it is; this is the first day in a new world.

On the dresser, she sees the photograph of a person she recognizes: a surge of love rises. She thinks of the Native belief that an image taken of someone captures and entraps the soul, imprisoning it forever. She knows now that this is true; the man in this photograph is alive, his eyes reaching out of the frame to her. She sits up in bed, gripped by his silent regard. He is wearing his favorite corduroy sport jacket and a striped shirt. She can see those clothes in the closet, just to the left of the photograph, and can't understand how they can be in two places at the same time.

What is this feeling that threatens her, the living silence before a tornado? She busies herself quickly, standing, walking, picking up around the room, making the bed. This is better; it stops fear that rises like sap.

She tries to take stock: it is July … Tuesday morning; she doesn't have school today. As she passes the window, she notices both of the children's cars in the driveway. Backing up to stare, she wonders what they are doing here. When did they arrive? Leslie had summer work at the college, and, well … Pamela can't clear her thoughts. Something dances and circles behind them, something vast struggling to be known, but she needs to avoid this thought at all costs.

Pamela walks to the closet to get her wrap. His robe is on the hook on his side of the closet. The question arises: "Where is he?" She takes the robe in her hands. Scent floats around her, and he is there, completely; the memory of him finds her, a guided missile exploding in the present. She doubles up as her knees land hard on the floor.

The word of what happened begin to silently chant: Dead, dead … dead. He has died. Her husband died last night. But the word "dead" doesn't hold any authority as of yet. It will deepen, the understanding of this word. Deepen in the endless minutes, hours, days, and years to come, teaching her what the word really means. Just now, simply, it means, "He is not here." The seed of this word has been planted and has begun to grow. A new commandment has been struck. Andrew, her husband, can never, must never, will never, reach beyond wherever he is to touch her—or speak to her—ever again in this house of time. She wouldn't have believed he could have agreed to this command in his love for her, but somehow he has. She is dizzy, knowing she cannot find him on this earth, and after all these years of being his wife, she no longer knows who she is.

Pamela Iverson is dissolving here in the bedroom where she has slept with this husband of twenty-four years: right now as her children sleep off the tragedy of yesterday … right now as neighbors go to get their newspapers on the front porch … right now as coffee begins to perk in sleeping kitchens in this once-safe little world … right now.

Back on the porch, Pamela stands and wipes away tears of revelation. The monarchs on Drakes Island … their migration on that day was a mirror, a reflection in which she was shown this reverse world. Prophets, the colorful harbingers, had forecast her future, but she hadn't understood.

She takes several slow breaths preparing to reenter the house, preparing to play the part as the widow in her fast-disappearing identity. She will not be on this porch for long. Today is both the beginning of something, and the end of something else. Tomorrow is the first day of another life.

CHAPTER 2

EASTSIDE MARKET

Providence, RI
1998

Bud Carey slowed the bus for his first stop, brakes squealing in the July heat; it was eight o'clock. On days as hot as this one, passengers rode the Rhode Island Public Transit Authority buses anywhere for free. Bud liked free rides, even if it meant the buses would be crowded; no change to make. All he had to do was man the doors, keep the peace, and drive safely, which, on Providence's loom of narrow streets, was a challenge in any weather. He cranked the AC up a notch as the temperature on the Citizen's Bank clock inched past 90 degrees.

Driving this route for seven years, Bud knew his regulars, "his" people, and watched them to see how they were doing. Some boarded each day buttoned up tight, not wanting to be public. Inter-sprinkled with those, he had his exotics, those wearing outlandish getups, tattoos, behaving conspicuously. Many dramas played out on board his bus: drunken displays, marital rages, just plain rage, pick-pocketing. One time a guy had pulled a knife on someone. Bud called 911 to get him taken off. No matter what though, he remained steady at the wheel—captain in charge, calm, usually smiling, approachable.

She had piqued his interest on the first day she boarded the morning run out to Eastside Market. Since then, she boarded at the same time every day, then again on his last run each evening for the return trip to the bank stop, around six o'clock. She was always alone, never paid attention to others, was polite to Bud, asking how he was, commenting on the weather or some tidbit of local news. Bud guessed early on that she was a live-in shopper, a whole classification of folks who spent the entire day in malls or supermarkets killing time. There had been others like her on his bus before, mostly women. They disappeared for the whole day, reappearing later with little or nothing to show for the time spent. There were men who lived that way too. A lonely way to spend your time, but who was he to judge? These folks were harmless enough. They made him appreciate the wife and kids he went home to every night, even though home wasn't always peaceful, especially around the supper table.

The mystery woman introduced herself as Pamela Iverson the first time she boarded. He wasn't really sure it was her name. A lot of people liked being anonymous on public transit. She dressed attractively, casual: V-neck sweaters, slacks, long coats in winter. She was self-possessed, well groomed, and her fifty-plus years (he guessed) lent her seriousness. She didn't fit with the riders on his bus. She stood out as demure and reserved in the class of people that rode public transportation. Her hair, shoulder length, brown-interlaced with hints of silver, framed a pretty face on which channels had begun to deepen around her eyes along with a fine network of lines. She was thoughtful, had a serious demeanor and moved easily, posture perfect. Whenever she came on board in the morning, a cloud of lavender enfolded Bud in freshness as she passed.

On her way home from the market, she sat quietly, looking out the window, as if she was someplace other than on the bus. Glancing in his mirror, Bud read sadness around her. When her stop rolled up, she always thanked him, walking away briskly in gathering dusk.

She had ridden the bus long enough for all four seasons to come and go twice. Her destination was always the same: first stop, the Eastside Market. Her return stop was Lafayette Avenue and the safe harbor of home somewhere down that street. What she did with her evenings, Bud had no clue, but he never saw her other than these two daily boarding times.

On this hot morning, the woman stepped from the protective shade of trees as soon as the bus approached, waiting for the loud, puffing vehicle to stop. Bud leveraged the pneumatic opener deftly, and the doors parted for his first rider of the day. Ascending out of the bright glare, she greeted him with, "Morning, Bud. What a hot day. I almost envy you your job in this cool bus."

He replied quickly, "One of those scorchers! You be careful of getting overheated yourself, Mrs. Iverson."

She pulled a fare out of her purse, extending it to Bud.

"Put your money away. RIPTA will pay today."

"Bud, are you sure?" she questioned, as if this was a favor he was doing especially for her.

"Mrs. Iverson, you just take your seat and enjoy the ride—our treat. It's dangerous leaving people sweltering outside. Money's no matter today."

A few more patrons appeared and climbed on behind the woman, putting an end to their conversation. She smiled, accepted his word, and put her money back. Bud closed the door on the hot air spilling into the super-cooled bus and watched for his customers to seat themselves. Then, all safely stowed, Bud engaged the gears, and accelerating noisily, pulled out into the Sunday street with no traffic.

Steadying herself, Pamela sank into a seat mid bus. She let her head fall against the headrest and closed her eyes, shivering a little in the AC. When she turned to the window, her face was reflected back to her. The woman she saw was a stranger, with a disappointment so sharp it hurt her to look. Pamela turned away. Today was her fifty-fourth birthday but she moved past that thought quickly, avoiding the always present, always compelling invitation of the past. The bus accelerated, gears meshing rhythmically, as Bud threaded the labyrinth of small streets over to the Eastside Plaza.

Pamela Iverson *needed* to be in the Market, especially today. Powerful anxiety rose in her, a nameless fear playing with her breath, making her stand too soon; she lurched forward when the bus braked for its stop, stumbling down the aisle. After wishing Bud a good day, Pamela stepped into the hot, empty parking lot focused intently on the doors of the Eastside Market.

Bud watched her determined pace through the hot morning air. *Her home away from home*, he thought. Compassion stirred in him. *What does she do in there all day?* He shook his head almost imperceptibly, and then turned his attention to the sparsely peopled plaza, looking carefully outside and around the bus for anyone waiting to board. Seeing that no one was around, Bud pulled the door lever shut and drove out of the stop, leaving Pamela Iverson to her fate. He would see her sooner than he could know.

In her too-enthusiastic approach, she almost walked into the glass as the automatic doors opened a little too slowly. Stopping abruptly, she waited for them, a bit irritated, then stepped inside, relief washing over her in the spooling AC currents.

The cool breeze rustled the leaves and blooms of the flower display in the vestibule. This lovely arcade of bouquets and plants welcomed shoppers. Music drifted in the circulating breeze as the Bee Gees begged the question, "How Deep Is Your Love?" Pamela knew the lyrics, sang along under her breath, asking the question over and over, receiving no answer. Entering the song's swaying mood, she slowed and stopped in the center of the aisle as the present dissolved into an inner landscape of happier times. She lost track of where she was until the audible frustration of a shopper trying to push his cart past her brought her back. She quickly apologized to cover this conspicuous lapse of decorum and moved out of the way.

Pamela always rebounded in the hopeful world of the Eastside. This wasn't her first market, but it was her preferred one. Inspecting the aisles on her first round this morning, she felt a troupe of memories expand, unruly and dangerous. She had zoomed back to the one crushing moment in Aisle 5 of her hometown market. Baking Goods—where she had abandoned the cart right where it stood, and ran, lit out for illusion, escaped the reality she couldn't live. This realization that there was, and would always be, nothing here for her had occurred on a Wednesday morning. Since then, oddly enough, it had become the world of supermarkets that she took refuge in, hid out, and pretended everything was normal.

Here, in the Market, people were in the trusty trance of shopping, glazed eyes searching shelves, unaware of what could happen in the blink of an eye. This was the difference between Pamela and her fellow shoppers: she knew the weight, the heft, and the danger present of each moment's innocent advance.

Pamela had become relatively secure in her safe, carefully constructed life here in the Eastside Market. She knew no one really saw her. Searching for items on shelves and in bins, checking lists, comparing products, shoppers were oblivious to those who appeared in front of them. Here, she believed she was living an ordinary life, every day, day by day, like everyone else who came and went from home. Here, she was just one more shopper.

After this morning's heat, Pamela needed to refresh herself before the market got crowded. She walked toward the ladies' restroom, looking both ways, checking for anyone watching. She stopped to read a label on a package of pasta to give herself a chance to run some surveillance on anything or anyone suspicious; nothing was detected. Once inside, she opened each stall to make sure she was alone.

When she turned on the tap, a burst of cool water rinsed over her wrists as she studied her reflection in the mirror. She looked normal, she thought, although she didn't really know what "normal" looked like anymore. Reassured that she was unremarkable, she reached into the basket of artificial flowers on the washstand and smiled when she felt the small bottle of cologne she had lodged in there a few days ago. The "tester" bottle had "Try Me" written on its label. She never would have thought of taking it home, but stowing it here didn't seem so wrong. She intended to enjoy it for a while, and then replace it on the shelves of the cosmetics section. She had also "borrowed" a magazine from the periodicals rack and placed it under the cushion of one of the booths in the café. These items, hidden where only she knew, made the market feel more personal, like she belonged here.

She withdrew the bottle and gave the plunger a squeeze; a cloud of lavender scent spritzed into the septic space. Closing her eyes, she inhaled, replacing the bottle just in time as the door of the washroom opened and a pair of young women, talking intently, entered. They didn't remark on the thick fragrance in the air—or notice her smiling exit.

Out in the market, the Bee Gees had segued to Paul Anka's "Put Your Head on My Shoulder," slowing her progress as she walked down the aisle. She came to a full stop at the coffee display just as ghosts from her past floated toward her. In an unconscious move to mask her fantasy, Pamela picked up a bag of Colombian coffee beans, and pretended to study the label. But she had already been transported to the backyard of her childhood home on Pine Street in Milton, Maine. It was late July, somewhere in the 1960s and she was having a birthday party.

In the dim light of a hazy moon, Pamela danced with Dave Richie, one of Milton's bad boys. The couple moved in uncertain, intimate steps on the uneven lawn. Pamela heard herself wondering what magic had brought this boy to her. He wasn't the kind of boy Mother would allow her to invite, but here he was, holding her in the dark perimeter of Mother's terrain. Before she could ask him this question, he eased her behind the lilac tree and kissed her softly. That kiss seemed to last forever; she felt it now. Somehow knowing her willingness, Dave asked her to go steady with him. Pamela trembled as she looked up into his inviting eyes and breathed, "Yes."

"She Loves You, Yeah, Yeah, Yeah" broke her reverie as the Beatles brash tones climbed the air. The memory faded, leaving Pamela standing at the organic section, coffee beans still in hand. Looking up at the overhead sign, she smiled. "Wild Harvest" it read, and she smiled at the double entendre. Wild harvest indeed!

Later that morning, she was startled again by a man trying to get to the bin of sweet potatoes she was blocking, still deep in a mental lapse. Pamela apologized, scurrying away. She'd learned how to vanish, to stay under the radar. Pamela was having trouble knowing what was real and what was not.

Unsettled by these spinouts, and chased by the past, she moved quickly down the aisle. Even in this isolated existence, Pamela trusted that the possibility for returning to some sort of life still existed … was sure of it because of the huge space its absence punched in her heart. There was nothing to anchor her to her days, nothing but her connection to the market. Pamela rounded the corner onto Hope Street, an aisle named for an actual street in Providence. As an organizing theme, the Eastside had posted the names of Providence's streets at the beginning of each aisle: Angel, Benefit, and Hope were street names that reflected the compassionate Providence that the city's founder, Roger Williams, had once imagined as a land of kindness and refuge. The street names helped Pamela imagine she was navigating the town.

Smells of warm, golden-brown baking goods from the café drifted down to her as she strolled. The spicy cinnamon of rolls, and the comfort of buttery crusts, leaked into the air mixed with the dark, bitter aroma of coffee. Breakfast called, and Pamela's hunger arose to greet the call. But she hadn't yet acted on the plan she'd made for this morning....

Pamela reached into her purse for the prayer card she had put there before leaving home today. She dug to the bottom, into the tangle of everything. When she felt the card, she pulled it into the light. But what she held in her hand took her breath away; it was a photo from Christmas years ago. In this snapshot, the angelic faces of her daughter and son looked out at her, red wrapping bows stuck on their noses like Rudolph's red light. At first the humor buoyed her, but confusion and uneasiness quickly followed. She leaned her arm on the shelf beside her to let these feelings fade. How could that photo emerge from her purse today? There was no connection between this place and the distant world of that photo. The fragments of those days had been boxed and stored away for years in an attic at her daughter's home, far away in Wells, Maine.

Another marker was surfacing. These incidents told her that she was either losing her mind, or had adopted some new operating system, one with no regard for details of cause and effect; one that was taking over her life. She couldn't trust anything to stay put anymore. Pamela stood tall, and again, forced herself to shrug it off. She didn't have the composure to think about it now. She plunged the snapshot back into her purse, then breathing deeply to settle down, she continued to dig, feeling for the sliver of paper she knew was there. This time, she pulled the right card out into bright market light.

The image of The Christ with velvety-hued rays of light streaming from his heart, returned her gaze intimately. On the fragile card, His eyes were streaming with compassion for her. She pressed the card to her heart, bowed her head right there in the aisle, and risked emotions in plain sight before she felt ready to move on.

When she had recovered her composure, she walked down the aisle marked "Angel" to the vestibule, the card in her hand. As she walked, the aisle expanded with the grandeur of a cathedral. The nearer she approached the flower display, the more she felt the sacred presence of an altar.

But the ever-present fear of danger surfaced as she felt someone watching. Pamela's gait slackened. She moved slowly, looking to each side, terrified of being discovered. She knew any incident could tip off the management to her constant and invasive presence. Fear delayed her for the moment.

Pamela was aware that many women relied for living on deceptions like hers, cruised local stores, creating lives of shopping. Like her, they were vigilant; conscious always of someone watching, eyes staying on them too long, the same people appearing around them repeatedly. In an attempt at diversion just in case she was being watched, she detoured quickly to the Benefit Street aisle, approaching the floral display using the outside perimeter of the store rather than a main aisle.

Once she arrived at the altar of flowers, Pamela stopped and looked both ways. Then reaching up gently to the fourth row of blooms, she lodged the precious prayer card in the space between two pink freesia plants and miniature red roses, directly below a cluster of brilliant-blue irises, and just above the trembling trumpets of snowy-white calla lilies. The bouquets around the card seemed appropriate, and they, in response, seemed to brighten.

Her task complete, Pamela backed away into the vestibule, her attention rapt on the image of The Christ in his bower. Moving backward, she bumped into a shopper, almost knocking him over. She helped the man regain his balance and apologized; then felt she had to walk away as quickly as possible. When she was far enough removed so as not to be associated with what she had done, she looked over her shoulder to view the power of the image as it spun out to her, a dynamo within blossoms, blessing all who entered unaware. At the end of the aisle, Pamela—a lost

woman on her fifty-fourth birthday—bowed her head and whispered a
prayer of supplication that came to her on the spot.

"O Divine Wisdom, I am confused and unsure, lost in the darkness
of this life. Shower light into my heart that I may see a path before me
in the wilderness of this day. Give me the courage to live again, quiet the
voices of fear that confuse my judgment and cloud my vision. Grant me
the gift of Your eyes to see with, and Your Love to embrace me on this
hot, fearful day."

Finishing the prayer, Pamela turned her steps to the haven of the café,
suddenly hungry. There she would relax, be one of the regulars. Even if
the staff offered her the occasional pleasantry or remembered her favorite
pastry, it was of no matter. There was enough of a cast of characters to
make her daily visits unremarkable.

As this was Sunday, Pamela wore a spotless white blouse with yellow
linen slacks and black flats. She had chosen a flowered scarf for accent,
even though the day was hot. As she stood in line at the bakery, she was as
in a communion queue, and had become that young girl she used to be.
She proceeded with the decorum of a queen: polite, calm, and composed.

Having gathered her breakfast items and turning to search for a table,
she thought again about the photo in her purse. Its appearance unnerved
her. She sensed a hidden self within, watching just below the surface, one
barely able to keep the riptide of feelings from erupting into the present
moment. Pamela knew this woman as herself, knew also that this twin was
so fragile that she could self-destruct in a moment. This morning, a battle
for control was raging, upsetting the flimsy balance she hoped to rely on.

Settling her tray on her table, Pamela noticed that a cappuccino had
been substituted for the tea she ordered. Not wanting to make a fuss, she
accepted things as they were, moving the cappuccino and muffin from her
tray to the table. She folded her napkin, tucked it to the left of the plate,
and then paused a moment to offer a silent grace over her food.

After the first few bites, she suddenly remembered the prayer card
four aisles over, nestled within the colorful blooms. She smiled as she
saw the uplifted arm of Christ welcoming all. But her smile faded when
recognition of her vulnerability in the Eastside roosted within her, ruining

her peaceful breakfast. Pamela became uncomfortable. Putting that card in a public place, especially taking into account its subject, wasn't keeping a low profile. What if someone had seen her, that phantom *someone* she'd sensed watching? It might be prudent to retrieve the card sooner than later; then there would be no possible connection to her.

Her coffee cup rattled in its saucer as she rose abruptly from the table. People looked up at the noise, startled. She tried not to rush and draw more attention to herself. Navigating the aisles at a normal pace seemed to take forever. Finally, she rounded the last corner and started down Hope Street toward her altar.

She caught herself just before gasping out loud at what she saw. She held her breath as a cloud of monarchs, flitting just above the card in circular orbits, peeled off in formation to come down the aisle in a queue toward her. Pamela stood, disabled by the sight. What could this mean? Images of Drakes Island and the beach visit that had warned of Andrew's death years ago zoomed back, bearing all the heft of a miracle in progress.

Then, monarchs became a phalanx behind her, surrounding her, fluttering strongly until she got the message. She was to come to the altar. In halting steps, the cloud following behind, she approached.

There, where the simple one-dimensional card had been, was the Christ, enlivened, arms raised, gazing steadily at her, his image glowing and wavering on air as if lit from within.

Pamela dropped to her knees and felt the jolt of divine regard surf her body. Their eyes met; she knew she was known.

Tears fell as she knelt mid-aisle. Approaching shoppers entering at the door, parted like water around her, and turned to see what this woman was looking at; wondering why she was crying here in the Eastside Market on Sunday morning. And still the woman knelt in the middle of the entry, staring up into the floral display, looking for the entire world to see like Bernadette of Lourdes.

Then, as a gust of hidden wind blew around her she knew this was the answer to her prayer of only minutes before. Pamela lowered her eyes, no longer daring the encounter of the knowing recognition from within the tabernacle of leaves. There she remained still, as minutes ticked by until the noise of the onlookers around her broke her notice.

As she lifted herself back into the world of the present, fear compromised her. She had to disappear quickly. She stood clumsily with twenty or so people watching, their attention bouncing from the flowers to Pamela's tear-stained face. The main event seemingly over, the crowd dispersed, slowly drifting into the aisles of the market; baskets hung on their arms to collect what they had come for. When she looked again at the site of the vision, afraid of what she would see, only the ordinary, small, flat, card was there. The butterflies had flown; now the diminutive Christ of cardboard raised His tiny hand over her head.

Nervously, Pamela approached, and reached gingerly into the tiers to remove the card. Inadvertently, she grabbed the leaf of a lily along with the card, pulling it off its perch. When the lily tipped, plants on either side tumbled, upsetting the balance of the entire display, which now crashed to the floor, pot after pot, vase after vase, strewing dirt, broken pots, and mangled flowers in a wide swath around her feet.

Trying to avert the disaster, Pamela jumped into futile action, but it was already too late. The noise and chaos had brought the dreaded moment of detection upon her. An angry cleanup team holding mops menacingly moved down the aisle toward her. Still hoping for escape, Pamela picked up the innocent card, stuffing it in her purse, turned, and walked quickly and anonymously away from the littered vestibule, skulking back through the aisles to her muffin as if nothing had happened.

Though she was shaken, she sat, avoiding the looks of those around her. She was halfway through her breakfast when Mr. Moikens, the manager of the Eastside, slid into the seat across from her. His expression said everything and suddenly her once delicious muffin turned to dust as she tried to swallow. The cappuccino, midway to her lips, spilled from her trembling hands, brown liquid dribbling down the front of her crisp, white, top, staining it, then, onto her slacks. Her cup clinked loudly in the saucer when she put it down. Everyone was watching.

Mr. Moikens stared at her, letting tension build as he held off his anger a few moments before speaking. When he began, his tone was level, suitable in volume, but his words were sharp as knives. "Mrs. Iverson. Oh yes, we know who you are... I will speak civilly, but there is absolutely no room for negotiation in what I am about to say. We have been watching you. We know about the perfume in the ladies' room and the magazines here in the café. That is stealing, Ms. Iverson! We are aware that you come here every day to use our store as if it were your own property. You have been observed handling merchandise, arranging shelves, and getting in the way of our patrons. The list of your offenses goes on and on ..." he paused, as if waiting for a response, but Pamela sat silently, not daring to breathe. "Today's incident in the floral department is the last straw. Are you aware of the cost of the mess that the crew is cleaning up right now? There is no excuse, no explanation you can give that would change the decision I have made."

Pamela swallowed hard, trying not to cry. Rigid and silent, she looked at her accuser, wondering what she might possibly say or do to make this man understand there had never been a choice, that she had been compelled to come here every day. It meant survival. She attended to him sadly as he took her world apart, turning her carefully created fragile existence to something flawed and silly.

He continued his rant: "Finish your breakfast. I won't deprive you of items you actually bought. But then I want you to walk to the entrance of the store and leave. You are not welcome here anymore. In fact, if you return to this store, I will call the police and have you arrested for shoplifting. Is that clear?" He paused impatiently, and waited for her response.

A remorse more painful than poison spread through her veins. Pamela could see herself clearly; the veil had lifted. She was a fake, a pretender, and now it was obvious to everyone. Her carefully constructed yet hopeful facade had been pulled down in front of her eyes, and worst thing of all, she had done this to herself. When she tried to shut out the leveling stare of the man, tears ran down her face onto her stained blouse. Pamela nodded in agreement. Mr. Moikens stood to leave, rapping the table with his knuckles before he walked away.

Bud Carey's bus rocked into the CVS entrance, air brakes whooshing. He had finished his second loop around and back to the plaza. As he glanced toward the market, a solitary figure emerged, a woman walking fast—almost running—toward his bus. Pamela's feet seemed to be moving on waves of heat so palpable that they held her up. But from where Bud Carey sat, she walked not on the earth, but on air....

He recognized Ms. Iverson all at once and knew something was wrong, very wrong. Reading tragedy around her, Bud punched the brakes tightly and leaped out of his seat leaving the bus unguarded, knowing full well this was breaking the first rule of his employment.

She saw him coming toward her and rushed to him, her unsteadiness growing as she ran. Bud reached her just in time, and held her up with his strong arms. Retreating quickly across the stinging macadam, the two disappeared inside the cool bus, and the spectacle ended. Jumping back into his seat, Bud pulled away from the stop, carrying Ms. Iverson away from the Eastside for the last time—and into the maze of Providence and beyond.

Bud offered escape for the moment, and Mrs. Iverson accepted it, though she knew the reprieve was temporary. Already, the scenery of her life had shifted; something new was beginning. For Pamela, the answer to her prayer had come, but she couldn't know that now. The thin existence she had shaped to hide within vanished in the blinding light of this morning's events. Now, in the bus, she sat, but going where, she didn't know. Despair loped in her veins, gathering momentum as the Eastside faded from view.

In the purse beside her, the smudged image of her Savior had His hand raised still in blessing.

CHAPTER 3

ED LACASSE

Drakes Island, Wells, Maine
Christmas Eve, 1999

Ed wondered when Sarah had stored this ceramic Christmas tree down here. She had been gone five years now—five years—and he had just found it in one of the storage bins in the cellar. His brow furrowed as he tried to think back to that last Christmas with Sarah, but there were protective gaps in his recall, and too much sadness. He remembered it all began with *The Bad Year* ... the year Sarah spent in deadly, silent denial while cancer grew inside of her. They might have beaten it if they had started treatment earlier.

When Sarah finally told him, it was too late. What it came down to was that she was ashamed that cancer had happened; happened to her... Ed had heard others talk about this when he took her for her chemotherapy; chatting with others approaching death most always gave folks the license to tell the truth. Bottom line: shame was as deadly as cancer. Growing up French Catholic in a small Maine town, shame lurked everywhere. It kept you guarded, wary of things, things that should have been natural, free. Whether shame was levied on you by your mother at home—in fear of what the neighbors might think—or by your Father from the altar and the confessional, or by your friends from the neighborhood who sat in judgment and betrayal, shame took root inside you; it was a constant companion that looked out of your eyes with suspicion.

And yet somehow, just before she had become so sick she couldn't even walk, Sarah had decided to stash this tree, her favorite Christmas relic, out of sight? He was amazed, and couldn't imagine why she would have done that. Holiday decorations in their household were always stored in the spare bedroom closet, and Sarah had been a woman of neatness and routine. Maybe he really hadn't known her as well as he thought he had. In the dim light of the cellar, this tall, slender man of sixty tried to imagine her carrying the heavy, unwieldy little tree down steep stairs. It just didn't sound possible.

Ed hadn't celebrated anything since her death. They had no children, so there was no one to celebrate with. His family was mostly gone except for a few distant cousins up in Maine. Christmas was now, and always had been, quiet; just an ordinary day on Blueberry Lane, in Drakes Island, Maine.

Ed LaCasse's cottage was one street back from Beach Avenue; there was little traffic in winter, and precious few neighbors stayed over through cold weather. Something, probably his own desperate boredom, had made him come down to the cellar to look for his long-neglected radio equipment this morning. And he had found this old treasure from another day.

He lifted the ceramic tree out of the bin carefully, pushing his glasses up on his forehead to inspect it for damage. He and Sarah had bought it years ago while in Germany on one of their Coast Guard vacations. He and Sarah—he liked thinking that. He and Sarah, in the fullness of their lives then, when they were healthy and busy, had traveled some. Ed's memories tugged at him, and he let himself return to those days when he had shipped out to sea two weeks out of every month. Still in this dim cellar of today, Ed could hear the long-distant echo of staccato telegraph keys clicking in his ears, and he felt the floor heaving under him. As a decoder, he had to have perfect hearing and fire-fast dexterity on the keys. His better-than-average math and physics skills, plus a command of electricity, made him a respected man onboard; the ranking officer in the dispatch room.

Ed, eyes closed now, felt the floor under his feet pitch as phantom winds from the past roared off a roiling sea. In his memory, the excitement of being on board ships as big as cities, steaming across heaving seas while dealing with life-and-death situations, was easily relived. It was too easy for Ed to step back into the past tonight. Coming back to this empty present was much more of a challenge.

Ed and Sarah had first moved to Drakes Island together as part of their retirement. Once here, Ed had spent countless hours in this cellar listening to worldwide transmissions on his ham radio. Reception by the ocean was as good as that on the water, and Ed, a master of code, was adept at reading the bursts of energy and answering back with precision. He had operated here on Drakes Island with no interruption for a good while. His communications from this new location flew on the same precise, but invisible, routes as had his official responses; over the same shifting seas he now lived beside and called home. Lately, his ham radio had gone silent. He had just lost interest.

Wrapped in reverie and still holding Sarah's precious tree, Ed felt the dismay of his prospects for this day. He shook off the time travel of the last few minutes, let the wooden top of the bin drop, and watched as a ruffle of dust rose visibly into the dim, stuffy cellar air. Turning to head up the stairs, with the little miracle tree still in his hands, he quite forgot his errand to find his radio equipment. Shutting the cellar door, he brought the prize—as good as any Christmas present—into his messy kitchen. He had to turn the lights on since the skies were darkening, even though it was just late morning.

Looking at the tree filled him with nostalgia. He would dust it off and light it tonight for Christmas Eve. Sarah used to send him after it every year, thrilled when it was finally installed and lit in the bay windows. It had been important to her: Germany first made ceramic trees to save their woodlands from the deforestation of the Christmas appetite for evergreens. She told Ed this year after year. She would have been classified as a tree hugger today, he thought.

As he worked at cleaning it, Ed's thoughts strayed to the development of Morse code by Samuel Morse in the early 1800's. A tragic story, it was one Ed sympathized with on a deep and personal level. As he'd heard it, at the time, Morse was in Washington, working on a portrait of Lafayette. A messenger on horseback delivered a letter from Morse's father, informing him that his wife, who had been ill, was getting better. But that letter was followed shortly by another messenger the next day. This second message informed Morse that his beloved wife had died suddenly overnight. Bereft, Samuel Morse left Washington immediately for his home in New Haven, Connecticut, but by the time he arrived, his wife was already buried. In his intense grief, he was inspired to develop an unprecedented system of communication, Morse code, one that communicated with the speed and dependability of electrical signals. His hope was that his invention might keep others from experiencing the painful fate he had endured.

In this empty December kitchen, Ed felt Morse's pain. Morse code had played a major part in Ed's work life and had bettered the lives of uncountable millions all over the world. But it couldn't save Morse.

Ed speculated that the tree would most likely need new bulbs after all these years. He resolved to get some in town this afternoon before the stores closed for Christmas. He chuckled at the small thrill of purpose this little errand caused him; he was grateful for anything that could get him out of the house. Sometimes it was so quiet here that the steady tick of the clock sounded like a gong. Ed welcomed any chore that needed him.

Setting the tree on the counter, he dusted and polished it until it gleamed as Sarah would have wanted; it was two and a half feet high with dark-green, snow-frosted boughs. The family antique was a fine example of its species. Small spires of artificial candle flame on the tips of the boughs would glow in all colors when it was working. His surprise was audible when he plugged it in, and the lights sparkled to life.

"Will you look at that?" he said to no one in particular, as the tree brightened the small room with its rainbow hues. Ed was mystified and delighted that it worked; he still had something from all the years of happiness with his girl. The tree connected him with a jolt to his past as it stood on the counter. It seemed to exist in both worlds at once, past and present.

Ed noticed how dark the sky had become in early dusk in contrast to the bright blaze of color in front of him. He wanted the tree to stand where Sarah would have put it: on a table in the bay windows. He carried it into the living room, looking for a clear spot to set it down. The dust on the end tables reminded him that he had let things go. He knew Sarah would have been peeved about his lackluster cleaning and would have said something. Ed set the tree on the floor, clearing magazines and a few cold, clotted cups of coffee away, then placed the tree on the table and plugged it in, hoping his moving it hadn't damaged it. Once again, the tree sparkled into the dull light of the living room and out beyond, shining on this dark island in Maine just as it used to so many years ago.

He was happy with the cheery effect on the dull day, and decided to leave it lit, even though he was going out. The little tree would welcome him home later.

He checked the time and saw it was getting late for his town run. If he was going to do his errands and get dinner tonight before the storm set, he had best be going. Ed went to the hall closet to reach in for his coat, causing a jacket on a hanger beside it to fall to the floor. Reaching down to retrieve it in the jungle of old coats and shoes, he was surprised to feel the buttery leather of his old Coast Guard jacket. "Where had this come from?" he thought. He hadn't seen it in years. Just like the tree, another refugee from the past. The weight of it in his hands, the smell of old leather, and the lamb's wool lining—perfect for tonight's forecast of bad weather.

"Wonder if it still fits?" Ed spoke aloud without even hearing himself. Going to the mirror near the front door, he tried it on, backing up to see its effect. He liked the way it looked, liked the way it felt. He would wear it, do some shopping, then go for an early supper at the Maine Diner before coming back to wait for midnight Mass. He did a lot of waiting, often forgetting just what he was waiting for. This emptiness of his life was expected, especially on Christmas Eve when families gathered. He wasn't a man to complain. The next day, Christmas itself, Ed would spend alone—nothing new there. He had books, scotch, coffee, firewood, plus a few cans of soup. Those were all he really needed....

As he backed the Jeep out of the garage, he rolled to a stop and watched the door bump down snugly in a beginning snowfall. He was ready for whatever tonight brought; the fire already set in the hearth, and his little Christmas tree, shining away once again, gave him something to look forward to. The little tree … how important it seemed: the first gift of Christmas. It brought a smile to his face as he sat in the idling vehicle.

The radio blared suddenly, warning of a Nor'easter approaching sooner than expected this afternoon. He paused for a moment before engaging the gears, brought back to a time of enduring storms on the deck of a Coast Guard cutter. Days on end, Ed would be in a dark room below deck, parsing icy-green probes of radar that forecast danger; warnings of objects and conditions just ahead in the dark. His skill and attention had changed the fate of people in those days. Tonight, his dim life asked him for reasons to go on, to move ahead. He shook off the thinking and shifted strongly into reverse. The car moved in response, but, faltering, he lost heart. The Jeep rolled to a stop again and idled. Ed's eyes closed as a powerful wave of emotion overrode the emptiness of this night. Something painful roiled deep in him; his life was a prison from which he needed to break free.

The tree in the cellar, the jacket—found tonight after years. The storm, coming in with such power …. These unconnected but overlapping details brought Sarah back to him, smiling encouragement and hope into his eyes from somewhere he couldn't quite reach. Ed threw the Jeep into reverse with more energy than it needed, and turned to look behind him as he backed out onto Blueberry Lane. He wanted to be that man again, wanted to reach out, change things, make some difference on this weary globe before it was too late. The need to be seen, to be counted on in some way, was so powerful that tears welled in his eyes.

Moving ahead at last, Ed drove past his cottage toward Island Road, looking into the rearview mirror for the glowing tree in his window which was quickly disappearing in snowfall behind him. As he did, his foot came off the pedal for a third time when he thought he saw Sarah standing beside the tree, waving him off as she had liked to do. Knowing this couldn't be, he refocused his gaze and accelerated to the end of Blueberry Lane, and continued on his way. In any event, he would be back at home before the brunt of the storm came in. There was no place else for him to go.

CHAPTER 4

CHICK'S CROSSING

Wells, Maine
Christmas Eve, 1999

Pamela stirred in her sleep. Snow sifted against gray tree trunks imprinting the cold air with a soft shushing. She knew these woods; they spoke to her from a time long ago. The soft rustle of boughs in wind, the fall of snow, the breath of the living forest—all together, they welcomed her.

Light glowed just ahead; tender, fragile light revealing the arching limbs above her. Wanting to be in the embrace of this warm radiance, Pamela walked toward it; she was drawn by its gentleness. The solid peace of the place held her up, silent and deep as the snow. She looked down to see that her feet were cushioned in the white carpet, but she wasn't cold. Moving on toward the light, she floated, amazed. But sounds from the house rose around her; the dream came apart, little by little; ripped fragments of a photo floated away, then faded to nothing.

When she opened her eyes, she knew where she was and shut them again; wanting, trying to stop this dawn from approaching. From over the treetops of the forest, she heard the Downeaster's train whistle howl like an anguished animal as it loped through the winter-barren woods of Southern Maine on its way up to Portland. She heard Leslie calling Robbie down to breakfast. The clock ticking on the dresser spoke in loud seconds, her pulse spiked within the now-familiar disappointment of this life.

Turning over, Pamela willed herself to go back to the dream—tried to knit it up again—but it was too late; it had already passed out of memory. She opened her eyes to the small familiar bedroom on the second floor of her daughter's home. Weak December light wanly illuminated blue flowered wallpaper, spreading without confidence into the corners of the room and onto the floor. She pushed herself up to sit in the bed, and then moved to the side, feet resting on the cold floor. She knew she must slip her life on, wear it like something found in her closet; something that seemed to belong to someone else.

The useless minutes of morning ticked by and piled up around her. Without warning, clouds obscured the light in the room, dimming what little December sunlight there was. In her mind, she hurtled back to that first Christmas. Her breathing went cold and shallow; a warning spread within her: This was a place she knew not to go; this memory mustn't be allowed to take over today, this first day of Christmas.

Pamela thought to attend her morning ritual, to head to the shower, but dizziness encompassed her, and she stopped and just stood still. The thinness of her spirit was no match for the power of memories. She walked past the mirror, glancing into it. Andy … she and Andy and Christmas … were all there together, whirling and spinning …. She could feel him near, returning through an unnoticed door, somehow unlatched and open. But she had felt the hurt of this place before.

In the kitchen, Leslie had left her coffee brewing. Pamela appreciated her daughter's kindness. Today, the simple evidence of her thoughtfulness brought tears to her eyes. These emotions were so close to the surface they frightened her. Was it because this was Christmas Eve?

By habit rather than desire, once the hot brew was poured, she stood with her cup for a moment, looking out onto Chick Crossing's Christmas landscape. Displayed on the bare front lawn, a family of artificial reindeer bowed their heads to nibble at the withered remains of summer's grass, and then raised their heads again, haltingly, only to gaze off into the horizon, and then repeat the empty motion over and over. They were so vulnerable in this daylight; defined by spindly connections of wires, intertwined with small glowing white lights. The effect was canceled out by the gathering gray. Pamela forced her eyes away from the hypnotic bowing of their heads, and back into the warm kitchen. She chose a blueberry muffin from the stash of pastries Leslie had put out for the holiday, warmed it in the microwave, and sat at the table; her Maine Diner mug filled with cooling coffee. Closing her eyes for a moment, she prayed as she had on many days since that day; praying for the strength to just get through. Outside the window, the morning's tepid sun disappeared beneath the lid of heavy overcast.

Like wind visible at the tops of trees but not perceived at ground level, a memory moved within her. She stood motionless, her hands flat on the table beside the untouched muffin, as the landscape, the house—everything—disappeared, and the past arose into the room.

Had it all begun then? Something deep inside *this* person at *this* table on *this* morning; cutting like glass, transparent, defying naming. She was in danger, swimming against a cold tide. She must just be normal for their sakes, she thought. That word, *normal* … she despised it like a poison. It meant something she now was forever denied. Somehow, on that day, the thief had slipped in and taken him and everything all in a one breath. It had happened because she wasn't watching. She had been warned.

After his funeral, everyone left for lives in places where people thought about other things. Once alone, Pamela swept the floors, packed fragments of twenty-four years of life in that house into cartons, and consigned them to storage. That done, she put the house on the market and moved out; out of her house, out of her life—just *out*.

Her children and those closest to her felt betrayed; she was to have been a place marker in the chaotic, distorted world that took over with his death. As long as they knew she was there, on the street they had grown up on. Maybe then they could go on with their lives … as long as they could call her, and hear her voice from the same kitchen phone next to the window that looked into the backyard where he had set the compost on fire that night. The firemen, she remembered, had raced to the rescue, tromping down the garden in the dark.

If only rescue were available this morning. *If only—if only* …. The choice had been hers. She could have done as others did, and made herself

busy in the community where they lived together for so long. She could
have walked the path from home, to library, to church. She could have
joined groups, visited his grave every weekend, talked with him in his
hidden world. But running away felt better—was better—better than
living within the fading outlines of what had been.

Pamela had found an apartment in Providence, Rhode Island.
Providence was the city that Roger Williams had named after "God's merciful
Providence." There she sought forgetfulness and anonymity. It had seemed
logical then though it made no sense now. She knew no one in the old sea
town. That was the most appealing thing of all; she would be a stranger
there. No one would recognize her or offer pity. She could rebuild a life.

Then there was the supermarket—the Eastside. Just how her obsession
with this place took over, she didn't know. She knew only that she was
drawn to the activity of shopping, of being in the crowds, of spinning
around the aisles in a centrifugal force. There was the ritual of the carts,
the *do-si-do* of bowing in aisles, of pushing ahead in the thoroughfare
of stocked shelves, of shoppers moving in a trance, of reading coupons
like maps, of the rows of colorful packages whispering subliminal caring;
it was all so comforting somehow. The shiny surfaces of freezer cases
reflected her image back to herself like fun house mirrors. She had fallen
under the spell of this great White Way; the distraction was hypnotic,
appealing, numbing....

But that world too had imploded on the morning she was asked—no,
forced—to leave the Eastside and never return. As the doors of her gates of
Eden closed behind her that day, she saw what she had become: a person
of no substance at all, a woman bearing no resemblance to the once careful
and caring wife, mother, teacher, and friend of earlier years.

Leslie was told about her expulsion when Mrs. Bisson, a Providence
neighbor in Pamela's complex, got her daughter's address, and called to
tell about the events at the Eastside. Leslie called RIPTA to thank them—
and especially Bud Carey—for rescuing Pamela. Bud had painted a
painful picture of the life her mother had been living there. After that,
Pamela Iverson had to leave Providence, and returned to Maine in a
protective custody.

Mrs. Bisson had meant well, but her interference forced Pamela into a nervous tenancy with Leslie, who insisted that her mother come back and live with them for a few months to get back on her feet. Pamela had no recourse. The Eastside Market forever closed to her. She owned up to her vulnerability, packed up her small crowd of furniture and belongings, and returned to the shadowland she had tried to outrun.

At first, moving into the snug, bright house—with Leslie, her husband, Paul, and her adored two-year-old grandson, Robbie—made a nice difference. Everyone relaxed a little as color slowly returned to Pamela's face. She began taking an interest in the daily running of things, and the world of this little boy. She took over the role as coffee expert, and she began cooking again; a talent that had developed into an art in earlier years. But now, today, the fog had begun seeping in; she was drifting again.

The sound of the ticking clock broke through her thoughts. She was stunned at how irrelevant this day felt. It was as if she saw herself from a satellite circling above, a pinpoint of black in the expansive gray landmass of this jagged state.

The clock in the dining room struck eleven. From the radio, a serious voice warned of a storm approaching: a Nor'easter with potential for dangerous winds and tides. In her tumble of thoughts, Pamela registered none of it. She lifted the coffee to her lips only to find it already cold.

Upstairs, sounds of Robbie and his mother wrapping gifts flowed down to the kitchen. Shushing each other and giggling, they were in deep intrigue about the special first gifts of Christmas, to be opened just before bedtime on Christmas Eve. This was a precious ritual in this family.

Looking ahead to the evening, Pamela shivered. With her emotions already in tatters this morning, she couldn't see how she would endure the evening; emptiness had burrowed too deep. In one tick of the clock she yielded: the allure of running—*running*—as she had when the silence before had taken over and sent her in motion, running for her life.

Standing abruptly, she jarred the table and spilled her coffee. She watched in horror as the dark stain spread into the Christmas tablecloth that Leslie had just put out this morning. She grabbed the cloth from the table, and rushed to the sink to flush it with cold water. She scrubbed, praying the stain to lighten, but it was too late. The coffee had set too deeply in the snowy-white cotton and she remembered the coffee that stained her cotton blouse that last morning at the Eastside. And now— *again*—it was an echo telling her it was time to leave.

Her courage already waned, she couldn't face the consequences of even this minor misstep. Leaving the cloth soaking in the sink, she walked toward the coat closet, got her jacket, picked up her purse and keys, and moved quickly to the door before she could think about what she was doing.

Calling up the stairs toward the sound of her daughter and grandson's voices, she fought to keep tears out of her voice. "Leslie, I need to go out for a little bit, some errands to run. I'll be right back." Before Leslie could respond, Pamela opened the outside door and shut it firmly behind her. The heady freedom of escape was now in command.

Under collecting clouds, Pamela backed her dark-blue Subaru onto Chick Crossing Road, and drove out of Wells Highlands toward a sea already rising on the storm's winds.

Pamela drove, her attention fixed on getting out of Leslie's neighborhood. She let the road lead her like a chain pulling her car along—away. Adrenaline filled her blood, its burst familiar and welcome. She had been here before, and recently.

She was thinking of Bud Carey as she drove, of driving into the Eastside parking lot every morning on his safe bus; this present state of alertness had ridden the bus with her, keeping her wary, disconnected. Only when she got through the doors of the market did she relax into thinking she was anonymous, and that was just what she wanted. If she were not herself, then, the past could not have happened. This had been her defense until the day it wasn't anymore, until the day she ran up against a wall of reality in the person of Mr. Moikins, the manager of the Eastside.

Route 1 came into view at the Junction of 1 and 99. She panicked. Where was she going? Where *could* she go to get out of the whole sad parade of the days of Christmas? Where could she go where no one would remember her?

Pamela sat for a red light. In front of her was the Wells Police Department building with its blue light blazing in the dim morning; it seemed to offer shelter, but she knew better. When the light changed, she signaled a left hand turn, then, took it having no reason not to.

The usual December traffic in Wells streamed around her, amplified by last minute Christmas shoppers. She was carried along in this path of least resistance until she realized she was heading for Kennebunk...she froze. No, no, no, she would not, could not go there where every street, every shop, everything held some memory of before.

Then, the blinking yellow a few cars ahead offered her a place to turn off, to change direction. She accepted gladly and turned right, leaving Route 1 behind. After a few hundred feet, she realized she was on Drakes Island Road, familiar territory. Here, she had spent summers on the beach with the children and had run the three mile beach up and back on most weekends. The contours of this place were so familiar, so like they had been then that she teared up following the straggling tendril of road that led to Jetty Beach.

She piloted the car up and over the hilly entrance into the large parking lot, driving down to the beach to stop by the huge granite boulders of the jetty placed side-by-side and stretching almost a quarter mile out into the sea. There were no other cars in the lot.

Finally arriving somewhere she could be alone, she put the car in park and sat. The waves were spilling over the rocks, foaming quite close to her. She saw how gray and low the sky was. A storm enthusiast all of her life, Pamela felt engaged by the dramatic setting. A thick gray shelf of clouds was advancing up from the south, quickly overcoming the lighter cloud deck. She seemed to have found a place that was a visual match to the stormy emotions within her. She turned up the heater and settled back letting her head drop against the headrest. Eyes closed for the moment, comfortable, she let the morning's angst calm.

Within minutes, she was dreaming about other days, days here at Jetty Beach. Sinking deeper into sleep, she was living a day years ago, a day when she had come here to run...a small smile played on her lips. It had been here....

Stepping out onto the parking lot, she is momentarily dizzied by the depth of a cloudless autumn sky, a tent of cobalt pitched above the sea, with no horizon visible. No one is on the beach; that's unusual for Drakes Island. Most weekends, even fair winter ones, families tug children and hold kites and dogs into the always-blowing wind. Today, the landscape is empty.

Taking off her jacket and tying it around her waist, she moves into her warm-up. And then, the monarchs. . . .

Part Two

CHAPTER 5

MISSING PERSON

Wells, Maine
Christmas Eve, 1999

A river of golden light flowed east just above the surface of the Maine Turnpike and up to the evergreen shoulders of Canada. From there to the North Pole, ever brighter and stronger as it rode the crest of the earth, the river widened until it disappeared over the top of the planet. Jimmy Casey could see it all; he was skimming above this undulating highway of light, the precious earth revolving reliably beneath him. His weightlessness held him above this river. As he flew, he recognized Wells and his house: his small, dark home below him. He had escaped. He could see unhappiness leaking from its windows and doors like heat; he didn't want to go back. Spinning effortlessly in his flight, he felt like a boy again, smiling in freedom, until a loud ringing invaded his dream. Raucous tones disturbed him. Jimmy hovered between the two worlds, fighting to stay here. Then he awoke.

The clock beside his bed shouted in the dying light of a winter afternoon, the red digits proclaiming 4:00 o'clock. The dark already in the room told him dusk had fallen. He rubbed his eyes, sat up and looked around, searching for something of the dream. The bad weather forecast for later tonight was already here: the curtainless windows of his bedroom were dusted with snow, and shaking in strong gusts of wind.

The phone was still ringing. Jimmy knew there was a problem at the station. The call had to be about the storm; social calls to Jimmy's number were few and far between. His mind cleared the hurdle of sleep, and he knew he was going to be working tonight, though Chief had given him the night off. "Christmas Eve off," Chief had said. "All of it!" as if it mattered to Jimmy. "Spending" Christmas was a joke anyway. All this holiday meant to him was a few beers at a local bar with others who were alone for the duration. Jimmy had nothing and no one to "spend" Christmas on—or with. Most years, he was the last to leave the Maine Diner before it closed. He held on as long as he could. Jimmy's Christmas Eve featured a microwave supper in front of the TV topped off with sleep before the empty hours of the next day. Was there any day longer than Christmas Day? No traffic, no crime, no familiar places open, nothing to distract him. Typically, he'd run to a movie as soon as the theaters opened for business on Christmas night. Once there, he'd buy popcorn and soda, and would sit to watch anything that wasn't his life.

On the other end of the line, David Farrell responded quickly to Jimmy's gruff "Hello." "Casey, man, sorry to interrupt your night off, but we got a missing person's bulletin going out, and Chief wanted me to call and tell you. With the storm in already, we're shorthanded, and bad roads are going to make getting through the night without you almost impossible. Sorry. But Jimmy, I have it on good sources the Chief wants *you* in *now*."

The young officer's voice telegraphed his mounting anxiety as he listened for an answer on the other end, prepared for Jimmy to come back with his usual blast of irreverent bravado. But silence held longer and longer until Farrell got nervous and began adding details he thought might entice the seasoned cop into action.

"Woman left home this morning to do some shopping and hasn't come back yet. She's been missing six hours. Storm's come in early. We have to kick-start a missing person's protocol ASAP. I'm due to go off duty in a few minutes. There won't be anyone in with any experience on dispatch. In fact, the whole crew on tonight is rookie status." He drew a quick breath and held it, waiting.

Both of these men knew that anyone out in a full blown Nor'easter had no chance for survival unless he or she was dressed for the full assault of killing winds and freezing temperatures, and had food and shelter of some sort. The person had to be as tough as the storm itself.

And still Jimmy didn't respond, forcing Farrell to sit through the long pause. Jimmy Casey was the only person in a radius of fifty miles who could navigate the demands of this night. His somewhat vulgar, but always confident, voice on the radio directing the search would make a difference in how things went. He knew who to call, what to say, and what to do.

Jimmy had to admit to himself that what he was feeling was relief in this call to work, even though the storm told him things were going to get complicated. It was more by default than desire that he had accepted the time off anyway. In the seconds between the request and his response, Jimmy's peculiar sense of humor floated the image of the abandoned toys in *Rudolph, the Red-Nosed Reindeer,* the cartoon he had watched on TV over and over. He could relate; he *was* abandoned, stuck here on the "Island of Misfit Toys," stockpiled and broken.

Finally, the cop snarled a response, "Okay, Farrell, I'll be there soon's I can get up and dressed." He heard Farrell's relief over the phone in a whoop.

Fully awake now, Jimmy took over immediately, asking questions, giving directions, entering the situation fully. A lot depended on the actual state of the missing person. Her physical condition was key: "How old is this woman? Who reported her missing, and what do we know about her health, especially mental? What the hell's she doing out in this storm? Does she know what conditions can be like in the middle of a goddamned blizzard? You find that out for me, Farrell. Christ, makes me mad to think of how stupid people are."

What danger a rescue under these conditions might entail was no joke. "How was she dressed when she left home? What's the make and year of the car she's driving? Does her family know if there was a full tank of gas in the vehicle? Get me those answers before I get down to the station."

Jimmy had seen storms like tonight's blizzard sling whiteouts so intense that everything disappeared into them. Snowfall rearranged itself into unrecognizable landscapes in minutes. Any sense of where you were could be lost. He had seen powerful winds blow up seas that could throw chunks of granite ten feet onto land. If this woman was out there too long, especially anywhere near the beach, the probability of rescue was next to naught. Risks included everything—from drowning to freezing to walking blinded into a snowdrift so high she would never get out.

Officer Farrell added that Benton was scheduled to be on duty tonight. Silence greeted this piece of news; Farrell didn't need to explain. Jimmy knew Benton. He was a nice kid, but he wasn't up to conducting a rescue, even in the best of weather, never mind a Nor'easter.

"Okay, buddy, we need ya," Farrell said. "Get the hell in here." With those words, he hung up and turned to a call-board lighting up like a Christmas tree with storm situations.

Jimmy stayed quiet for a few minutes, trying to recapture the giddy glide of his dream. Minutes ticked by before he could force himself off the bed. When he turned on the overhead light, his cluttered bedroom coalesced out of the dark, reminding him of how little he cared about anything. It was depressing. He stepped over the piles of clothes, scattered video cases, and stacks of old newspapers. He chastised himself for his own discomfort at the sight.

"Get over it, for Christ's sake. Get ready for work." His rumpled uniform was on the chair in the corner where he had thrown it last night: brass tacky and pants shiny from being over worn. He picked them up to dress quickly but not before closing the closet to avoid looking at himself in the mirror. He knew he had put on weight and needed a haircut; knew the lack of attention to his life was beginning to show. It had been too much effort for quite a while now. He would shave, though. Chances were, he wouldn't get home for a few days.

Jimmy snapped off the overhead light in the bedroom and walked the narrow hall to the kitchen; he lit the kitchen light and recoiled from the cluttered counters that emerged showing the obvious disregard he had lately for anything. Though chaos was not unusual here, it had become a disease tonight. Months of neglected mail lay piled on the shelf by the back door, dirty dishes littered the counter and sink, and discarded jackets and shirts from as far back as fall hung on chairs. Gingerly, he picked up a grimy cup, ran it under hot water for a minute, and then filled it with yesterday's coffee. Putting it in the microwave, he tried to revive the stale beverage. It was hot and bitter.

Jimmy leaned against the wall, sipping the brew and preparing himself for the night ahead. He rubbed his neck, trying to sharpen his wavering focus. His thoughts were muddled and confused. He would have to move fast to leave them behind, but he knew how to do that.

As he busied himself with arranging his equipment, a pain bloomed suddenly in his chest: a thorny red flower directly over his heart. Steeling senses against it, he leaned heavily on the counter, breathing slowly. It felt to him like a heart attack. He had attended plenty of those, people having these symptoms. But it couldn't be happening to him....

He sank into the chair by the door and closed his eyes. Waiting for the pain to subside, he let his head rest on the wall behind him. He considered calling rescue but simply didn't want the bother of it ... especially with this storm. While he waited it out, images from his dream returned. Somehow, this pain and that dream converged, and for a split second, he was back in that airy chamber, suspended over the very earth.

In this enforced state of unusual calm, the memory of the night Melissa left came out of somewhere. That night, she finally had enough of his not being home, his always putting his work first ... that night it was all too late. It had been too quiet when he got home: no television, no radio, nothing. He saw the crumpled paper on the counter and full ashtray by the phone. He knew right away. When he straightened the paper out, he saw it was a bus schedule with several connections circled. He knew then she was gone. He had feared it. He had known it was only a matter of time, but still, he hadn't done anything about it. The echoes of her complaining and their fighting were still deep in the walls of the house. Melissa had simply packed up and caught the Blue Line down at the junction. That was how it ended, almost silently.

While he was at work, she made the decision and took action, changing their lives forever. Seeing her in town with her suitcase, some of his friends asked him the next day where she was going. What could a man say when his wife had left him? It took him months to admit, even to himself, that she was never coming back.

After that, it was winter in this house. In time, if he moved fast enough, he realized her actual absence didn't matter that much. She had left months before anyway. The ache of coming home came back sometimes, and he felt regret; he hadn't known she'd felt this bad, had never asked. He'd just hoped things would improve. He hadn't done enough. Her silent, growing unhappiness had scared him, made her a stranger. He just didn't know how to talk about feelings. These were things that weren't discussed in his family. Jimmy had just turned his back on the obvious and kept on working, hoping that would be enough. He had been wrong.

After the shock wore off, he canceled their bank accounts (she hadn't tried to use them), changed tax forms, car liens .... He did all the paper work; reshuffled the badges of ownership so he looked like a man in a single life. Then the transition to living alone began. In the end, he found he really didn't mind. Here he was today, still alone in the same house in the Highlands of Wells, Maine. When Melissa contacted him for a divorce a few months later, he never even asked why; he simply complied, taking the route of least resistance.

In all the years since then, nothing had happened to make him step out from behind this blind he created to keep things balanced, at least from the outside. He counted on his career as a cop to keep him from feeling much. He was unfree, unwilling, unable to enter that place of vulnerability, afraid it could happen again. That was the difference below the surface. Even though people had no idea, Jimmy had become a hidden person. He had lost hope—or optimism. Which was it? Some people knew what to do, what to say, how to act ... but not him. And it was way too late. After all, he had to be himself: a fifty-four-year-old man, a dispatcher at the PD, a cop on the town workforce. It was safer this way.

Tonight, in this kitchen reverie, the roar of wind increased in the trees behind his house, reminding Jimmy that there was a person out there, lost. The pain gripping his chest gradually loosened; Jimmy breathed more easily. He couldn't let this, whatever it was, interfere with his presence at the PD tonight. He did, however, lodge a thought about scheduling a visit with Dr. Stewart up to Kennebunk before too long.

Standing up, he rubbed his chest area that had hurt so. Probably heartburn, he thought. He convinced himself that he seemed okay; maybe he was just a little over-sensitive. His will to move on overcame caution. No matter what, Jimmy had to get on the road. Time was no one's friend tonight.

He opened the closet door to get his boots. They went on hard and felt tight when he laced them up. He would need them, so he ignored the discomfort and strode heavily back down the hall to the bathroom for a quick shave. He rubbed his eyes with his big, square hands, trying to snap himself out of this funk. He grabbed for the stiff towel on the hook. When he looked in the mirror, he was shocked by the puffy skin and ringed eyes in front of him. Days and months of stress, bad food, and no exercise had taken their toll. Even he could see that a change was needed—and soon. He turned away while he readied his razor. After a quick, cursory shave, Jimmy dried off.

He wondered how this would end. He knew men who lived up in the woods along the Sanford-Wells town line. Representing the law on occasion, he had been in their slipshod homes for every reason from drunken episodes to drugs and suicide attempts. He saw tonight that his home was taking on the ramshackle appearance of those cabins. The possibility that he was becoming one of these men, aging alone and getting more and more silent, set off an alarm in his head. He was grateful for the storm, grateful for the job, grateful to have someplace to go and something else to think about.

Moving back down to the kitchen door, Jimmy grabbed his bag of emergency equipment which was at the ready on the hook, and switched on the garage light; the snow was falling heavily in fierce winds. He reached for his parka, checked for his gloves, a hat, and then took a moment to remember anything else he needed to turn down or off in the house. That done, Jimmy the Cop consigned himself to what the future would unveil.

He thought about all the Christmas events that would bring people out tonight. And tomorrow, all driving would be on what were sure to be treacherous roads. These folks were counting on people like him to keep things operating. All over town, workers were packing lunches, kissing kids and wives good-bye, gearing up to plow, sand, and salt—and yes, to go on an almighty search for a lost woman.

Jimmy felt a surge of enthusiasm. This was what he was good at. He was looking forward to the welcome of the busy station tonight. As he backed the police cruiser out of the safety of his garage, he was smiling. Jimmy clicked the door closed and drove toward the ferocious sea which was already licking at the land.

CHAPTER 6

SHELTER

Drakes Island
Christmas Eve, 1999

A cramp twisting up her leg startled her awake; Pamela writhed with it until it ran its course. Disoriented from the pain, she sat up, trying to remember where she was. A roaring wind sent a surge of warning through her body. Outside the refuge of her car, she vaguely saw huge waves rise in angry, black hills, coursing powerfully down the jetty and crashing onto the parking lot only a few feet away from her. Pamela shifted her focus to the inside of her Subaru, recognizing it gratefully. In the next second, another punch of wind shook the car in its great hands. Her drowsiness cleared quickly and Pamela remembered how she'd come here. She remembered the desperate flight from Leslie's house (*had it been just this morning?*), the turnoff at Drakes Island under a flashing, yellow light, the drive down the narrow road to Jetty Beach. She intended to be home long before dark; this deepening dusk meant she had been here too long.

It was so easy this morning to grab her keys and to run to the moments of happiness she had known here. She had followed her heart, but what lured her here a few hours ago would have consequences now. Dire consequences ... Leslie, Robbie, and Paul were waiting for her on Chick's Crossing in the home they so graciously shared with her. They would be afraid for her; afraid she had retreated to a place where they couldn't reach her.

Pamela realized now that this breakout today was against the "rules" of her arrangement with Leslie and Paul. In the past when she had been in this dark place, she'd driven the perimeter of the small town in an attempt to outrun the crushing sadness, but she had always gone home again, her broken heart concealed. Today, she knew she had clearly gone too far.

Since the Eastside, someone was always watching her, waiting for signs that trouble was coming. She felt like she was under surveillance. Her need to be alone, to have time to reflect, to just be herself away from the caring but anxious eyes of her family, had brought her here. No, she couldn't put the blame for this on those dear people. She was here because of her own fear; fear that it was all too late. And the ferocious presence of this storm told her it really might be. This time she may have acted in a way that would mark the end.

Pamela's attention snapped back to winds pushing clouds of snow which were beginning to encompass the pathetic capsule of her car. Though the roads home would be treacherous, she must drive them. The keys were still in the ignition. She gave a quick twist and heard the whirring of metal, then a singular, loud *click*—and then silence. The quiet that followed screamed of unthinkable possibilities.

Pamela slumped against the seat, her head snapped back in quick despair. This couldn't be happening! Pulling herself up again abruptly, she flicked on the interior lights to check the gauges. Light responded quickly, and her hopes with it. The instrument panel blared out, telling her she had gas. But within seconds, the lights fluttered and dimmed, plunging her into an even deeper darkness. She thought hard. *What could be the problem?* she wondered. Within seconds, she understood: she had fallen asleep. The heater fan pumping full blast, she had drained the battery ....

This was bad. The miles of exposed marshland stretching between her and Route 1 paralyzed her thoughts. It would be impossible to walk that distance in these stinging winds. From her years living here, Pamela knew there were few opportunities to find shelter on the island tonight. No one stayed during winter, and even if someone was here, he or she wouldn't be out in this storm.

The car rocked violently once more, from both wind and the thundering tremor of waves filling the parking lot. The storm was intensifying and would continue; it had really just begun. Waves crashed closer still to her car, splashing up on her back windows. Frantic, Pamela sat up and grabbed the keys, turning them with all the force she could muster as if she could command the start. But still no response—just the deadened click of metal.

It was time to assess the options she had before her. No one knew she was here, miles away from Route 1. Dressed in corduroy slacks, a V-neck, and a light jacket, she wasn't prepared to be out in this weather. The storm could last days; that had happened in the past. Abandoning her car seemed the only action she could take, but actually doing it would take more courage than she believed she possessed. She wasn't ready to abandon this fortress of metal and glass for the world of sea, snow, and wind. It would be so easy to get lost in the whiteout boiling just beyond her windows.

Her mother had told stories about getting lost between the house and barn in the storms up in Prince Edward Island, when she, as a little girl, had to go to feed the animals. Her father had strung a rope from the kitchen door to the barn door for her to hold onto. Pamela would have given all her worldly goods for a rope to safety tonight.

For just a moment, Pamela wondered whether she could make it through the night by staying in the car. It would get cold, but maybe she could survive that, at least until the light of day showed her in which direction to walk. As she thought about this, another wave pounded onto the jetty, closer still. Pamela rolled the window down, hoping to see something to help with her decision. A white wedge of icy snow blew into her face on the freezing blast. She recoiled against the stinging snow, rolling the window up quickly.

The decision came to her fast; she had to get out of here, had to walk into this wild night of snow to any refuge she could find. She had put gloves and a hat in the glove box this fall when the weather turned cold, a small mercy now. She found them and put them on.

Before committing herself to leave the car, she ripped a scrap of paper from an envelope in the glove box and took a pen from her purse to write a note. If someone found her car here, she wanted them to know what she had done, although she didn't know herself what would come of her efforts. By the dim glow of the one streetlight in the lot now filling with snow, she wrote, "Whoever finds this note—battery's dead. Have gone to find shelter. Will walk out of parking lot, keep to right, away from the sea, walk to cottages. Please help! I am cold but all right. Pamela Iverson." She would leave the note on the driver's seat. Doing just this little thing made her feel less alone. That someone might find the note during the storm was only a remote possibility, but it gave her something she could actually *do*.

She said a silent prayer, zipped her jacket up, and pulled her hat over her ears. After a few deep breaths, she opened the door into a solid blast of cold wind. She shrank back when the frigid gale blew into her face, blinding her. In a swift reflex, she swung the door closed, breathing again in the relative warmth of the car. But she knew there was no other way.

Pamela opened the door again and stepped out quickly, turning her back to a phalanx of bluster that raked her clothes and threw her off balance. The wind slammed the car door shut, leaving her standing on the surface of the moon. There were no recognizable landmarks under this shifting carpet of heavy snow.

Her back to the wind, she held onto the car to keep from being blown away. Looking over the hood, she saw mountainous waves curl high and tight, then race down the massive granite stones as if they were a garden path. Hills of water surged into the parking lot, fanning out under the car, pushing her away.

A prisoner in her small circle of vision—no more than two feet in circumference—Pamela began to walk. Confused about what direction to go, she knew to keep the sea pounding at her back, to keep moving away from danger. Memories of summers here with the children flooded back as she walked; including long afternoons spent on this beach they had all loved. Templates of a life from another time, she welcomed these thoughts and used them as map to guide her tonight.

The old rotted pier among the rocks that her son used to jump from in high tide must be on her left. Thomas had named his stunt "Riding the Dragon," swimming the waves like dragon scales that glinted under the sun. She heard his laughter ring in her memory and called on those days to power her tonight as those dragon scales, the size of small buildings familiar no more, rose up behind her. But the sunlight of those summer days had given her something to reach for tonight: direction and courage. She would walk by memory. She was walking for her life.

Eyes nearly shut by biting, wind-driven snow, Pamela stepped warily, feeling the ice under the snow. She felt the angle of road descend under her feet. In her mind, she reversed the direction of her drive here this morning. Any miscalculation could lead to the endless marshes in the center of the island. When she arrived here this morning, the road had veered off to the left and up a hill, the same hill she was going down now. Suddenly, her feet gave out from under her, and she fell, sliding down into the accumulating snow that had softened her landing. As she got back on her feet, a snow-covered shape appeared ahead, huddled just off the beach at the corner of the parking lot and the road. A cottage!

She turned toward the snowy outline and stepped up her pace. As she approached the cottage, the lanyard which was snapping on the flagpole beside it, thrummed, as it was plucked by the furious gale. Scooping snow out of her eyes, she made out the stairs leading to a porch, a place out of the full force of wind. Pamela quickened her steps as the invasive cold began to penetrate her clothing. She would break into the cottage with no regard for any law.

Pamela climbed up snowy stairs on her hands and knees until the screen door stopped her. Snow had clotted in the screen, forced through by wind off the beach. She pounded and pulled at the thankfully wooden frame, assaulting it until it gave way. It opened in, and she crawled onto the porch and found a small area, pressing her body tightly against the solid wall of the house. She blessed the kindness of the wooden clapboards, which blocked the wind and eased the full force of the snowfall.

After a few minutes of rest, Pamela felt the cold seep deeper. She had stopped moving, and her body warmth was plummeting. Numbness nibbled her feet and hands. In the few minutes she had allowed, she began to feel drowsy. This was her new enemy: hypothermia. Pamela kick-started a rebuttal to its presence on the spot. "Notice details," she said aloud. "Keep awake; your life depends on it."

She thought about Leslie, about what was happening in that house up on Chick's Crossing. Anguish rose within her, quickly submerged in the wind. She cried out for the pain she was causing—had caused. And although the cry was heard by no one, it canceled any self-pity that might have cloaked her actions. She had to survive; had to call forth every ounce of energy and brains she had to stay alive. In this moment, she could either take charge and move on, or give herself up to weakness. She closed her eyes, willing herself here fully. Now—as *now* was all there was or ever would be. Again and again, she repeated to herself the details of her story: she was on the porch of a cottage on the southern coast of Maine, and she was alive. If she could stretch her courage to fit this challenge, she would be all right. She could entertain no fear, no anxiety, only presence. She asked the protection of any angel or saint available to help to give her strength and to keep her calm *now*. The prayer spiraled up with the wind.

After a few moments, calmness took over, and her fear ebbed away. In its place—in this extravagant, desperate situation—peace came from somewhere. As a child, she had been lulled to sleep at night by just such roaring winds. Ancient pines outside her bedroom had often whispered to her child's heart. They were speaking to her again now. She had the courage she needed. Pamela inched her way to the cottage door. Breaking into the house was her one purpose.

Before she took on the more solid door, she looked beyond the flimsy screening of the porch to the snarling sea foaming over dunes and headed her way. Seeing this, Pamela gave herself permission to do whatever was needed.

The kitchen door had a window. She peered in but could see nothing. Taking a few breaths, she prepared herself for the assault. She knew the penalties for breaking rules. She clearly remembered that morning in the market, the angry reproach of the Eastside's manager and the look of meanness in his eyes. She had broken the rules that day and paid dearly for it. Here she was breaking the rules again, but there was no other way to get through this vicious night.

Pamela took off her hat, wrapped it around her gloved right hand and made a fist. She jabbed strongly at the glass just above the doorknob. She had seen this done on television countless times. Tonight, it was happening for real.

The glass fractured in a webbed pattern but didn't give way. On the second blow, glass skittered both ways, out onto the icy porch and into the kitchen. Her hand still wrapped tight, she reached in gingerly, then dropped the hat and felt for the lock. Feeling it immediately, she turned it until she heard a click, and then withdrew her hand carefully.

Trusting that the door would open, she reached for the knob and turned it easily. When she put her weight behind it, it gave so quickly that the force she mustered to open it caused her to slide across the kitchen floor on shoes caked with snow and ice. She skated into the middle of the room and landed, sitting with her legs out in front of her. Her relief at being inside, even inside a frozen house, was so great that she actually felt tears. She got up off the floor, and closed the door, retrieved her hat and put it on. Then she turned back to the quiet world of this relatively safe place.

After leaning against the refrigerator for a minute to rest, she prepared to search for a source of heat. It was just possible that whoever owned this cottage had left the electricity on to heat the cottage just enough for floors and dry wall. She needed a flashlight; one couldn't be far away. People in Maine were always prepared for weather, summer or winter. She could barely make out the counter in front of her, but it looked promising. It had lots of drawers for storage. She stepped to them carefully, opening the first drawer. Taking off her other glove, she felt around and found the flashlight, where some very wise person had surmised it would be needed. She picked it up and pushed the switch, and a sword of light cut the heavy dark into pieces.

Holding the powerful wand, she peered around the room. Having just learned a lesson about batteries, she snapped the flashlight off, sending the kitchen tumbling back into the dark. "I have to use this carefully," she said aloud. "The most important thing is heat. If I can find heat, I can get through this."

Afraid to walk on the slick floor, she bent and took a moment to get the rest of the snow off her shoes. The temperature in the house was below freezing; nothing was melting. She stamped both feet on a rug by the sink and walked out onto the floor to test her stability.

Thinking about Leslie, Pamela knew she would have called the police when her mother didn't show up, but no one would have had any idea she was down on the island. She snapped the flashlight on to look at her watch. Five o'clock. She had been gone since ten this morning. There was no use thinking about the foolishness of her actions now.

Again, she tripped the switch and aimed the flashlight around the kitchen. Was it possible that the cottage owners had erred in her favor? Maybe these people came down on the odd weekend to spend time here and had left the utilities on for just such visits? Pamela prayed to every image of any saint she could dredge up for this to be so. She saw a wall plaque and moved toward it, sliding out of balance on the slippery floor again. She lurched over to grab the stove. Carefully, she reached for the switch, praying as she moved. Her hand touched the switch and pushed; she felt it engage. But nothing happened … no light. Pamela pushed the switch again and again, hoping it would work. Nothing ….

There would be a fuse box somewhere with a master switch to turn the electricity on, she thought. Though the idea of finding this box was a powerful incentive, she was afraid she was too cold to search for it just now. She would find some blankets and warm up before she went on the hunt for heat.

Moving cautiously through the cottage, she saw what might be a bedroom off the living room. Entering, she lit the flashlight, spotlighting a pile of blankets at the foot of each of a set of twin beds. This seemed an answer to her prayer. She took three blankets back to the kitchen, searching in the small circle of light for a spot that might be comfortable and secure. She wanted to be near the door in case someone passed the cottage—as unlikely as that was—given the conditions.

As she swung the light around the kitchen, the beam revealed what looked like an enclosed area, a cave between the refrigerator and the stove, with just enough space in which a person could wedge. It spoke safety, and was opposite the door through which she had broken. This protected space appealed to her, buttressed as it was on each side by the heavy appliances. She doubled up a blanket and placed it on the floor, then carefully crawled in. Next, Pamela wrapped herself in another of the three blankets, placing her precious flashlight carefully on the floor beside her. She pulled the third blanket over her shoulders and up over her head as a hood.

Once warmth began to collect, Pamela felt a profound weakness from the anxiety of her flight. In childlike submission, not thinking beyond this minute, she settled into the little refuge of blankets, safe for the time being. She knew she had to be alert for any possible rescue, but her eyes kept closing, closing; and finally, she allowed them to close completely.

Maybe a little sleep would be all right, she thought. Her body was exhausted, and her spirit, battered by the last hour's labor, wanted nothing more than to rest. Instantly, she drifted away from the dangerous present.

CHAPTER 7

WELLS POLICE DEPARTMENT

Wells, Maine
Christmas Eve, 1999

As Officer Casey drove the familiar roads to the PD, he was flying somewhere above himself, seeing the white whirligig of this Nor'easter from space—the deep effects of his dream ….

The two-lane roads of this rural area were disappearing in the now strong fall of snow; trees whirled in a familiar circular dance, the embrace of a Nor'easter. Temperatures were falling through the twenties threatening ice. Way too cold for December to his mind. His thoughts kept returning to the woman out alone in this white nowhere land. *What's she going through? Why the hell would someone be out in the teeth of a storm like this, especially on Christmas Eve?* Something wasn't right. This was too desperate an act to be an accident.

Because of his years in the PD, dangerous behaviors irked Jimmy. He was especially irritated by people who put others at risk with their lapse of judgment. It seemed irresponsible, though he felt sympathy for her all the same. No telling how this story would end, assuming they even *could* find her.

Cold air from the low pressure of the storm pinched Jimmy right through the heavy clothes he wore. This was going to be a doozy on all fronts, made more difficult because there hadn't been much advance warning.

Arriving at the parking lot behind the PD, the telltale crunch of snow under his wheels told him that snow had accumulated a lot in the hour or so since its start. He parked where he guessed his usual spot was, though he couldn't quite make it out tonight. One of the two Wells' cruisers was idling by the back entrance; the other had already gone out on some assignment. Other than that, the lot was empty. Out behind the PD, at the DOT, a queue of trucks lit like lanterns in the dark revved their engines, vying for the essential load of sand and salt. The boys would be restless tonight, jockeying to get a head start on their all-important work.

Jimmy heard a loud horn blast repeating above the wind and turned around to see Taddy Stevens standing on his truck runner, third truck in, waving to him for all he was worth. The telltale cigarette in his mouth gave him away. Jimmy chuckled in redneck collusion with his friend. Shaking their heads simultaneously, they commented without words about the blizzard, inciting excitement about the night ahead; they had been through this before. Jimmy knew Taddy—knew he loved riding out in these extreme storms, duking it out with road conditions and weather as bad as it could get. The worse the storm, the better the story it would be when they finally sat down for coffee the next day, exhausted, triumphant. Out on the road, these boys did by rote what most people couldn't do in their finest hour. This was going to be a "goddamned good old Christah'," Jimmy muttered to himself, chuckling at the absurd accent the Maine saying demanded. The wind whipped the words out of his mouth and flung them up.

The police station buzzed with waves of calls frustrating the small crew on hand. He stopped before fully entering the room to inhale the tension in the air, feeling at home. The racket of the trucks out back over howling winds died out as the door closed, and Jimmy, fully present and now awake, walked down the hall through the honeycomb of offices to Dispatch. Reports were streaming in about deteriorating conditions: accidents, disasters, lost animals. The anxiety ratcheted up with each call. This suppressed panic was music to Jimmy's ears. In the PD, he always knew what to do next.

The boys who worked the PD knew who lived in what neighborhood, knew it was crucial to communicate with the people, help them stay safe on awful nights like these. The most demanding sector of town was where the rich out-of-staters lived. They were always quick to demand entitlement for the hefty taxes they paid. Jimmy surmised they not so secretly wished they could build a wall between themselves and Route 1, a wall that would shut out tourists, beach-goers, and traffic from the public parking lots.

He'd had to officiate a few times when the residents actually put up "Private" signs on *public* streets, just to keep people from driving down "their" roads. Once, after Jimmy had taken down these signs, he had been warned that "they" weren't above forcing a court case for exclusive rights to the beach if *things* didn't suit them. Jimmy had seen people with icy stares challenge folks simply for driving on public streets: *Just what are you doing here?* The egalitarian soul of this cop stepped up and glared back, wearing some authority. It was lucky that most of this breed couldn't make it through the long, cold Maine winters. By the end of November, they closed their fifteen-room, forty-window, five-door "cottages" and headed south to even larger houses. They weren't Jimmy's favorite citizens.

The merchants up on Route 1—businesses stretching from the town line of Kennebunk on the north side to Ogunquit on the south—were another group. They were middle class, living comfortably, welcoming to tourists and visitors, and encouraged folks to frequent their shops. Tonight they would be concerned about plowed parking lots and sanded sidewalks. They needed to be up and running, open the day after Christmas for the post-holiday sales. They usually got on fine with the police force, since they needed them in many practical ways.

Wells Highlands, Jimmy's neighborhood, was nestled northwest of Route 1; a residential district, housing middle to lower-class families. Zoned for agricultural use, there were small farms, subdivisions, small homes, plus one small golf course at Merryland Farms. For the most part, people who lived up there were descendants of the original Wells families who sold their land on and near the beaches years ago, when ocean-view real estate offered more money than those folks had ever even thought possible. In the early history of the coastal plains, living on the beach, or even near it, meant you were poor … from "fisher folk." Things had changed.

Jimmy knew people from his neighborhood would take the prudent course and stay home tonight. He could count on their patience and reasonableness. He was proud to come from the Highlands himself. His folks moved up there right after he was born, selling the beach house they'd inherited from his grandparents to buy a small cape.

Jimmy had grown up with these long-standing families; his high school buddies had come from among them, and even today these friends were still around. Taddy Stevens over at DOT had been his friend all along, and being on duty with him tonight gave Jimmy the sense of belonging that he desperately needed after the dislocation he still felt after waking from that dream. Just thinking about it brought back the dizzy feeling of flying. He couldn't give it much attention here, though. Here, he had to be on solid ground to do his work.

Shaking it off, he picked up a mug, and poured from the eternal pot in the dayroom. He needed to prepare himself for the concentration his work would demand tonight. Fully entering the chaos of Dispatch, he settled near Farrell, listening to the back-and-forth of storm talk streaming in. Accidents on untreated roads around town were piling up. A few officers, already out in the area tonight, were registering that they were overwhelmed by the conditions. In the storm saga on the air, a rescue vehicle in progress up to Biddeford was trying to assist a Christmas Eve baby who had decided to be born into the world up on 9B.

Jimmy listened to silence as much as to words; silence between words held meaning in itself. He'd studied radio communications as far back as his badge in the Boy Scouts. Then he'd gone on to learn Morse code in his police academy training, parsing the "dits" and "dahs," translating semaphore, police scanner codes; he had learned them all. As a kid, he'd loved secret languages—loved having something no other kid had— something that singled him out as capable in his own way in the crushing isolation of being a teenager and a Wells Maine redneck.

Tonight, here in the dim, littered office, the words of the last transmission that had ever used Morse code came to him. Issued in 1997, it was spoken by an officer of the French Navy. As he prepared for this night ahead, dots and dashes floated in front of him, and he translated that message silently, to himself. *Calling all: this is our last cry before eternal silence.* The words circled in his mind as he sat watching Farrell at the board. Suddenly he remembered the lost woman out there in the blizzard somewhere. *Last cry before eternal silence?* A chill passed through him. He sat up, preparing to take over for Farrell with renewed purpose and energy.

As though Farrell could read Jimmy's thoughts, he wheeled around and stood up to give him his seat as he approached. "Jimmy, the real crisis is the missing person. She left home this morning, lives up on Chick's Crossing with her daughter and family, said she was going out for a few gifts but hasn't been seen or heard from since."

With this declaration, Farrell bent toward Jimmy, looked around the small space for anyone listening in, and added in a whisper, "Her daughter confided in us that her mother, Pamela Iverson—that's her name—has been distressed for a while now. Distressed to the *extreme*.... Actually, she was banned from a supermarket down in Rhode Island for loitering. She got kicked out about a year ago and has been living with her daughter since. She seemed to be doing all right until today. That means, Officer Casey, we don't know what the hell we're dealing with."

Jimmy snapped his head up and whirled in the seat when he heard this. "Jesus, Farrell, this is what I was afraid of. We could be dealing with a suicide here, a person out of hope and lookin' for something like this storm to help them out. And we are already in emergency operations because of the blizzard, goddamn it! We can't waste any time. Someone'll have to go up to Chick's Crossing and get a clearer picture of how crazy this woman really is."

Farrell, already knowing there was no one else who could accomplish this tonight, looked back at him and asked, "You up for it, Jimmy?"

"Jesus Christ," Jimmy began, "I'm begging off that one, Farrell .... This woman is endangering everyone who gets involved in this rescue. She's spent no time thinkin' about how her family will get through all this. I don't think I'm the guy to send up there; they aren't likely to enjoy my view of things. I'd do better taking over for you. Where the hell are we supposed to find her anyway? Talk about a needle in a snow bank! She must be from away." The Maine joke about not being born in state didn't even bring a smile tonight.

Farrell saw right away that Jimmy wouldn't be the one to send out as a representative of the Wells police in a situation as sensitive as this one. He couldn't leave the phones himself until he thought Jimmy was settled in for the night's protocol, so he rang the chief to ask for someone to assist him out to Chick's Crossing. That call made, he connected with the truck crews heading out on the roads. He tapped a pencil in nervous counterpoint while he waited for the maintenance dispatcher to answer. Spikey Tolman picked up at the barn.

"Spikey, we got a missing woman tonight ... you boys keep your eyes open for a Subaru Outback, year 1994, dark blue. Pamela Iverson, fifty-five years old, used to live around here in Kennebunk, so she knows something about the roads. No explaining what the hell she's doing out in this weather. Been gone for over seven hours now. Best scenario, she is stuck somewhere, maybe taken shelter with someone, maybe not, but any of those scenarios could be a disaster tonight. Worst case is she might want to check out, and this is how she's decided to do it. Keep your eyes out for her when you plow; she left home to go shopping." In response to Spikey's disbelief, Farrell quipped, "Yeah, right, right... OK. Now, pay attention. That Subaru won't show up in the dark, but snow will help. License plate is Maine registration, 4142 RAF. We've got someone going up to her home to get more information from her family—that'll help; I'll send it over as soon as I get it. Your drivers have to be my eyes and my ears. Next time you call in, Jimmy's going to be on Dispatch."

Whatever Spikey shot back was insulting enough to make Farrell laugh, but he still kept one nervous eye on Jimmy to see if he had heard. After a few more inquiries about accidents already on the board, Farrell hung up. Rescue operations in any small town were networked between all departments, from the plow crews to EMT rescue personnel, to the guys who actually had to get out and shovel. Success depended on all of them cooperating; each guy was as important as the next tonight.

The young officer hung up and stood stretching, his slim body causing Jimmy a moment of envy of the kid and disgust for his condition. Farrell hoped to go home to his wife and young son waiting for him on Harrisecket Road.

Sensing Farrell's need to be released and head out, Jimmy said, "Okay, kid, get out of here. Go on home to Sandy." He playfully elbowed the young cop out of his way, picked up the earphones, and settled them on his head. He dialed the state police, and while he waited for them to answer, he opened a notepad and uncapped a pen. As an afterthought, Jimmy covered the receiver and asked Farrell to stay at the board until he could make a run up to the diner for food. He had to promise the now-off-duty officer a cup of coffee and some blueberry pie for the favor, but the bribe worked. Farrell agreed, adding that Jimmy had better not take too long.

When the call connected, Jimmy was ready: "Merry Christmas to all you poor bastards on duty tonight. This is Jimmy Casey down here in Wells." He waited for the reply and laughed when it came. "Is Trooper Conner on the road tonight? Is anyone crazy enough to be on the road tonight?" he asked. "What's going on down there?" After waiting for what seemed like a long time, he began to sputter. "Shit, you guys, I am serious! We got an emergency MP bulletin coming out. Is Conner in the station?" he demanded a second time. When Conner came to the phone, Jimmy spat out, "Conner, listen up. We got a missing person down here." At this he put his hand over the speaker and directed a question to Farrell. "What the hell is her name?"

Farrell picked up the pad, quickly wrote the details of the missing woman, reached over, and placed it in front of Jimmy.

"Name's Pamela Iverson, fifty-five years old, widow, lives up on Chick's Crossing with her daughter, Leslie Collins. She left the house to go shopping this morning around ten and hasn't been seen since. Seems to be some doubt about her mental state. That fact could change everything. Family has no friggin' idea where she is, but with almost everything closed for Christmas Eve, she doesn't have much of a choice for refuge 'cept a gas station or something. License plate's Maine registration, 4142 RAF,

Subaru, dark blue. I'll fax the rest of the details to you boys as soon as we get them from the family. She could be anywhere, and with this storm looking like it's going to howl for a while, we have our work cut out for us by this blizzard."

Jimmy listened as Conner, broadcasting on his scanner, spread the word up to Portland. As he listened, he did some inner calculations about the woman's chances. Jimmy could see that Pamela Iverson wouldn't make it through the night unless she found shelter. He paused briefly, and then continued: "Yep, we got the number for the family. Name's Collins. Leslie Collins, up on Chick Crossing Road." The phone number passed from one to another, and the circle of rescuers widened.

Jimmy hung up and handed the headset back to Farrell. He stood to stretch himself, but remembering what shape he was in compared to Farrell, he stopped himself. He was suddenly hungry—very hungry—and wanted food before the night's work began.

Before leaving, Jimmy walked on down the hallway to the chief's office and peered in as he leaned on the doorjamb. Chief Hooper didn't see Jimmy right away. He was just sitting at his desk, head in hands, looking glumly out at the snow that occluded his window on to Route 1. Traffic lights swinging over the junction of 99 and Route 1 switched in two-minute intervals from green, to yellow, to red, suffusing the falling snow with bright, seasonal colors. Lost in thought, the chief's dismal manner proclaimed the fact that going home for Christmas Eve with his family was out of the question. He would be a champion of public safety tonight; here for the duration of whatever Mother Nature had to throw at them.

In spite of the blue mood in the chief's office, Jimmy dared a comment. "Merry friggin' Christmas, Chief … and many happy returns, you old sea biscuit."

The man jumped a bit at the irreverent greeting, swiveled in his chair, and smiled. "Hey Jimmy, glad we got you to come in. It's shaping up to be a wild one… Farrell clue you in about the missing woman?" he asked.

"Yep, I'm yours for the night Chief, you lucky bugger. I'm going down to the diner for some supper before they close. Guess it won't hurt to pass on the word about this woman. You got any theories about where she could be?"

"The possibilities are endless, Jimmy, and none of them are good. She could have slid off the road, run out of gas, had a heart attack, or worse. We don't know where to begin, but tell Farrell to post a bulletin on the airwaves stat, okay? We are definitely going to have some storm surge from high tide around midnight. God, I hope she's not anywhere near that."

"He's posting the bulletin now, and I already called the state troopers. Anything special you want, Chief? I know you're in for the evening. Your wife's not going to be too damn pleased about that, I bet."

The chief sighed and nodded. "Doesn't matter, Jimmy. Doesn't matter a damn. You're right; wife isn't pleased at all. In fact, she's pissed. Bring me a sandwich and some pie. Surprise me. We got work to do here. Welcome aboard and merry friggin' Christmas to you too. And by the way Jimmy, thanks for coming in. I got a little somethin' to make a toast when we make it through the night." With that, the chief patted his top drawer and grinned.

"I wouldn't be surprised if we need it *before* the night's over." The two men laughed companionably, both turning back to their tasks, feeling the crisis deepening as night descended.

Jimmy retraced his steps, put on his winter gear again, and left the station by the back door. The spinning white snow blinded him for a second; even he felt unsure which way to walk to his car.

The thought of her, the Iverson woman, out there alone and what she might be facing became a 3-D image as he looked around. His senses reeled with the impact. It was getting to him; there was sure to be terror up on Chick's Crossing. Unused to prayers, he offered a homemade request: "Jesus," he uttered, "you better send some help down here tonight, birthday or no. This lady is in danger. We all pray to put us in her path—or her in ours, either way...."

With the makeshift entreaty released, Jimmy raised a mittened hand and scooped snow off the windshield. He then cleaned the back and side windows, got into his car, and drove up Route 1 to the neon-lit oasis of the Maine Diner.

Part Three

CHAPTER 8

THE MAINE DINER

Wells, Maine
Christmas Eve, 1999

The neon rim of the diner clock spun color into the dim room; tints of red, blue, and green pooled on plates like gravy. Along the counter, folks talked amongst themselves in subdued conversation, the excitement of this Christmas Eve's storm gathering momentum. People here read skies, knew that the color and heft of clouds were heralds of particular weather. They knew this approaching storm would be one that postponed holiday events. A marker storm: The Blizzard of 1999, a Christmas Eve to be remembered for years. Lots of folks went out for dinner whenever natural events like this approached.

Ed LaCasse was already thinking about his drive home on treacherous island roads that ran parallel to the sea. He glanced toward the always opening door to see that the snowfall had increased. This storm would bring discomfort—even danger—on their heads, but the people of Wells wouldn't be intimidated; they had built lives and friendships around difficulty. Tonight there were neighbors to shovel out and check on, cars to rescue, and power outages to deal with. Yes, tonight would be a night to draw close. In this sea town, people endured this hardship for the privilege of living on the edge of the blue Atlantic highway.

With his acute professional hearing skills honed in the Coast Guard, Ed sensed a lull in conversation cresting around him; the loud clink of dishes filled up the small space. He touched the leather of his long-lost old coat, bemused. It was as thin and creased as his aging skin. He shrugged deeper into it. He was surprised to be wearing it, since he had thought it long gone.

Ed turned on his stool to watch folks around him chatting about plans for Christmas the next day. The fragrance of the famous food here made him hungry. The offerings at the Maine Diner featured real New England cooking at its best: lobster stew, blueberry muffins, baked beans, chicken pie, lobster pie, pot roast, all accompanied with rich coffee or the occasional glass of wine.

The scent from his old jacket overrode aromas of food for a moment. Instead of finding the scent offensive, Ed found the mothball fragrance reassuring. This jacket would keep him from the cold tonight as it had done for many years on the ships he'd sailed. But that wasn't why he had chosen it. Tonight, this fragment of other days reminded him that he had lived other lives, been to other places, and known other people. Tonight, Ed needed to remember that he wasn't the singular person he seemed to be at this counter, a man who could lose track of whole days at time. After Sarah's death, Ed held to the well-etched routines of the life they had lived together. He tried to pretend he wasn't lost without her. Tonight he was ready to concede that he was losing that fight.

The aging Coast Guard officer looked back at the menu, his blue eyes scanning the appetizing lists, even though he knew them by heart. He had decided what he would order before he left home. Now he patiently waited for Darnice to notice him as she ran between her overcrowded tables. The skeleton crew on for the holiday had been overwhelmed by diners who came through the door in droves. Everyone wanted to eat out when a storm pushed up the coast, needed a last chance to see neighbors and connect in the anticipation before the white lid of snow came down.

Dusk had fallen on Route 1; the day was gone. Ed, trapped in his forgotten life without the energy to escape his age, sat at the counter, watching the white curtain of snow fall outside of the windows. Though the winter solstice had happened a few days ago, it would be months before the early dark of winter rebounded in spring's advance. Tonight was the waiting period. The *stasis:* no gain, no loss in the amount of daylight; a moment when movement stopped, but only for a moment. Nothing stayed the same for long.

As he waited for Darnice, memory took the reins from the present. From Ed's attic of memories, the scenery of the diner wavered, thinned, and Sarah was there, brushing her hair, letting it fall in a mahogany cascade over her shoulders. Smiling courageously across the dinner table at him, she transformed as he watched her from the young girl he'd adored in the beginning of their forty years together to the middle-aged wife of organization and thrift she had become. Sarah, his suffering companion, was here—Sarah; who needed him beside her in the deep disappointment of her last days. She was, in the end, most familiar and beloved as the Sarah of pain and courage, enduring all her suffering patiently until her death. In this last vision, the space of her absence expanded in his chest until he couldn't breathe. With no children and few friends, his road ahead stretched dark and desolate, like Route 1 under the threat of tonight's storm. He gasped for breath and forced himself away from these thoughts.

A familiar voice from above him offered connection. "Ed, I'd better get to you 'fore they quit in the kitchen. No one's gonna stay here long tonight. Know what you want?"

Looking up, Ed gazed into the warm eyes of Darnice, comfortable Darnice—Ed's favorite here. Darnice served compassion along with coffee. Tonight she wore a headband sporting deer antlers with bells. The mighty effort of keeping her customers in chowder, biscuits, and coffee had left her dark hair in ringlets around her cheerful face. The gray stealing in at her temples gave her the distinction of modest age. She was positively glowing in the steamy room. Though girls here dated customers, Darnice hadn't. A single mom for years, she was more conservative than the younger women. Over the years, she and Ed had shared laughs and a few good talks. He felt she knew more about him than most folks except Jimmy Casey, and he felt he knew her as well.

Speaking with the peculiar dialect of this region, a requirement in the diner, broad *ahh's* peppered her greeting. One could not be from "away" and feel totally at home here. Still standing in front of Ed, coffeepot angled over his cup, a concerned expression lighting her hazel eyes as she asked, "How about a bite to go with the coffee?" When she received no response, she frowned a little and said, "Ed ... you listenin' to me?" With her insistence, he sputtered his assent, and his trance mercifully passed.

No one knew, but tonight marked the twenty-second anniversary of the departure of the boy Darnice had married. He left his young family and his life with her behind on Christmas Eve. How he could have gone— this night of all nights—with two babies waiting for Daddy to come home, had been the question of her life so far. She had to deal with that memory every year, especially on the night itself. When she allowed herself to look back, which wasn't often, she didn't recognize the naïve girl she had been in those days. Tonight, a forty-two-year-old woman about to be an empty nester, Darnice was still living in her mother's home; the home to which she had run for refuge when he left.

She hid her sadness under a patina of being cheerfully "busy" until it had become the truth. She had worked a collection of jobs that kept her and her children in necessities, adding whatever she could to her mother's income. Darnice was proud of her kids and her life, thankful. Tonight she would take the short ride up to Stephen Eaton Lane after work, as she did most nights; the children and her mother would be waiting for her with dinner and the bright tree. It was enough.

Darnice had known Ed for as long as she'd worked here at the diner, knew there wasn't much more than his little cottage down on the island waiting for him. She had known Sarah as well, remembered when she died a gathering stack of years ago. Here at the counter now, sensing his loneliness, she took the time to offer a smile and pat his hand as she waited for his reply.

Ed repaid her gesture with a smile of his own, then replied, "How about some lobster stew, a few muffins, and that lonely piece of chocolate cake over there." He gestured toward the gleaming display column of the diner's celebrated desserts. "How's about I do it a favor ... unless you're saving it for Santa?" Ed's voice reassured him; allowed him to remember who and where he was. Before Darnice could answer, the door opened, seasonal jingle bells ringing above the hum of conversation.

Darnice looked up to see Jimmy Casey entering out of the storm, a gust of snowy wind wrapped around him. Everyone knew Jimmy: a native of Wells, he was the epitome of the good cop, devoted to justice in the community, true to his word, courageous in the line of duty, and very much a Maine son. Those who knew him called out greetings with a few friendly insults. Jimmy raised his hand in acknowledgment as he headed toward the counter and his friend Ed, whom he had spotted from the door.

Darnice had waited on Jimmy for years, knew him as well as she knew the whole cast of characters here at the diner. In a small town like Wells, folks' lives followed paths that intersected at points here and there. Jimmy's divorce had caused gossip when it happened, especially because he was a police officer, but that was years ago now. Since then, he had emerged as a personality on his own. Darnice and Jimmy had seen each other by default at restaurants, and at town events that came and went in a yearly circuit: Chili Fest, the Christmas Parade, concerts down at the Wells Harbor gazebo, town meetings; all the usual venues where small-town life happened. It was probable that they had noticed time change them both from afar without special interest.

Tonight, as Jimmy proceeded toward the counter in a slow advance, stopping from table to table, talking about the storm, it felt to Darnice as if he were some hero, arriving in the nick of time. She stood a little straighter as he approached, suddenly worrying that the antlers she was wearing looked silly.

Jimmy looked up to find the two friends watching him. He waved and called for Ed to save him a seat. As he did, he was caught off guard by Darnice's unspoken attention, a welcome that felt warm. Jimmy stopped at a few tables on his way, exchanging greetings and jokes while she and Ed watched. A wake of laughter floated behind him as he moved forward. Darnice became uncomfortable. She could see how alike they were, she and Jimmy; both had started life in hope but had been damaged by disappointment. Their lives were shadows of what they had hoped for.

Arriving at the counter, he unbuttoned his coat, took off his hat and gloves, and sat, smiling first at Ed, and then looking up at Darnice. She was regarding him intently, dared a moment's gaze into the man's eyes, coffeepot still in her hand. The blind she erected for her customers was breached. She felt exposed. Though this cop had walked into the diner hundreds of times—in all weathers and seasons—tonight, the honesty between them brought rising tears to her eyes

For Jimmy, his eyes met hers, and the gaze locked between them with the power of radar. He was dizzy in her attention, his internal balance shifted. And in that moment, the dream flight of just hours ago zoomed into his thoughts. The same marvelous weightlessness flashed through him, spinning Jimmy off kilter. He dropped his eyes, and took a few breaths before he dared lift them again. When he did, Darnice was still there, eyes intent and open. Jimmy felt she had seen something in him he wasn't aware of, something new, fresh. His feelings churning, he silently questioned himself about the power of this moment: why so powerful? With that question, a shift took him over like a deep breath—like a window opening. Light flooded in, and he began to laugh for no reason.

The moment continued to roll out like a movie: two minutes, three …. It continued between the two actors at the counter as no one spoke. Ed felt the emotional disturbance from where he sat and wondered silently what was going on. But being Ed, he kept quiet. And still, here they were: Darnice with the coffeepot, and Jimmy looking up at her as if he wanted to say something—but couldn't remember what.

Jimmy was the first to force himself away from the paralysis of the moment, his embarrassment bottoming out. He wished he had taken more time to prepare himself for tonight, of all nights. To cover his discomfort, he turned to look at Ed, greeting him. "Merry Christmas," he began, hoping that somewhere in talking to his friend he would remember who he was. He went on, speaking too loudly, "You old bugger. Merry Christmas and Happy Blizzard to you!"

Darnice, confused and flushed, broke out of her part of the trance to swing into action. The coffeepot she held gave her a clue about what to do; she backed up automatically, grasped an empty mug for the coffee Jimmy would undoubtedly order, and then poured.

When he looked up to acknowledge the coffee, Jimmy found her gaze disabling his senses. After the cold, dark drive up here, this Darnice-spell felt like stepping into a patch of sunlight; he let himself stretch into it, smiling. The silent, intense connection of the two resumed. It was a minute or two before Jimmy could stop looking at her. He retreated to the comfort of stirring his coffee. The spell momentarily broken, Darnice turned away to fill filters with fresh coffee, even though it was very nearly closing time.

"Darnice ...." Her name came out of the small delivery window, and she moved to collect her orders from the kitchen. As she passed, Jimmy forced his courage up and spoke to her. "Darnice, darling ...." The term, one he had never had a problem saying to her before, sounded so dangerous now, it took his breath away and made her blush. He wanted to tell her he had a "to-go" order, but when she looked at him, plates of food in her hands and a smile playing on her delightful lips, he forgot what he wanted to say. Then ... the enchantment started all over again.

Jimmy, trying to normalize the moment, said, "Jesus, Darnice, don't you know 'nough to go home? Or is this home? It's the only place I see you." In trying to sound normal, he'd flubbed it up terribly.

"You come here for some other reason than to insult me?" Darnice shot back, knowing that what was said wasn't what was meant. All the 'real' talking between them was being done with their eyes.

Ed, part of this confusion, took pity on the two friends, stepping in gently to remind Darnice about his order. "Don't forget my stew. You people are likely to close up any minute, and I'll be skunked. There's not much down at the cottage to keep me going for the duration of this storm."

Jimmy echoed Ed's order for lobster stew and added a slice of blueberry pie; then he tried again. "Darnice, the crew down't the station will need some food for the storm watch tonight. Gonna be a bitch." Not one to watch his language, he regretted it now. The word sounded clumsy in his own ears. He tried to amend them quickly. "Sorry 'bout that, Darnice. When you get a breather, I've got a to-go order ... keep the police happy tonight. Thanks, darlin'." And again, the once-familiar and comfortable term bit him with its implied intimacy. They were both blushing now, but Darnice managed a response.

"Sure, Jimmy, I'll be right back."

Darnice walked away to deliver her orders; Jimmy turned to Ed only to see his amusement at the last few minutes forming a question in his eyes. To ward off what he had no answer for, Jimmy hurried to change the subject; his duty to inform folks about the missing woman becoming very important. He stood up and signaled for the attention of the whole diner, his booming voice overriding the conversations in the room.

"Listen up folks. I'm Jimmy Casey, representing the Wells PD. We have a missing person: a woman's out in this Christer of a storm. Left home this morning around ten on a last-minute sprint for a few gifts, so she said, but hasn't been seen since. Last her family knows, she was going downtown for a few minutes, but that was over seven hours ago. They have no damned idea where she is. If it wasn't for the weather, nobody'd be so worried, but Jesus H. Christ"—the dispatcher was warming up— "Goddammed Christmas shopping on this night and in a storm? She must be crazy to spit in this wind. We'd appreciate it if you spread the word. No tellin' where she is, but if you see anything out of the ordinary, get to us at the station."

After his announcement, the diner was quiet for a few minutes, folks digesting the news Jimmy had given them. Slowly, diners turned back to their companions, speaking in softer tones. Though he was regarded fondly (more or less) for his outrageous humor and language, Jimmy's presence and experience always commanded attention. His aggressive and usually successful way of handling trouble was welcome. He had become an impresario of the airwaves at forty-six: the Howard Stern of Southern Maine. He'd even been written up in the *York County Coast Star*, the local newspaper, as a coastal "character;" an honor he staunchly disavowed.

The exhausted kitchen crew of three peered out of the small window opposite the counter, listening to Jimmy's announcement. There was concern on their faces as well as on Darnice's. She stared at Jimmy again, and in her warm attention, everyone else in the room faded away. Her eyes seemed to see right through him, spawning emotions he didn't trust. This wasn't the way he was comfortable being with people, this flush of warmth. When he finished his news brief, he turned to Ed to steady himself.

After a few minutes, Darnice returned with their food and set their orders in front of them, making sure they had plenty of butter for their muffins, crackers for the stew, and fresh coffee. Then she moved off quickly to attend to her last customers of the night. The steaming bowls of stew simmered in front of them, too hot just yet for digging in. They lifted chunks of lobster and potatoes from the creamy broth, blowing to cool them, watching the fragrant steam rise. This was food up to the task ahead: hardy, savory, warming … a celebratory meal in the finest Maine tradition. The customary blueberry-corn muffin, buttery and warm, would sop up the juices to the end. Ed and Jimmy ate in companionable silence.

Her orders taken care of, Darnice returned to get Jimmy's to-go list. He got lost in his words a few times while he ordered, but stayed fairly steady. The list of sandwiches, pies, and hot coffee put in to the kitchen, she leaned on the counter beside the men as they finished their food, listening to Jimmy expand on the details of the rescue effort. Darnice empathized with the woman immediately. Her tender feelings about this—on the anniversary of being abandoned—made her sorry for anyone in pain.

Jimmy talked about the particulars, and the vicious conditions someone could be in out there in this cauldron of weather. Sleet, high winds, whiteout potential, high seas, snowdrifts: a person could go off the road up on the Highlands, slide into the woods, and not be seen for days.

The two men understood each other without words. Ed knew Jimmy was telling him the details because, with his training, he might be able to help in the effort if it came to that. Ed asked Jimmy questions, clarifying the details in his mind. "What kind of car was she driving? Was she dressed for this storm? Do they know that, at least? Who put out the missing person's call?"

Jimmy took a few sips of his coffee before replying. "She's drivin' one of those foreign cars." As he spoke, it occurred to him that he should make these details public as well. He turned to the diner crowd again, stood up, and rapped on his glass with a spoon. Alerted by the sound, the talk died out, replaced again by uneven quiet. The clank of dishes in the kitchen stopped as well. Only the roaring of the wind outside continued under Jimmy's strong voice.

"Okay, people, when you leave here, keep your eyes peeled for a Subaru Outback, license plate Maine 4142 RAF, dark blue, which will be damned hard to see tonight. We're pretty sure it's gotta be somewhere close around town. Woman driving is Pamela Iverson, mid-fifties, fair condition … had some hard times lately, some preexisting conditions, and she may be distressed. Ahh … really upset, if you get my meaning. Call us down to headquarters, 646-0012, or 911 if you need to. She has got to be found. We don't have a full staff tonight, and we need every person we can to be on the lookout. Spread the news; keep your eyes open. Okay? If you don't know me, I'm Jimmy Casey. If you call the station, I'll probably be answerin' the phone." Jimmy sat back down.

The hum of conversation picked up again, people nodding their willingness to be of help. Many, including Ed, wrote her name and the license number down on napkins. They had heard the plea for help; they would keep an eye out for the woman as best they could.

Jimmy asked Darnice for his "to-go" order and just a little more coffee; any excuse to put off going up the road and leaving this warm place.

Before he left, Ed leaned toward Jimmy with a question. "What's that bit about 'had some hard times lately'? What the hell does that mean? Sounds like there's something you aren't telling us."

Jimmy looked at Ed and thought for a moment. This was where knowing the people you lived with counted. He could trust Ed with what Farrell had told him. "Seems this woman was almost arrested in Rhode Island a few months ago for loitering and alleged theft. Had to move up here with her daughter in a family 'asylum' situation. You know … surveillance … lady gone nutty is the picture I get. So there could be more to it than just being lost … maybe ran away, or worse. Don't say anything to anyone … I don't have a Christly clue what's behind it all." He stood to leave, taking out his wallet to pay up, and then put a generous tip under his cup.

Darnice was waiting at the cash register and took his money. When she gave him change, she took and held his hand along with his attention. Leveling a direct look to him, she said, "Jimmy, anyone out in this storm tonight is in real danger, and that includes you. Be careful yourself. Wells would never be the same without you. You're an important part of us here." While she said these words, her confidence wavered, but she kept her eyes open to his. "Tonight's going to be a long one, Jimmy. Check in early when we open after Christmas ... I want to know you're all right. If I can be of any help, you know where I live up on Stephen Eaton Lane. I'll be there."

Jimmy teetered on the edge of saying something he couldn't remember how to say. He wasn't used to this flushed feeling around his heart; her words left him unwilling to go into the night, unwilling to leave the place where he could see her. But the press of time away from responsibilities prodded him hard. Again, the two stood face-to-face for another minute of pleasant confusion. People approached the register with checks and cash in hand, but shuffled around and backed away, willing to wait their turn after whatever was going on. After all, this *was* Christmas Eve.

Darnice broke the spell first, lowering her eyes and turning back to the register. Jimmy had no recourse then but to turn and go. He put on his hat and moved toward the door.

Ed watched from his seat, marveling at the events of the last few minutes. He was stunned by being a witness to the impossible, at least *improbable*, happening before his eyes. Jimmy just wasn't that kind of guy. Just before he went out of the door, Jimmy looked over at Ed, who blessed him with a grin that spoke much. Jimmy acknowledged this with a wave. All he knew was that he would definitely be back here early on the twenty-sixth, and until then, he would wait anxiously for time to pass.

The meanness of the storm assaulted him as the door closed behind him, deepening his wish to stay here. Jimmy felt a freshness, a warmth— and he wanted more. Had her smile been as personal as it felt? Was it really him she was speaking to? He was going to have to do something about his weight and the way he looked. He might join the gym. Maybe he had just needed some attention tonight—so much so that he had imagined what had happened; or at least imagined it meant something.

These thoughts were whirling in his head when he opened the door to his car. He placed the take-out bundle on the passenger seat and pulled the keys out from under the floor mat. When he looked up, accumulated snow on the windshield blocked his sight. No wipers would be up to the job. He muttered a good-natured complaint and got back out into the weather. Using his large gloved hand, he swept the snow off. It fell to the ground in soft mounds. When he got back in the car, the smell of the food sent him off again, marveling in the glow of what he might hope.

Driving along, Jimmy replayed the scene over and over again: Darnice smiling at him, her hand in his…. Was this making him dizzy, or was it just the swirling snow?

He was glad to be going to the station; he needed to feel connected after that interlude, more than ever. All those pleasant thoughts flew out the window when he remembered the missing person, Pamela Iverson. The sharp contrast between his excitement and her peril cleared his head.

The radio played familiar holiday music. Traveling Route 1 slowly, Jimmy journeyed to his past; through his personal landscape down the long line of Christmas Eves behind him. There were only tatters left; childhood images … toys, a tree, and his mother.

Darnice's raid on his heart tonight had upset his comfortable oblivion. With one touch of her hand, his armor had failed. His mother was gone now, and he hadn't been in touch with his brother for years. Harry had moved out of state early on in Jimmy's career, and though Jimmy knew where he was, he hadn't visited and had never written to him. "Let's face it," he said aloud, "I'm embarrassed about who I am and what I have let myself become."

Jimmy let himself admit that Harry had tried to be in touch at the beginning, when he first moved away. He had even called. But Jimmy hadn't responded. In the middle of this slow train of thought, he heard the Downeaster sculling through woods on tracks parallel to Route 1. "Even in this weather?" he said aloud. "I guess folks have to keep trying to get where they are going."

Darnice's touch opened a door Jimmy had locked long ago. Anything could happen now … and then, it did. When he saw the monarchs, his foot came off the pedal. He blinked, pulling up to full attention, and let the car roll to a stop in the empty road. Jimmy peered into the mesmerizing snow. The fragile creatures were etched on dark air, backlit by headlights; bursts of pure color, swirling orange and yellow. They circled directly under the cone of light dropping from the Drakes Island's turnoff signal light. Somehow, in spite of powerful winds, they stayed in formation, swarming in front of his car in air that should have frozen them.

Jimmy watched for some time; he didn't know how long. He could come up with no explanation; this was foreign territory. Even if this had been one of the wonders of the world, which it assuredly was, after a long vigil, there was nothing else he could do but move on down the road. As this thought entered his mind, the butterflies rose in a gust and shot off down Drakes Island Road, disappearing into the dark.

Jimmy still sat, watching where they disappeared to, wondering about the how and why of what he had seen. There was no answer, and he wasn't going to chase a cloud of butterflies into the storm. He searched his rearview mirror as he moved ahead, looking to see if any trace remained. Only the dim of the signal light was visible, and even that was quickly swallowed up by the snow.

Looking for some answers, Jimmy made an internal audit of what he'd had to drink and eat over the last few hours. He thought about sharing this experience with the guys at the station … but, no way. He laughed aloud. Who would believe such a thing? He would never hear the end of it. The police station wasn't the place to announce that Tinker Bell lives. He decided to say nothing and be safe.

Within ten minutes, he turned into the lot and parked. Retrieving the still warm food, he inched his way toward the station door, the wonder from the events of this night holding him tight. This was proving one for the books. Opening the door awkwardly, he mused on the happenings of the last hour and muttered, "Jesus, Christmas Eve miracles everywhere." And he wasn't thinking of butterflies in snow.

CHAPTER 9

HOMEWARD BOUND

Maine Diner
Christmas Eve, 1999

The diner dimmed when Jimmy closed the door behind him. Most customers had left in the last half hour, but Ed sat still at the counter full of envy for Jimmy and his work tonight. With nothing but the meager commitments and tasks needed to live his life, Ed's life felt invisible beside the lives of others. He was still sharp, could decipher and phrase code as rapidly as ever, and had kept himself current in radio developments, but it was clear he wasn't needed these days. Always a strong man, he'd felt his physical strength slipping too. He walked the beach and neighboring streets every now and then, took care of the little house that was all he had in the world, but years of inactivity were telling on him. He might as well sign on to bag groceries down at Hannaford's Market for all the good his Coast Guard training was doing him.

Ed had loved his work. Barely touching the radio dial, he'd heard people think and speak all over the world. He saw a world made of energy shimmering in the airwaves. He understood words floating in air; deciphered emotion and meaning within tempo and tone. With Morse code and semaphore as specialties, Ed could still feel the signal flags in his hands sometimes. Sometimes, on the wind-raked beach of Drakes Island, his arms automatically rose to form the geometric arcs, writing letters confidently; he imagined someone could read him on passing ships. But all that didn't make much difference tonight as the minutes scrolled down to mark another Christmas Eve he would spend alone.

Ed listened to sounds in the diner with professional attention. Darnice's voice was like a bell as she wished people Merry Christmas, a bell ringing with new, bright tone. The banging and sloshing of dishes in the kitchen was calming, and was a signal that the rituals of closing had begun. The hum of voices declined and flattened as folks left, everyone ready to hunker down in the oncoming front. Ed surmised that this powerful, innate run for shelter was a sure prediction that something powerful approached just overhead.

The evening Ed had planned lost its heart. He would have to wait it out; hold out on this freezing night. He was stranded on his island. He sat very still, not wanting to leave. At least he had the little Christmas tree to light his arrival home. His thoughts went back to it now, the tree gleaming from his windows as he last had seen it. And there was Sarah beside it again. He shook his head to clear the sad image.

As Darnice cleared the last of the tables, she replayed the past few minutes' marvels. Her thoughts were unflinchingly on Jimmy Casey. The surprise of him, of seeing him the way she had tonight, warmed her body and thrummed in her pulse. She came out of her daydream when she saw Ed still at the counter; she could read his hesitancy to leave so she moved toward him, preparing to respond in some way—but not quite knowing how.

On one of his lonelier nights, Ed had trusted Darnice with an intimate story, told her about the day his mother sent him, a boy of twelve, to a neighbor's house to borrow a cup of sugar. His mother had given him a cup and clear directions of what to say. But hours later, when he hadn't returned, she tracked him down to find him sitting on the neighbor's porch, empty cup still in hand, too shy to knock on the door. Darnice was one of the few who knew the heart of the man, and she saw his loneliness tonight. He was the boy on that porch, still waiting.

Ed was well liked out on the island. Here, in the diner, he had only to clean his plate and make small talk. Cooks were the major cogs in the wheels. Looking on through the pickup window into the small universe beyond, they knew where their food went, and it made a difference that they felt appreciated. Ed ate heartily, was pleasant, appreciative, and tipped well; he was always well treated. He didn't participate much in the doings of the town. He didn't like going out alone, or driving in the seasonal crush of summer people that made traffic impossible.

Darnice was always glad to see Ed and she let him know it. He usually sat at the counter in her section. She had found just the right mix of familiarity and space to suit him. Although the diner was officially closed now, she lifted the last brown triangle of chocolate cake onto a plate and placed it in front of him. He took up his fork and cut into the dark sweetness.

Leaning on the counter, she took a minute to talk to the last diner. "So, Ed, what're your plans for tonight? Probably get changed anyway by the weather ... I can't help but think of that woman out in this blizzard. Hope Jimmy finds her." Darnice's face lit up as she said his name. Ed smiled at her, letting her know he could see what had happened and that he knew her little game—knew she was holding tight to the encounter of a few minutes ago.

When Ed didn't answer immediately, she looked to him and found her thoughts revealed in his eyes. Her voice died away, and they shared a close, quiet smile. Then, feeling vulnerable, she broke into the soft laughter that belied her pleasure; Ed joined with her for the moment.

She asked again about his holiday. This time he answered. "I thought I'd go to midnight Mass over to St. Mary's, but maybe I'll have to reconsider. ... I'll wait 'til time comes to decide. The deer on the island get penned up in heavy snow. I'll tend to them, play Santa, and bring 'em apples and carrots. That's if I can get out my door at all." Saying that, he sadly knew the time had come to leave. The simple truth was that he was going to be alone tonight and tomorrow, and probably for longer than that. He turned away, but not fast enough. Darnice had seen into his sadness.

Empathy moved in her to allow his slow exit. She couldn't quite let go, and so she spoke to delay him a second more. She asked, "How many holidays you spent on the coast here, Ed? Seems like you been here as long as me: forever?"

"I've been here over twenty years." As he spoke, images of what he loved about the place—ocean landscape, cliffs, marshes, birds lifting into gray skies, the booming of powerful surf—filled him up. Ed and Sarah had come to Wells from the western mill town where they had been born and spent their working years. Since then, they'd treasured seeing the great ocean roll in across Maine's rocky shoals, and breathing the marvelous salt snap of sea air.

When Ed traveled Route 1—either south or north for groceries, meals or appointments with doctors—the original land showed itself to him in the few isolated places not yet destroyed by real estate greed. Stands of pampas grass, wild aster, Queen Anne's lace, and cat-o'-nine-tails bordered the labyrinth of buildings and waved in sea winds. Wells, Ogunquit, Drakes Island, Moody Beach, Kennebunk ... was all this sweet, dramatic land to be subdued by pilings, Tyvek, timber, and ownership? Here and there he glimpsed the merest hint of the magnificence of the landscape of earlier days when land was land for all, and not for just the property owners.

He came out of this reverie to find Darnice waiting patiently for his answer to her question. In her expression, he saw that he was stalling for time she really didn't have tonight. She needed to get home. The roads would be worsening by the minute. She slid the bill—minus the chocolate cake—in front of him. "You have a nice one, Ed," she offered, then covered his hand with hers for a moment.

Ed smiled his thanks to her as she moved on down the counter, polishing with her towel as she went. He looked at his bill and stood to call her back about the absent cake when he realized she had meant it as a gift. Ed picked up the napkin he had written the woman's name on to put it in his pocket. He looked at it, saying the name aloud: "Pamela Iverson." He felt connected to her now that he knew her name. He said it aloud again: "Pamela Iverson." Then he reached for his wallet, even though most of the cake was still on the plate. He had lost his appetite.

Ed wanted to delay leaving, delay getting into his Jeep, delay going home. He could drive to Blueberry Lane blindfolded most nights; tonight he would need to use caution and courage to face it all. He began driving the roads in his mind. The blinking light on Route 1 would be swinging in howling snow winds off the sea, signaling his turn. He would brake carefully, descend the small hill, and then cross the marsh. He could see all this ahead of him, was ready for it, but he didn't know what to do when he arrived.

He backed off the stool, crossing to the register to pay. Darnice took his cash and wished him a Merry Christmas for the last time. He nodded, and then reached deep to find the energy to send the wish back to her. But he couldn't find it. He only turned away and opened the door into the storm.

The cheery voice of the bell was lost in pelting winds. Buffeted by a powerful scouring of snow, Ed stepped sideways, head down, snow stinging his neck as he moved toward his car. He turned the lamb's wool collar of his jacket up around his face. His Jeep, one of the last vehicles in the parking lot, needed to be brushed off before he could drive. He reached into the back seat for his broom and busied himself with the task as he pushed back from steady gusts.

As Ed cleared the windows, the tremor of strong surf on the beach rippled up through the earth into his body. He had seen the gray silk waves of a roiling ocean lift and shatter before; had seen the sea in its many moods. The storms always ended. The sun always returned. But the question always remained, "How much damage would it do before the end?"

Ed settled in the driver's seat, windshield clear for the moment. When he turned the key in the ignition, the heater pumped still-cold air into the cab. As the warming air from heater vents began to circulate, Ed reached for the gearshift. The driving couldn't have been worse. But then he remembered: Pamela Iverson. It could be worse! There was a woman out there alone in this fury. That thought of her exposed in these lethal conditions pushed him toward the safety of his cottage. Ed drove out onto Route 1, south toward Drakes Island.

CHAPTER 10

THE SUBARU

Drakes Island
Christmas Eve, 1999

The headlights spun a tunnel in thick snowfall as he drove. Conditions were bad; this was a narrow, two-lane road in the best of weather. But tonight, Route 1 was an iced luge. The first lumbering snowplow had yet to pass, leaving the road surface covered with mounding, drifting snow. A white dance of flakes reminded Ed of Christmas snow globes in local tourist shops, only in this one he was the trapped Santa Claus. He switched the radio on to hear the prediction of another fourteen to twenty inches before the storm ended.

The Jeep moved slowly on this disappearing path to home. Once again he thought of the missing woman. "Pamela Iverson; that's her name," he spoke aloud. He reached into his jacket pocket to retrieve the napkin. In the light of the dash, he confirmed the name: "Iverson." Ed tried to imagine how she could have gotten into this situation. Hadn't she heard the forecast? Jimmy had said she was in "distress." Funny word to choose. Ed suspected there were reasons for her "distress." People didn't realize how you could wander into distress unwittingly and become bound by it. It was a familiar story to him.

Landmarks lifted out of the snow as the beams of his headlights revealed them. Along Route 1, there were mostly signs to attract tourists into one of the many shops or restaurants. Ed thought of them tonight as bread crumbs in the storm; bread crumbs leading to his cottage: Big Daddy's Ice Cream, Litchfield's Restaurant, The Wells' Donut Shop, The Bull and Claw ... parking lots empty and dark, with signs swinging crazily in the bluster of wind. In his slow progress, Ed mused over the garish transformation these businesses had gone through, all to get the tourist trade. This stretch of Route 1 in his early days here had been rustic and simple, bearing only slight resemblance to the upscale strip he drove by tonight. Litchfield's Restaurant, once a small family-owned clam and lobster shack, had a particularly ugly sign; the "surf and turf" logo displayed a dolphin's graceful body weighed down by a steer's head. The charming coastal Maine that he and Sarah had moved to had morphed into a vacation playground that crowded out those who lived here year round.

His musings were brought up short as the back wheels of the Jeep spun out; the vehicle careening out of its lane, heading for the field on the other side. Ed's quick, light pressure on the brakes stopped the skid short but left him straddling the middle of the narrow road, headlights aiming off into space, lights revealing wild wind and serious, hefty snowfall. Getting home was going to require his complete attention. He was a skilled driver, but he surmised this night could prove his equal.

He sat back, quiet behind the wheel, and paused for a moment before straightening the Jeep in the empty road. Again, his mind wandered; this solitary journey home tonight mirroring the feel of his life. He spoke aloud again. "No need to hurry. No one's waiting for me anywhere. Anywhere in the whole world ...." The local station had switched its programming at five o'clock on Christmas Eve to Christmas music. Playing now was "Jingle Bell Rock." It finished and was followed by the peaceful, reverent "Silent Night." Ed could feel the whole town listening in the stormy dark; their thoughts mixing as his were with Christmas past, present, and future.

"Sarah?" He breathed her name right there, in the middle of a storm, in the middle of the road. And then came the only question he had left. He asked it aloud, "Where are you?" There was no answer, only the sound of snow and wind outside his softly lit cab. After a moment, he pushed the sadness aside to put attention to getting home quickly.

As he peered ahead in his slow progress, the yellow light at Drakes Island turnoff lifted out of the dark. Ed braked carefully, knowing this road by its feel. He turned left and eased down the gradual hill toward the sea. Gusts of snowy wind came off the beach in great clouds, clogging and slowing the metronome of his wipers. He felt the first of the three speed bumps on Drakes Island rise under him. He counted them, and then the Jeep's tires echoed across the small bridge. He was on home ground. As he drove, it became clear to him that a trip to St. Mary's on Eldridge Road for midnight Mass was out of the question. He bet they'd cancel it anyway. He tuned the radio to a Portland station to hear cancellation lists that aired between Christmas music. Almost immediately he heard, "St. Martha's, Kennebunk, Maine: all Christmas Eve services, all Christmas Day services—canceled. St. Josephs, Biddeford: all services—canceled." The list rolled on. St. Mary's Church aired last, finalizing his isolation; not even a Mass to attend.

Jetty Road came into focus out of the snow, rising on the right faster than he had anticipated. He tried to slow for this turn but braked a little too hard. For the second time tonight, the Jeep spun out beneath him. His trouble in judging the conditions shook him up. To go off the road here miles from help and from his cottage would be to risk his life. Ed doubted he could make it home walking if something happened.

The car had stopped its slide and left him sitting cockeyed in the road again. A swift anger at the lack of control instantly flared up from somewhere. It rose in him and boiled over, disabling his usual calm. Ed slammed the gearshift into park, the car rocking with the force. He felt the burn of adrenaline in his veins. Within a few minutes, the anger deepened to a despair that shocked him with its depth. The uncomfortable truth of his useless life flickered like a movie in front of him. "What the Christ am I supposed to do with this night—with this life?" He rested his forehead on the steering wheel, closing his eyes against the emotions boiling up. He wanted to be allowed back to the dull but comfortable acceptance of just a few hours ago.

After a few minutes he surrendered. His Coast Guard training taking over, the potential danger of his situation called him back to caution. He didn't have time for self-pity; he had to get out of here and to the safety of Blueberry Lane fast. The rage softened; competent Ed took control. He straightened the Jeep out, shifting between reverse and forward until he could resume his journey. At least there was no traffic and no danger of being in someone's way.

Before moving on in his journey home, wary from the two spinouts and the intensifying cold and winds of the weather outside, Ed reached in the back seat to make sure the emergency gear he'd stowed for winter was where he had left it. The gear at hand in the box included a hat, gloves, a scraper, a can of deicer, flares for emergencies, rope, and an antique—but still usable—folding shovel. He rummaged around for his hat. He hoped he wouldn't need to get out of this car before he reached home, but if he did, preserving body heat would be essential. Once he had the hat in hand, he glanced into the rearview mirror to settle it on. Pulling it down over his ears he then turned his attention to the road.

Ed shifted the lever into drive and spun the wheel carefully as he moved forward. As he did, his lights illuminated something in Jetty Beach parking lot. Something that didn't look right to the old sailor. He stopped mid-acceleration, bothered by the impression of a snow-covered mound down by the edge of the sea. Ed twisted in his seat, trying to see out the side windows of the car. Whatever he had seen before he couldn't see now, but he wasn't quite ready to let it go. He backed the Jeep up and swung around until the car's headlights shone directly into the beach parking lot.

His lights quickly found what had troubled him: Ed saw the snow-covered hump of what could very well be a car way over by the jetty. There was no reason for any car to be out here tonight. And then it hit him … *the missing woman!* Could this be the Subaru Jimmy had asked about? Was her car here on the island? Ed's miserable night spun on the dime of possibility.

Filled with new energy, he put the car in reverse, spun the rest of the way around, then drove into the parking lot; his conviction that this *was* the missing woman strengthening as he drove. His headlights sparked the brake lights of the silent vehicle. They flashed out at him, a signal of distress. Wind had blown snow off the license plate, and the numbers were clear: 4142 RAF. The chilling recognition of those numbers rose in him:

those were the numbers he had written on the napkin. This was Pamela Iverson's vehicle.

When he got close to the car, Ed took his foot off the gas and sat, holding the wheel tight and letting all this sink in. What should he do? He had to open the car door. He had to see if the woman was still in there. There was no outward sign that she was, but then ... he remembered what Jimmy had said about the reasons she might be here. A dread rose in him. It was possible that she wanted to end her life and had chosen this way to accomplish this. He would just have to open that door no matter what he felt. He was the man on the scene tonight. The PD was too far from here to alert Casey, and there was no way to call for help.

Ed wheeled his Jeep in beside her car as close as he could, and then rolled his window down to listen for anything he could hear over the wind. But there was nothing: no sound, no movement. As he sat listening, an innocent cuff of snow collected and was blown to the ground. The motor wasn't running. The car was dark and silent.

Calling courage from somewhere, Ed forced his door open, fighting wind all the way. "O Come All Ye Faithful" seeped from the radio, the powerful words lifting into roaring sea winds along with escaping heat from his Jeep. He said a quick prayer against what he might find. The first sharp sting of cold air woke him up completely when he breathed it in.

Ed stepped down from the car into islets of snow floating in fairly deep sea currents overrunning the jetty. The ice-cold flux crested over the tops of his boots, spilling inside. He braced in the sting of cold water as he made his way over to the small vehicle. Ever polite, Ed rapped on the glass, calling her name. "Pamela, are you in there? Are you all right?" He knocked again and waited for a response, but there was no answer, no sound.

He knew he had to open the door. The moment had come. Ed pulled hard on the door handle and the door gave way easily, revealing an empty interior. Quickly, Ed felt relief. A trace of fragrance flowed on the winds. Ed bent to look into the car. There were books on the passenger seat, a tray full of change, an umbrella ... nothing remarkable. In dim streetlight from the parking lot, Ed caught sight of a scrap of paper fluttering on the driver's seat. The relative tepidness of the air in the car told him it hadn't been vacant too long. He took the paper, put it in his pocket, closed the door, and then stepped gingerly through the deepening sea river to his idling Jeep.

Once inside his car, Ed flicked on the lights, took off his gloves, and read the note with shaking hands: "Whoever finds this note—battery's dead. Have gone to find shelter. Will walk out of parking lot, keep to right, away from the sea, walk to cottages. Please help! I am cold but all right. Pamela Iverson."

Ed opened the car door again and stepped out onto the runner board of the Jeep. He looked in all directions, trying to see through the impossible snowfall as if he might find her walking. He was in shock from these developments. She was here—on his island—trying to find refuge?!

As if he needed reminding about the power of this storm, a wind gust nearly blew him off his perch. He turned to look back at the jetty just in time to see a surge of water cresting over the granite blocks behind him. Quickly, he folded his long frame back into the Jeep and slammed the door out of the hands of the wind. He knew he was one of only four islanders who wintered on this small boat of land. He knew that most summer residents had shut down their heating systems, if they had them, which meant 90 percent of the cottages would be frigid. No—if Pamela Iverson was going to be saved, it was up to Ed to find her.

"All right," he said aloud to himself. "No feeling sorry for yourself. You have a mission to pull off tonight. Question is, where have you gone to, Pamela Iverson?" Ed, the Coast Guard guy, fixed his focus peering through the boiling chaos just outside his windshield intent on rescue.

CHAPTER 11

DARNICE

Wells, Maine
Christmas Eve, 1999

The lights of the diner rippled, fading quickly in dense snow. Darnice checked her watch … just past seven. The rhythmic chant of wipers sounded in counterpoint to the rush of warming air swooshing out from the vents. She accelerated carefully, keeping the car moving ahead slowly on deserted Route 1. Only a few miles ahead, home waited—down to Cole's Corner, right turn on Stephen Eaton Lane, and left into the driveway and into a safe garage. There was plenty of time to think as she drove. When she realized her route home would pass the police station, a pulse of excitement surprised her.

Until tonight, Darnice hadn't even been aware of being in the same world that Jimmy Casey inhabited. After this evening, he had taken center stage. She felt like a teenager; a subtle difference coloring everything because of the last few hours—and the town cop. A laugh escaped her. The terrain of her thoughts felt as unrecognizable as the terrain outside the window.

Darnice's thoughts turned to the gifts she had accumulated for this Christmas. She hoped her small family would like them. It had taken her a few years to establish security for her kids and herself again—years during which she had given up the options of being young, of dating, of education or travel. She had given up anything and everything for her kids. Darnice had come to terms with her role as a single mom. She made doing it right the most important part of her life. Amy and Danny suffered still from the rejection of a father who had never stepped up to any of his responsibilities. She hadn't been able to protect them from that.

For her, his being gone was easier than his being around. She had made all of the decisions herself. Of course, living with her mom made it all possible; her parents welcomed them into the small cape Darnice had grown up in. She still called it home on this very night. It wasn't easy to adjust to home again. She had once left this home with so much hope. In her mother's house, just barely big enough for all of them, she'd begun a new life, one that offered safety, loving care, and support for her children and herself—even when self-doubt battered her. Everybody was alright tonight though. All were safe and happy, awaiting her arrival home from work, waiting to celebrate Christmas together.

Amy, a senior at Wells High School, wanted clothes and money to spend during the Christmas break. She and her friends loved Filene's Basement in Boston. They devoted whole trips down there to try on discount hats and exotic gowns they had no need for. They even tried on wedding gowns. The girls laughed mightily to see each other transform from country girls to fashion plates. They stayed in Boston for lunch, and spent a few dollars on bargains to bring back to dull little Wells. Amy was a great kid who contributed to household expenses in the summer by waiting tables; working long, hard hours while trying to squeeze in fun. Her years growing up had been all Darnice could have hoped for her— minus the presence of her father.

Darnice's wish was for dinner at Varano's Italian Restaurant on Mile Road, one of the only places open on Christmas Day. Over her short day off, she didn't want to see the inside of a kitchen. The twenty-sixth rolled around fast enough and the luxury dinner out felt good. Being waited on was a rare pleasure for a waitress, although Darnice found she knew too much about what went on in the kitchen to relax totally. She had made reservations for the family at five o'clock tomorrow. Varano's overlooked the marshes, just up the road from Wells Beach. In her homeward trek tonight, she found herself anticipating the candlelit table, fire on the hearth, and glass of wine. She smiled in anticipation. But there was this storm to contend with first....

Danny had asked for help with his tuition at Seacoast Community College, and Darnice was only too happy to respond; watching her boy take on more and more responsibility was satisfying to her. An education hadn't been part of his parents' lives, but the desire for it for her own children was something Darnice instilled in each of them. On work mornings, he dressed carefully, took time for a bagel or cereal, and went to work at the bank where he was a part-time teller. Days off, he went to classes at the college. He studied in his room late, keeping up admirably with his classes. Though he had a favorite girlfriend (Darnice, too, was fond of Susannah), he'd committed himself to finishing two years of college before he let himself get serious. At least, that was what he had told Darnice in a recent late-night chat.

In spite of the fact that neither kid had any contact with their dad, they seemed all right with that now. Many times in earlier years, when Father's Day rolled around or when there had been no dad at their games or school events, they had come home in tears. Darnice's brother, Tim, had done his best to fill in for that lack, nearly always including her children on trips to local fun spots along with his own four boys. Mandy, Tim's wife, often asked them to come over and spend the night or come for dinner. Darnice was grateful she had a family who pitched in.

As her thoughts continued their assessments, Amanda, her mother, a jewel of patience and generosity through all this came to mind. She had sat with Darnice when there was worrying to do, when the kids were late or sick, or when the weather was bad. She loved Bingo, and went once or twice a weekend at the Masonic Hall up in Kennebunk. After dad had died, she had given over her days, her house, and her energy to the job of helping out.

She snapped out of her reverie as a push of powerful wind shook the car, dragging it into the opposite lane. Her interior musings had masked the deepening tension of danger out here. She checked her speedometer to see that her speed was almost thirty-five; that was as fast as she dared push it. On most nights, she could cover the distance from the diner to home in ten minutes. Tonight, she would err on the side of caution, no matter how long the trip would take.

Keeping her eyes on the road, she reached one hand into her purse, feeling around for a cigarette, a stolen pleasure. The car responded to her divided attention with another lunge out of the barely visible lane. Once a steady smoker, now indulging on the way home from work had become a buffer between the pressure of the workplace and the demands of the home front. She managed to pull the car back over into what she thought was her lane while lighting her Bic. Since she couldn't see more than a few feet in front of her, confusion mounted as doubt crept in about where she was. The limited vision, like the unknown emotional territory of Jimmy's visit earlier, left her disquieted.

Pulling smoke deep into her lungs, she held it, and blew it out in the now-warm car. She would finish this cigarette and hide the evidence before going in the house. She knew her mom and the kids could probably smell the smoke, but they never said anything. Darnice was conscious of the double message in this covert habit, but somehow she didn't want to stop.

Once again the thought of Jimmy invaded her musings, his face flickering in and out in front of her against a scrim of snow. She wanted to understand why the night's surprise interlude had so affected her. Why had she been so direct at the cash register? She had known him when he and Melissa Timmons married just after graduation, and she had known when their marriage ended. Melissa left quietly. It had taken most of a year for word to get around that she was gone. In the way folks do in a small town, Darnice had been marginally aware of Jimmy, watched as he became the PD heavyweight (no pun intended) as he frequented the diner over the years. Every now and then, she went out for a beer with friends to one of the local bars, and Jimmy would be there. Their acquaintance had never seemed personal at all, not until tonight. He was the joker and she just the waitress.

So why had she held his hand and looked into his eyes (something anyone who waited tables knew better than to do)? And why had it felt so good? As she reflected on this, a wave of the new but disarming feelings from just an hour ago swelled and spread through her. She drove, wrapped in its warmth, until the car kicked out, slurring sideways. Darnice steered into the slide, chiding herself for taking her attention off the road. When the car pushed off again, she rolled down the window to throw her cigarette out.

Cole's Corner, lit by traffic lights, came out of the snow. Pumping her brakes into action, she prepared for the upcoming right turn. The PD showed up on her left, its blue light tinting the snow falling around it. Taking a split second's attention away, she sent a thought to Jimmy, who was probably buried in situations by now. The entrance of the PD faced the junction of Route 1 and Route 99, the major intersection from the turnpike down into the heart of town. During the summer, thousands of cars flowed past the squat building daily. Tonight, red-and-green traffic signals pulsed in Christmas colors infusing the snowy road. All the flashing lights seemed to highlight the small building holding this new person. The thought made her laugh aloud.

Snapping on her turn signal despite no one being behind her, Darnice began rotating the steering wheel carefully. But mid-turn, she took her foot off the pedal and let the car roll to a complete stop. There, under traffic lights, something was moving in the wind, fluttering above the road. She wiped her eyes, trying to adjust her vision to explain what she saw. "Impossible," she breathed out in a whisper. But as she stared, there they were. As she sat in her car, the graceful monarchs descended and spun in a wheel, around and around, fast and tight, over the hood of her car. After a minute or so, they rose swiftly, fusing in seconds into a cloud of color that shot down Route 1, disappearing into the dark behind her. First, they were there, and then they were gone. After a few moments, Darnice began to doubt whether she had seen them at all.

What an odd night, and it had just begun; it was still early. Darnice tried to shake off the weirdness of the experience and force her attention back to getting home. She accelerated again with great care; Stephen Eaton Lane was almost in sight. A warm jumble of thoughts spun within her. Jimmy, butterflies … what was going on? Darnice could see him, headset on, barking orders out to the road crews. She would tell him about this vision—or whatever it was—or maybe she wouldn't. Could she trust him? Darnice wondered whether, in some way, Jimmy had something to do with those butterflies. Nothing seemed impossible tonight.

CHAPTER 12

SOMETHING EXTRAORDINARY

Drakes Island
Christmas Eve, 1999

Ed pulled the steering wheel left, then right, alternating between accelerating and releasing the gas pedal, forcing the car over the snare of icy ruts and out of the parking lot. The seriousness of the situation called for a rush of energy he hadn't felt for years. His pulse was up; he paid attention to every detail outside of the Jeep. A woman's life was in his hands and nothing could be clearer or more important. The instincts of his professional training zoomed back large.

Once out of the jetty parking lot, Ed eased the Jeep down the hill, and then paused, eyes scanning in front of him like radar—left to right, then right to left, down each side of Ocean Drive. Or at least as much of it was revealed in his headlights. How would he ever find her? Could the lights of the Jeep be seen in this dense snow? He hoped the woman, Pamela, had taken cover somewhere. Survival for any length of time out in the boiling whiteness was impossible. He couldn't—wouldn't—let his panic rule him. "Stay calm," he told himself.

As the car inched ahead, something about the sound of the wind and the movement of his car brought him back to the decks of Coast Guard ships during the hundreds of storms he had lived through; echoing foghorns warning nearby ships of hulking structures coming their way. *Horns … !* Ed slowed the car and sat up straighter. His two worlds came together in a flash of insight. Ed would use his car horn as a foghorn, blow loud and steady, and catch the woman's attention. That is, if she was within hearing distance. The idea felt like a long shot, but it was all he had.

Ed knew that there was no other possible place for the woman to go but into a cottage. Breaking in wouldn't be hard. Questions about her condition continued to surface as he inched along. "How long ago had she left her car? Was she dressed for this weather, and did she have the energy this walk would take? Was she mentally up to saving herself?" He started speaking aloud just to hear his voice. These details would mean the difference between survival and death. Ed tried to remember what Jimmy had said about her back at the diner. Could so much have happened since that bowl of lobster stew?

Snow blowing parallel to the ground indicated wind direction and hinted at a fierce wind speed. Ed felt the coil of anxiety winding around him as he began blowing his horn again and again in short, regular bursts. After a few minutes of this, he simply held the horn down steady and picked up a little speed. The noise was alarmingly loud inside the car, but he doubted its reach outside. Pamela couldn't have gotten far; she had to be in one of the first cottages.

The Jeep's wheels bit into the topsoil of snow as Ed peered out, looking in all directions for any sign of life in the mesmerizing sameness of white. He stopped as a bright-red octagon came into his lights: a stop sign was whipping back and forth like paper in the power of the wind. Ed recognized where he was by the sign. He was at the beach path where foot traffic crossed on summer days. He knew from years of driving here that when he looked to his right in summer, an enticing white sandy beach stretched out at the end of the path, inviting and visible through the dunes. Beyond that, a summer ocean broke gently on the shore.

He stopped, leaned forward, and rolled the snow-laden passenger window down to see that breakers, two to three feet deep, were coursing down and out of the path into the road as if it were a drainage channel. Ed was at least fifty feet away from the beach here, and the tide was in the road? The island would surely sustain damage from wind-driven water tonight.

Rolling up the window, Ed resumed the steady blare of his horn. He looked hard, and tried to focus on any detail that might tell him that someone had entered a cottage—or worse—was in the road.

When he saw them—the butterflies—they shocked him so completely that his foot came off the gas, and the car stopped as if he had braked. Spinning, they were over his hood, orange wings in snow, black-spiraled color riding night air like bright scarves.

Ed sat back staring, stunned enough to accuse himself of being crazy for what he was seeing. "You have snapped, LaCasse," he said, still watching the monarchs, which showed no signs of being blown away. It was impossible, yet they were in front of him. He watched for seconds, then a minute, his car still idling. They mesmerized him, but finally he remembered Pamela, and was able to force his attention away. He had to get a grip for her sake. He closed his eyes, rubbing them with the backs of his hands. When he was calmer, he looked back out through the continuing presence of the monarch escort.

"Okay then, let's just get through this. Show me the way," Ed said loudly as if they might hear him, sensing the apparition might be part of the rescue he was part of. His horn blazed out again, and his car inched forward. The butterflies moved with him, always in front and above, riding in the slipstream of the Jeep. Down the snow-filled alley of a street, the man and the butterflies progressed. After the initial shock subsided some, Ed felt encouraged by their presence. Something extraordinary was happening—and it had to be hopeful.

CHAPTER 13

LIGHT

Drakes Island
Christmas Eve, 1999

Pamela woke to the sound of a roaring train in the room. Cold air swirled around, reaching into her cocoon of blankets. But where was she? She opened her eyes into a small, dim space. The window across from where she was nestled rattled as if to break. As her thoughts cleared, she realized it wasn't a train she was hearing; it was the howling of the gale around the flimsy cottage.

She tried to move but couldn't; panic arose quickly and she began fighting wildly against her confinement. As she loosened the blankets and stretched her legs, she relaxed a little. Her sleep had been so deep that she had forgotten how she had come here. Leaning her head against the wall behind her, she tried to remember the details, but dozed off again. The window's intense rattling roused her again. This time, the memory came into focus: she had left the car, found the cottage, broke in—it all came back. How long had she slept? How long had she been here?

Pamela felt for the flashlight beside her—precious, precious light. Freeing her hands, she grasped it. She flicked it on and looked at the time, even though she didn't want to know how many hours had passed. Hours, minutes, and seconds ... they all meant that fear for her at Chick's

Crossing was growing. Leslie didn't deserve to have her Christmas in ruins on her account.

She tried to estimate the temperature in the house from the feel of air in the room: low twenties at best. At least she was spared wind chill. She drew farther into her blankets. A clock ticked on the wall across from her, reminding her of Leslie's warm kitchen this morning. She shone the light on its face; it was past seven. If only she'd had the courage to wait it out this time, to let the arrow-sharp emotions come, to sit with the pain. If only she had, she might be by the tree with her family right now. She had been here before. She'd been in this place where she would do anything—drive, shop, or scream. *Anything* ... and she'd do it fast to block the darkness of her feelings. She feared their power. She wanted, no—she desperately *needed*—another chance. But it would have to come tonight and it would have to come fast. She simply couldn't imagine what would turn this dangerous blunder around.

She checked the time again; a few minutes had ticked by. How could time move this slowly? To take her attention off the growing panic, Pamela assessed her physical condition. Her legs were cramped but warm enough. But her fingers and toes ached with cold.

Pamela closed her eyes while she ran a review of everything she had ever known about survival in conditions like these. She was desperate for some idea of how to get out of this alive. From the years she had lived here before, she knew she was almost three miles from Route 1. She concentrated, searching for an answer.

And then the day on the beach came back: That day on a beach with an ocean as broad as a desert; a jewel of agate blue shimmering beside her. It had been a Sunday, and she was running and running on the empty beach. Suddenly Pamela was there again. The day had dawned somehow, was happening again, fueling her with its energy. The memories sharpened into feelings. *September, Drakes Island*: She watched herself running; feeling each footfall on soft sand, feeling the muscles of her body contract and spring. On that beach, Pamela—or the distant woman now in her mind— was being followed by ribbons of color, ribbons that wound and unwound in the air behind her. The woman had stopped as she saw them. And then they came to her. The woman on the beach—she—had dropped to her knees under the magic of the butterflies.

But the dream out of time collapsed, and Pamela found herself back here in this cold kitchen, on this dark day....

Pamela struggled out of the cage of blankets, her comfortable lethargy suddenly hateful. She wanted to run from this place. *Run ...!* But she feared her cold limbs weren't up to the effort. She tugged and pulled, loosening and then tumbling out. Rubbing her legs and feet allowed her to—at very least—stand.

And the Holy instant came. It seemed so real that Pamela gasped aloud. "They're here again; they're here!" Her voice echoed in the empty room as the glow began, blossomed in the corner of the ice-frosted window. Crystalline ice scrolls ignited, flowed into a pattern, spreading from one crusted pane to the next, catching fire from the frozen outside; the whole window glowed gold.

This golden wall of glass was her sign. She understood suddenly that it was coming from outside, from the street. With all the mental command and energy that her cold, weary body possessed, she sprang for the door. Flinging it open, she plunged without reservation into the raging night— just as Ed's Jeep was passing the cottage.

CHAPTER 14

COLLIDING

Drakes Island
Christmas Eve, 1999

Ed was driving in the highest state of alert he had ever known, focusing on all he could see within the snow blindness. Proceeding slowly, he went until a loud banging on the rear of his vehicle interrupted the cadenced rhythm of windshield wipers and humming wind. Ed snapped to attention, imagining ice chunks tangled in the axel or wheel casings. The sound repeated, but didn't have the regularity of a mechanical cause. He had slowed some, was chugging along, and listening, when the noise stopped altogether. Just then, he heard a scream.

Ed jammed on the brakes; the car seized abruptly, rocking from the force. He was thrown forward onto the wheel, his seat belt cutting against his chest. At the rear of the car, a solid thump was followed by a sharp cry, then silence. Ed slammed the shift lever into park and was out of the car and into the storm in a matter of seconds. Wind hit him hard as he rounded the back of the Jeep, pushing him off course. He closed his eyes against the darts of ice. Leaning into the powerful blast, he regained his balance, sheltering his eyes with his hands, and peered ahead of him. He gasped when he saw someone kneeling in the road—a woman holding her head. Pamela Iverson!

Ed, fighting the wind all the way, went to her as quickly as he could, and knelt beside her. He became alarmed when he saw that the gash on her forehead was bleeding down the side of her face and into her eyes. He quickly understood what had happened; the noise had been Pamela banging on the back of the car to stop him. When he'd braked suddenly, her head must have hit the window—hit it hard.

"Okay, okay, Pamela, let's concentrate on getting you home," he shouted into the wind.

As Ed uttered the words, Pamela put her head in her hands, sobbing she was so grateful to hear a human voice. Ed felt the bite of freezing air in just the few minutes he had been out here. Pamela had been in the storm for hours by any calculation. The first thing she needed was warmth, and she needed it right now. He stood and looked around to get his bearings, the storm circling them like a hungry animal. Gently, Ed slid his hands under her arms and lifted her to her feet, exerting a little pressure to get her moving. Softly, he repeated, "You're safe now,"—over and over. They stumbled, clinging together toward the back door of the Jeep,

When Pamela saw Ed open the door to the back seat, she stopped him with a plea. "No, please. I don't want to lose sight of your face. *Please, please* ... not in the back." Ed nodded, sensing the panic immediately, and changed course, opening the passenger door. Blessed warm air seeped out, Christmas music embedded within it. Ed helped Pamela up over the high runner, guiding her until she sank into the passenger seat, a sigh escaping her. He leaned down, picked up a handful of snow; and though she protested weakly, he pressed it to the cut on her head hoping to staunch the flow of blood and counteract the swelling. From what he could see, she could be in shock. She let her head rest against the seat and closed her eyes. Ed closed her door softly; at least she was out of the cold.

Holding on to the car as he walked, he got in himself, and then reached for paper towels from a roll in the back seat. Layering a few on her head wound, he said, "Pamela, hold on to this while I drive. Apply pressure if you can."

She didn't respond, was very still, eyes closed.

He touched her on the shoulder; gently he asked, "Can you do this? We need to put pressure to slow the bleeding down."

Her eyes fluttered as she responded. She put a hand on the makeshift bandage. "Thank you … I can manage this. Thank you." The woman began to talk, her words slurring a little. He heard the confusion and trauma in her voice. "I don't know how this happened. I fell asleep in the car this afternoon, and when I woke, this storm …. Who are you? I'm so sorry to get you involved in this, Mr. … what is your name?"

Ed slowed, turned directly to her and took her hand. "Pamela, hold on, we are all right. You don't have to know anything but that you're safe. I'm Ed LaCasse. You're out of the worst of it. We've got to get out of here and get attention for that cut on your head. Stay with me now, Pamela. We can do this. No panic; you are all right. We are going home."

The wounded woman nodded slowly but kept talking. "I broke into a cottage … I was freezing, and thought I was going to die. My God, *my God*," she moaned.

Ed turned back to his driving, squinting ahead of him into the featureless world outside the car. Ed continued talking as he guided the trusty Jeep toward Blueberry Lane. "Come on now, Pamela, you're safe; don't rile yourself up and make the bleeding worse. We're getting out of this storm now; there's a remedy just up the road. My cottage is waiting with a good, warm fire and food."

Pamela looked over to Ed, encouraged by his sureness, his strength, and his kindness. His words had quelled any reluctance or fear for the time being. She let herself relax, breathed deeply in relief, and kept her eyes on the driver, trusting him to get her to safety. "I can't begin to thank you … I don't know *how* to begin to thank you. I have family on Chick's Crossing who are …." As Leslie and Robbie returned to her thoughts, she turned her face toward the window to hide the visible wave of her regret.

"Time to go home, Pamela," Ed said. "We'll have plenty of time to talk when we are out of danger." He engaged the four-wheel drive, and the surefooted car rolled on.

The events of the night still stunned Ed. He made a note to call Jimmy as soon as he got home to tell him about the mind-boggling rescue, and to call off the search team. Finding this woman had been the focus of efforts between a wide network of people. Moreover, the terror her family must be feeling on the Crossing and many were still at risk looking for her.

In the rush of events in the last few minutes, Ed had forgotten the monarchs. Remembering them now, he looked out into the snow for traces of his guides; there were no signs of the colorful companions. He wondered whether he should tell Jimmy about them. Imagine talking with Jimmy Casey about butterflies—not only that, but butterflies in a Nor'easter!

For her part, Pamela was dizzied with conflicting emotions. The heartache and turmoil she had caused her family were a fear within her that wouldn't allow her to fully accept the relief this rescue offered. She had believed—or feared at the worst of it—that her life would end tonight. But now, she was in a warm car being driven by a kind man to a safe place out the storm. She didn't deserve it.

Ed followed the faint path of his headlights. Pamela's breathing had calmed; she closed her eyes and let herself go, reliving the dream of monarchs in the kitchen less than an hour ago—the dream that had awoken her just in time to see this approaching car. He had appeared, after all, in a split second, and could have been gone just as quickly. She could have slept through it all. Somehow, the monarchs were meant to wake her. Pamela looked over at Ed's face, illuminated in the light of the dashboard, driving steadily through the hell outside the windows. She was so touched and encouraged by his calm, kind face, her eyes closed, and sleep overtook her.

CHAPTER 15

BLUEBERRY LANE

Drakes Island
Christmas Eve, 1999

Ed drove by his instincts toward where home should be. The white vagueness around him left him fearing that he had taken a wrong turn somewhere—that he was out, lost on one of the small lanes of the island. He drove, anxiety rising for what seemed a very long time, until a rosy patch of color bloomed in the left side of his windshield. He slowed the Jeep, tapping the brakes with restraint, peering toward the patch of color as it grew more distinct. "Hah!" he called aloud when he recognized the lights of the Christmas tree in his bay window: Sarah's tree. Something loved from their past had marked his home for him as surely as if it were a lighthouse. Ed navigated by the glow, only able to gauge where the driveway *should* be. The trusty Jeep rolled on through deep snow into the driveway toward the garage.

With Ed's tap on the opener, the door responded obediently, and he drove in, windshield wipers flailing in suddenly empty air. Gusts of snow blew in behind him until the door lowered, creating a barricade between Ed, his surprise guest, and the howling night. Relieved, Ed sat still in his seat, taking in the quiet of the garage for a moment, and offering heartfelt prayers of gratitude. The relief from the challenges in the last hour compared with the safety of home overwhelmed him. The gravity of having saved this person's life descended, and Ed was left deeply humbled and thankful.

Everything was as he had left it only a few hours ago: wood piled by the kitchen door, a shovel against the outside wall, summer furniture covered with tarps and stacked in the corner. In spite of the familiarity, the jarring events of this rescue made it seem like he was on another planet.

And still Ed sat in the warm car, looking at the woman beside him. Her eyes were closed, head against the seat. She was asleep or had passed out. He couldn't tell which. He knew he had to keep her conscious; the impact from the window could have caused a concussion. Ed would treat the wound, keep her warm, and try to keep her awake. It was a big order for a guy who hadn't had much to do with the world for a while.

The overhead light in the Jeep came on as he opened the door, and he saw that the gash on Pamela's head had continued to bleed, dripping back into her hair and down her cheek. But it seemed to have stopped now. She was so quiet that he was suddenly afraid for her. The trauma—including the two-inch head wound—freezing temperatures for hours, the physical and mental stress; anxiety and sympathy mixed and surged in him, pushing him to get her into the house.

The old Coast Guard man stepped out onto the solid garage floor, tempted to kneel and kiss it. He blessed it silently for being there as he went around to the passenger door. He opened it to put his hand on Pamela's shoulder, nudged her gently, and called her name. "Pamela, we're home. Can you hear me ... Pamela?" Her wan, silent face didn't change; she was in a deep sleep. He continued calling her, until thankfully she lifted her head, looking groggily at him. Just as she opened her mouth to respond, a deafening crack exploded very close overhead, severely shocking both of them. Ed ducked automatically, going to his knees on the floor. Pamela screamed, holding her head in her hands, bending forward in the seat.

"Jesus!" Ed shouted. "What the hell?" A loud boom answered his unfinished question. When he straightened up, Pamela had doubled over in the seat visibly shaking. He put his arm around her, massaging her shoulders, trying to reassure her. As gently as he could, he leaned in close to her, explaining calmly that, in all likelihood, lightning had struck somewhere, but that they were safe here at his cottage. Thunder snow was not unheard of in Nor'easters.

After waiting a few minutes, he put gradual pressure on the woman to stand and began guiding her toward the kitchen door. As they reached the three steps up, another sharp crack stopped them both. Pamela grabbed onto Ed, almost knocking him over with her fear. He encircled her with his arms to hold her up as the boom of thunder answered again. He didn't need to be told how weak she was; he could feel it in the support she absorbed from him just to stand. Just as Ed reached for the kitchen latch, lights in the garage and in the kitchen blinked out, resurged momentarily, and then went out with finality. Ed guessed that it was an outage from downed lines somewhere under the extreme weight of snow. That meant phone lines might be dead as well. He wondered what would happen next.

In the deep, sudden dark, Pamela grasped Ed more tightly. With a few soft words, he assured her that everything they needed was just inside the door and tried to keep her moving up the stairs. The fireplace, just steps away, seemed like a very lucky thing right now. He had set a fire for himself in anticipation of getting home, something he often did to hold onto the old life when Sarah prodded him to it. It would make a difference tonight.

They were only a few feet into the kitchen when Pamela's total weight slumped against Ed, shifting his balance so suddenly that he careened against the counter. Barely able to catch her from falling, Ed knew she had fainted. Thank God he knew this space blindfolded, knew where everything was. Without any hesitation, he picked her up and carried her, finding her light. He walked into the dark living room to the sofa opposite the hearth and lowered her carefully.

The air in the house was still warm, but that wouldn't last long with the furnace out. He had never felt so happy to be home in all his life. He sat Pamela gently on the sofa, holding her up until he could pile pillows to keep her head raised. Then Ed took the comforter that Sarah had knit that last winter, unfolded it, and stretched it over the sleeping woman. As he fussed to make sure she was totally covered, he marveled about tonight's surprising path. Years of sameness had plodded on, and then in a flash, there was a brilliant challenge. Things felt different. Emotions swept over him: hope, hope for her survival, and hope for something else he couldn't name. It wasn't just the same old house or the same old Ed. He was up to this night. He knew what to do and he'd give it his all. In the odd events unfolding tonight, he could hear the echo of the wish he had made just a few hours ago: The wish to be useful to someone ....

Having covered his guest, Ed knelt to light the fire, tending it until it caught, little orange shoots of light weaving up through the tinder. He smiled when he saw a repeat of the orange-and-black pattern of his recent butterfly visit. The room lit softly; the pleasant snapping of kindling against the wild storm providing a counterpoint to the wind and snow at the windows. Ed placed his hand on Pamela's forehead. She was warm and breathing evenly. He would have to treat the wound. He held her wrist to get a pulse. It too was regular ... strong. He called her name. "Pamela, wake up. You're safe here, now. The worst is over. I need you to wake up."

She opened her eyes and looked into his face. After a few minutes of focusing, she began, "Thank you, thank you ...." She mumbled her gratitude, expressing it in almost unintelligible words. Then her eyes closed, and she went out again. He watched her for a few minutes and then made a decision: he would take the gamble and let her sleep.

When he stood to go for the peroxide and bandages, he saw the little tree in the window; dark now with no power, but so important. He blessed it again, and blessed Sarah too for her part in this: her hiding it down in the cellar to be discovered today just when he would need it most. The odd layering of that old life onto the events of tonight left him a little amazed. It was as if Sarah had known and played her part in this rescue. He found himself smiling in the dark.

Part Four

CHAPTER 16

TOWN BOYS

The Wells PD
Christmas Eve, 1999

Jimmy doubled over in his chair when the sharp crack sounded. It was followed by thunder in a matter of moments. Dispatch went dark. Startled, all the staff stopped in their tracks; phone boards dead along with lights and radio. An uneasy wave of silence spread in the small space. Just outside, the storm still howled, seeming louder than ever. As auxiliary lights that were mounted over the exits snapped on, the space filled with a greenish artificial glow. The backup system had thankfully kicked in; thin illumination in the offices giving the impression of small, cramped caves deep underground.

Jimmy knew what this would mean for the night's rescue. A low growl was the prelude to his quick assessment. "Goddamned, friggin' power lines are down somewhere. We're finished guys ... couldn't be any Christly worse time for this to happen. Missing person, people all over the roads tryin' to get home for Christmas, and the power goes out leaving us in pitch goddamned dark." He grabbed a manual nearby and hurled it across the room. Farrell, who hadn't left yet, ducked as it hit the wall above his head.

The young cop stepped toward his infamous colleague. "Hey! Take it easy, Jimmy. We don't know if this is all over town. It could just be down here. Look out on Route 1 and see if traffic lights are still operating."

Farrell reached for the telephone on the desk and picked it up, but the fact that it was dead registered on his face. He replaced it gingerly.

Jimmy moved quickly, moving by rote down the dim hallway, through dark corridors, to the front of the building. He barged into the chief's office without even knocking to find the chief standing in an open door, peering out into the street, snow swirling in and all around him. "Well, are the friggin' street lights working?" he bellowed, paying no heed to the privilege of rank.

The chief closed the door softly and turned to Jimmy. "Officer, your evening—*our* evening—just sank a little deeper in crap than it was two minutes ago. We'll have to operate on emergency power, Jimmy. Christ, a rescue operation, people on the roads, emergencies headed for hospitals … it's enough to make a man cry." The station was in crisis without enough staff to manage what would come their way tonight. Everyone's stress level, including the chief's, had soared by double digits.

Hoping that the chief might have been mistaken about the lights, Jimmy reopened the door onto Route 1 himself. Trees bent double in protest to the Nor'easter's gale were gyrating in the snowy wind and blowing sideways. Traffic lights above the intersection were nothing but dark circles swinging crazily.

Chief shouted at Jimmy to shut the door, but he didn't comply immediately. He was with the monarchs—memory copies of them anyway. That didn't make them any less real. *What the hell is going on?* Jimmy thought. "Shades of, *It's a Wonderful Life*?" he muttered, pushing his head out through the curtain of snow, imagining Jimmy Stewart running down the street in … what was the name of that town? Yes, Bedford Falls ….

The night was getting stranger and stranger, and this assessment covered his interlude with Darnice. Every time that woman came into his mind, a rush of feeling pulsed through him—like right now—even though chief was howling at him to "shut the damn door." Jimmy wanted to just stand here, with the snow falling on him, and think about her. But duty was calling, and loudly. He shook himself out of it, closed the door, brushed the accumulated snow off his shoulders, and turned back to the real world. *Or was it … ?*

When he turned back to the chief, he saw that Farrell had entered the room. The two were bent over a map with flashlights surveying Wells' main and secondary roads. Farrell looked up at Jimmy and scolded him playfully. "Get your ass into the game, Casey." These words relaxed the three men the way pretend insolence always did; they even laughed a bit.

"Maybe it's time for a slug of that bottle you've got in your drawer," Jimmy suggested.

The chief turned to him, quickly reining him in with a look. "Not yet, Casey ... we've got too much work ahead of us. But later, man—later ...."

The chief walked over to Jimmy and put his hand on his shoulder. "I'm taking you off regular duty, Casey, putting you on the Iverson woman's case exclusively. She was in deep enough before the power blew; things are much worse now. Do you have any idea where the hell she could be? I mean it, Jimmy ... that's about the level of intelligence we have left—a guess! Telephone service is out from Portland down to Portsmouth. She couldn't get to us or anybody, even if she wanted to. Farrell—God bless the boy—will take over for you at Dispatch. You get out there and find her. Hear me, Casey? I got no one else who is up to this job. State cops are involved with traffic, and you know Wells better'n anyone here. I'm counting on you. I'm thinkin' her car's off the road somewhere. Maybe she has enough gas and sense to keep warm overnight."

Jimmy nodded a reluctant acceptance. "Before I go out, get me some more info from the woman's family about where she could be. They might have some idea about what direction she may have gone, based on her habits. Getting out to Chick's Crossing will not be easy tonight." He paused. "How long has she been out there? Ten hours now? Time is not on our side, Chief. The first twenty-four hours offer a decent window for finding someone; after that, leads get cold—real cold, real fast. That'll be the case tonight for sure. I'm going back to Dispatch for a little bit. Think this over; try to come up with a plan. Generators will've picked up the lines by now. I'll make a few contacts with guys out there and see if someone can swing up to the family home for information. We can't depend on our usual procedures with the phones out."

Jimmy turned and left the room, distractedly rubbing the back of his neck, anxious about his new commission. People who knew him knew he would use every means to get the job done. Tonight that was the only hope the PD had.

Farrell joined Jimmy in Dispatch a few minutes later. Jimmy was already talking with the state police, getting road conditions and forecast details. Farrell tiptoed over and sat, waiting for his direction.

Something he heard made Jimmy sit up in attention. He hung up abruptly and swung around to face Farrell, his face lighting up.

"Okay, Farrell, listen up. This is what I've been waiting for: There's a chance the Iverson woman might be down on or around Drakes Island. That was her go-to spot when she lived here before. Daughter's afraid; said her mother was really depressed and might have gone there ... you know *where* I mean! Farrell, I'm going out on the road with the plow crew; makes no sense for me to be drivin' on my own. The town boys can handle road conditions like tonight's. Their routes cover all the roads, down to the island and up to the Highlands. ... I'll countermand the route Taddy Stevens drives, ride along with him, and look for Pamela Iverson as we go. You hold the fort here, Farrell. With the power out, if we get any emergencies, you'll be the contact for hospitals and ambulances. You can keep in touch with me over DOT's radio in case you need me or you get some new information. This woman's a goner 'less she is rescued or has found shelter somewhere. I hope to Christ she has. You tell the chief what I'm going to do. I don't have time."

Without waiting for his colleague's response, Jimmy grabbed his coat, dressing as he moved toward his gear by the door, and headed across the yard to DOT.

"You be careful out there, Jimmy," Farrell hollered into the storm after him. "We're depending on you for the heroics, but be safe." Then, to amend his message, he added loudly to be sure Casey heard this request. "By the way, if Congdon's is openin' for coffee and doughnuts tonight for road crews like usual, pick up some on your way by. Apple fritters for me."

Jimmy, almost out of sight, turned and responded with a wave, then disappeared in the dark night. When the snow began to pile up inside the door jamb, Farrell closed the door.

As Jimmy walked across the lot toward the plow trucks idling, he found he was fighting wind and snow like an actual adversary. This had to be the height of the storm: it couldn't get any worse. He kept his eyes on the lights of the truck barn as he moved toward it. Somewhere in that walk, those damned butterflies got into his mind again. Maybe they weren't just an unexplained event. Maybe they had taken off for Drakes Island to get him to follow them. He had seen movies like that, but that kind of thing was only in the scripts—or was it? Maybe, just maybe, Pamela Iverson and those monarchs were connected. Jimmy had his heart set to buddy up with Taddy. He knew he could trust him, get him to break the rules and go for a look-see on the island right away. The collision of the monarchs and Drakes Island and Pamela Iverson left him with goose bumps, signaling that he may be onto something.

After a few minutes, Farrell heard the rumble of snow equipment advancing toward Route 1 and a few toots on the horn. Jimmy would be on that truck, redirecting Taddy down to the island, he guessed. He had to hand it to Jimmy; he had a plan anyway. Farrell dearly hoped Congdon's would open. He would need a fritter by morning. This was going to be a night to remember.

CHAPTER 17

DISCOVERY

Drakes Island
Christmas Eve, 1999

Jimmy and Taddy, now settled into the overheated cab of the mammoth truck, focused their attention on the shallow indentation of what they hoped was a road that spooled out in front of the headlights. Primary roads of the town were always plowed first to accommodate emergency vehicles. The going attitude toward secondary roads was that anyone foolish enough to be driving them in this weather deserved what they got. Accordingly, they weren't tended to until all the primary roads were clear. The roads out on the island were definitely secondary, even thirdly, if truth be told. Taddy would be out there alone making a first pass tonight.

The going was awful. Taddy's strong-handed control of the lumbering truck kept it centered, but they made painfully slow progress. A spinout with the big, heavy vehicle was always imminent. As they bounced along together in silence, chains on the huge tires chinked in the wheel wells; a metronome counting out each rotation. The crunch of the deep bites into the snow was music to the ears of men who drove these vehicles. As local men, they knew the seasons well and lived large in them all, especially in winter and on roads like the ones tonight—deserted and dangerous. These were their playgrounds; they plowed and sanded with great skill, windows down, pellets of ice stinging their faces, a deep camaraderie among them.

The trust that went with this job meant something to them. They were aware that not many men could be out here, didn't have the know-how. The men of the Wells DOT weren't businessmen, doctors, or lawyers; they were no kind of professionals at all. Those men were home with their families, depending on the skill, guts, and dedication of the road crews tonight. The town guys were a vital part of everyone's life. Because of their efforts and skill, folks could rely on being safe. They were known, appreciated, and respected wherever they went.

Conversation ping-ponged between Jimmy and Taddy, most of it pithy with lame attempts at joking around. Taddy began by teasing Jimmy about the "spare tire" he had picked up since he started doing more time at the desk. Jimmy pushed the envelope by retorting with a few wise comments about Taddy's smoking. He shouted over road noise, "It's easy to find your truck, my man. It's the one with a cloud of smoke where the driver should be." They laughed at the playful jibes. Jimmy took silent stock of what a disaster the cab of Taddy's truck was; empty thermoses of coffee rolled around on the floor, butts, still smoldering, filled the nasty-smelling ashtray. The back window of the vehicle was piled high with the paper work Taddy never bothered to read or file. No matter; Jimmy had picked Taddy to ride with in spite of all this. He knew this man was a fiercely competent driver. He was well practiced in navigating blizzard conditions, and he knew he would agree with Jimmy's mission tonight to head out to the island as the first order of business, regardless of whether he was ignoring orders or not. Most importantly, he knew him as a friend and felt a little more secure to be with Taddy on tonight's mission.

Time to introduce the mutiny, Jimmy thought as he turned to him. "Taddy," he began, his tone a bit wheedling, "you've got to get me out to the island on your first pass tonight my boy, like *right now*. State cops just checked in with information that Pamela Iverson—the missing woman we're looking for—may have been out there today. You've heard about her, right? From up on Chick's Crossing—woman in her mid-fifties, driving a Subaru? The details are grim, friend."

Jimmy continued, adding the facts they knew. Taddy kept on driving as Jimmy spoke, but was paying attention, looking over when the road would let him. The smile had left his face. He nodded gravely as Jimmy went on, letting him know he recognized the seriousness of the night's route. "The state guys finally got to the family home up at Chick's Crossing, found out she'd lived up in Kennebunk a few years ago. The woman left the area when her husband died, moved down to Rhode Island. Why *there* I don't have a clue. Drakes Island was one of the places she used to go a lot. Looks like we need to get ready for anything. Family said she was depressed when she left. Could even be a suicide here, Taddy. Hard to tell, but Drakes Island's the only lead we have."

At the word *suicide*, Taddy did a double take, cigarette smoke drifting in his eyes. "Jesus, Jimmy, you mean we could have a suicide in the middle of this bastard storm?" He quickly switched his eyes back to the road, using every bit of strength he had to keep the rig steady. Dashboard lights reflected up into Taddy's weathered and handsome profile. "That's all we need to complicate a rescue with all this weather shit to contend with." Thinking, he unconsciously stubbed the present cigarette out only to light another one a moment later, somehow driving true while he did it.

Drakes Island was always last on the plow crew's priority list. The news Jimmy had shared unsettled him to the extreme. Suicide was a different story. That would justify ignoring his work order. "Okay, Jimmy, you got my attention ... out we go." His expression warmed a bit in the collusion with this friend whom he loved.

Until now, they had been driving south on Route 1. With the new destination set, Taddy deftly turned the huge vehicle around in the parking lot by the movie theater, reversed direction, and headed north on Route 1. The Drakes Island turnoff was still five or so miles down the road, but Jimmy snapped the high-powered search light and aimed it manually to light the roadside as they lumbered past. Tightly closed shops of Route 1 appeared and disappeared in the spotlight. Snow pelted his face; every few seconds he had to reach with his big hand to clear the accumulation. Taddy chuckled, watching him, but soon both grew quiet. As much as they wished for a lighter mood, the real possibility of what they might find wouldn't release them.

When the Drakes Island turnoff came into sight, the truck slowed to a crawl; the men peering ahead for the yellow light that signaled the left turn. Jimmy focused the searchlight up in front of the truck; there was the blinking light, careening in wild winds. For a moment, Jimmy saw the monarchs of just a few hours ago in his mind; he wanted to see them again. But there was only darkness and snow and wind.

Taddy—using memory as much as sight—turned right, and then slowly, slowly descended the hill. With a vehicle the weight of this truck fully loaded with salt and sand riding behind you, every move you made had to be gradual, slow. Speed could tip the truck over in a heartbeat spilling the load. More than two feet of snow had fallen already; the headlights were dim circles in the powerful, thick fall. As they crossed the marsh, a wicked blast off the sea fought Taddy for control of the truck. On the best of days, this narrow road was a challenge. With the icy accumulation here, Taddy took extra care. Jimmy scanned the road and marshes for what, he didn't know. There was nothing out there to see.

As they approached the main road of the island, they traversed a slippery arc of road, wet with marsh runoff. Taddy doubled down on the brakes; a slow, cautious pumping. All manner of debris—seaweed, lobster traps, rocks—had been flushed up in what looked like ankle-high tides. Jimmy broke the silence. "Goddamn it, what a way to spend a Christmas Eve." Taddy nodded silently in agreement.

They were approaching the vicinity of Jetty Beach; at least that's where they thought they were. Teddy slowed the truck as they came around the corner to the entrance to the parking lot. Jimmy's light scanned all around as they drove up and into the seaside area. In the second arc of the searchlight, the men both saw a large, snow covered object by the stones of the jetty. Taddy took his foot off the accelerator, and the big truck slowed to an idle. Both men were stunned at the ease of finding what they suspected was the woman's car.

Taddy responded to Jimmy's arm-grabbing by accelerating gradually, inching along until the vehicle was launched into a long skid, the ice under seawater causing a treacherous free fall. Jimmy grabbed the dashboard to steady himself while Taddy held the wheel tight to the direction of the skid. It wasn't too hard to imagine going off the edge of the jetty. The truck came to a stop broadside, back to the entrance of the parking lot. The two men swiveled the searchlight to locate again what they thought they had seen, but the dark snow had swallowed it up.

Jimmy spoke first. "Taddy, there was a car in there. There ain't nobody out in this storm but us guys and maybe that crazy woman. It must be her. Christ, my heart's poundin'. I got to go there and open that door. If she's in there, we got to get her out before the tide takes the whole damn car out to sea. Or get rescue down here. No tellin' what shape she'll be in."

Taddy put his hand on Jimmy's arm in support to help his friend. "It just might be good news. She might have gone off to one of the cottages, you know, or still be in the car, waiting for a rescue. Let's give it the benefit of the doubt. I'll get you over there, but we can't stay here for long. The water's comin' up fast. You can't hesitate, Jimmy." The cop looked back toward the sea and nodded, the weight of what he had to do in his eyes.

Taddy backed the truck up until they saw what they thought must be Pamela Iverson's car. They drove ahead until the headlights illuminated their target again. They were stunned into silence a second time to see huge waves breaking over the jetty—almost onto the back end of what looked like the Subaru.

Stopping gingerly, Jimmy faced his fears by jumping into action. Taking a flashlight out of the truck's equipment tray, he buttoned his coat, put on gloves, opened the cab door, and lowered himself into the flooded lot. His boots proved no barrier to the freezing water. He clamped his mouth tight when the cold water seeped in, but continued moving ahead carefully, sliding along on the treacherous layer of ice under nearly six inches of seawater. As he approached the Subaru, possibilities roiled in his mind. He'd responded to suicides before; knew the images stayed with you for a long, long time. In his house tonight, before the storm started, some of those images resurfaced, with him playing the central character. He feared to add another picture to that gruesome gallery.

Jimmy hesitated only a second at the door of the car before taking courage from somewhere. Clearing off the snow, he opened the door. He bent to peer inside—prepared for anything.

CHAPTER 18

MORSE CODE

Drakes Island
Christmas Eve, 1999

Ed opened his eyes to the soft glow of embers on the hearth. His back ached. He shifted, trying to get comfortable. He'd been dreaming about windows: storm windows, old hulking storm windows; the kind taken up out of the cellar each fall and carried up ladders to shield against powerful winter blasts off the beach. In the dream, a younger man (maybe Ed himself—though it didn't look like him) lugged the windows out of the cellar, and climbed up high on an invisible ladder carrying the heavy load. He was trying to settle hooks into loops, to secure the windows, but the loops were loose, and wouldn't hold the weight. The windows slipped out of his hands and tumbled slowly through the air, breaking into a million pieces, and slamming onto the earth far below. And he—up on the ladder—didn't care. Then the dream faded and there were only a few of the ingredients left: hooks, broken glass, and a view from a very high place.

Ed shifted his weight as he rose toward consciousness trying to remember more, but the warm room lulled him back toward sleep until the question of why he was sleeping in the living room came to him. Reality finally overcame his drowsiness. He sat up to clear his head. Before he could completely remember why he was there, Ed saw that he wasn't alone. Someone was there on the sofa across from him. The floodgates of memory opened. The events of the past few hours played through his head. Was it possible? Pamela Iverson—the woman, the *missing* woman—was resting here, only a few feet away from him.

It still had to be Christmas Eve. Yes, it had all happened. He relived the jab on the brakes, and the jolt and sound of her head hitting the rear window. He remembered, too, the drive home with her beside him. In his concern for the woman, none of his customary hesitancy had held. She had been in the cold so long. The loud crack of lightning in his memory brought him back to the room. Most probably the whole town had been blown out from that powerful surge. They were all in the dark together.

Restored a bit by this memory of the events of the night, Ed stood and walked to her. He knelt by the sofa, watching her, watching and listening to her breath. *This was Pamela Iverson, the missing woman.* She seemed to be all right. She was still sleeping, covered by Sarah's quilt. He touched the bandage he had applied to her forehead after cleaning her wound. It was still secure; there was no sign of fresh blood. The temperature in the room was warm, maybe in the mid-sixties. They were safe, and morning would come—then he would see what the situation was and deal with it in daylight. A blizzard of this intensity couldn't last too long.

Ed looked toward the bay windows. The little Christmas tree stood in darkness but was still glowing in his mind. Sarah's tree had guided him home, had been his lighthouse on a rocky shore. He remembered the snug bump of the garage door, the feeling of safety. They were here on Blueberry Lane. The details of the evening's travel, the monarch butterflies, the lights from a long-lost Christmas tree—it had all affected Ed. It was connected somehow with Sarah. He spent a few minutes letting the warmth of that knowing rise up in him, rise all the way to his eyes, which were uncharacteristically filled with tears.

Fortunately, there was plenty of wood for the fire and food in the house. If this storm did keep up—and it had happened before, snowing for a week in February of '67—they could wait it out. Thunder cracked over the house. Ed flinched involuntarily. He'd heard of this phenomenon: thunder snow; another surprising thing to add to the list of wonders for this day. It was hard to understand that only a few hours ago, he'd left the house paralyzed by a wave of melancholy.

Ed looked down at his sleeping guest. Watching her, Ed wondered what could have caused such risky behavior. Something had driven her and overridden caution for herself and concern for her family. Jimmy had made reference to her being disturbed. Actually, Ed remembered Jimmy used the word *nutty*.

In the midst of this quiet moment, he realized she had become very, very still. The trauma of the night's events might trigger any number of reactions, he thought. Ed leaned over, took her hand, and listened closely for her breathing, relaxing a bit when he heard the slow intake of breath. He could see from her relaxed face that she was sleeping deeply. He put his hand on her forehead to feel her temperature. She was warm under his hand, a good sign. Pamela Iverson was going to be all right. Eying the ashy coals on the hearth, Ed rose to get a few pieces of wood, placed them on the embers, and ruffled the flames up a bit.

How should he proceed? When things had gotten dangerous in covert operations at sea, Ed had been in charge of the code room. He needed that protocol tonight. He needed his old, trusty, self-reliant self tonight. He needed the stamina of that man of the past—needed it now. These days, he rarely had to decide on anything more significant than what to buy at the supermarket, or how to live on his pension. Tonight's drama had challenged Ed's forgotten capabilities. A woman, whose life was dear to many—was in his home. And there were people out looking for her, putting their own lives at risk.

Ed took stock of the reliability of the house: air temps would keep in the sixties with the wood fire, his improvised bandage would probably hold until he could get her to the emergency room up in Biddeford, and there was plenty of food and water.

Still, he somehow didn't feel okay with waiting it out. People—his friend Jimmy Casey to be exact—would be in danger. How could he try to get word out without a phone? Suddenly, he realized that the phone's being dead was only an assumption. Maybe the outage hadn't taken the phone lines with it. Ed rose abruptly and went into the kitchen and picked up the wall phone by the stove. He paused a moment, praying, then picked up the receiver. There was no sound, no tone, and no connection.

From the kitchen doorway, Ed stood still musing as he watched Pamela, her profile clear in the firelight. She was thin, with delicate features, and from what little talking she had done, he judged she wasn't "nutty." From what Jimmy had said, she was somewhere in her mid-fifties. In the quiet of the room, he could feel her soft presence. No one else had been in this room in years. It felt different with her in it—warmer. Or was it his concern for her that he felt? He couldn't tell. When you are together with a person in a struggle for survival, distance disappears. Tonight they were together; he felt he knew her now.

Ed guessed Jimmy was probably cruising Route 1, searching for Pamela right now. With that, an idea sparked. Just this morning, when he was in the cellar, Ed had noticed some old radio equipment in the same bin as the Christmas tree. He had been meaning to get rid of the old stuff this spring at one of the flea markets around town. Although it was old, the equipment still worked, but it needed electricity to operate. Ed mentally kicked himself that he hadn't gotten around to buying a generator, the basic requirement for safety out here on the island. It was something he would take care of come the first business day after this storm. Tonight it was a moot point.

But wait a minute, Ed thought. His old relic of an ancient hand-operated Morse code transmitter was down there. It had been scrapped when they scrapped the Code, and Ed had bought it for a souvenir. He straightened up with that thought, a surge of excitement surfing through him. It might work! If he could oil the apparatus to get the shutter moving smoothly and find a powerful beam of light to fuel it, the "dits" and "dahs" of Morse code could be put to good use tonight. Question was, could it be received through this snow? And, more important, who would be there to receive it?

No one who had ever known or transmitted Morse code could forget the emergency SOS sequence; it was basic communication for the whole world. *Jimmy!* Jimmy knew Morse code and would know where it was coming from and who was sending it. It was just possible that Ed could put this entire plan together and get a message to his friend if he was near.

What were the odds that Jimmy was on the island somewhere? That, he didn't know. But it was worth trying. He keenly felt his part in this drama and had to act.

Sitting in the dark kitchen, elbows on his knees, he thought deeply. With eyes closed, he remembered seeing the bright bursts of light, discs of gold skidding through the atmosphere flung from the silent continent of his ship on dark waters. An SOS would go out again tonight if he had anything to do with it.

There was a drawer full of batteries in the cellar, probably still good; he would not run out of energy. If he could get the old shutter to send, he might save everyone a lot of grief. He had to go for it anyway; couldn't just sit here and wait anymore. Even if it was an antiquated method of communication, it might work tonight. It *had* to work tonight! Ed went to Pamela's side. She was still peacefully sleeping. Reassured now that he had a plan, Ed swung into action.

In the kitchen, he dressed for the cold, hoping against hope that Jimmy would head for Drakes Island. Or maybe the road crew would see the light. Ed felt sure Jimmy would recognize Morse code if he saw it, even if it came from a flashlight. Would Jimmy put two and two together and realize it was Ed trying to get his attention?

Dressed for the storm, Ed went back into the living room to tell Pamela what he was going to do. He spoke to her softly, even though she was asleep. "Pamela, I've got an idea. I'm not leaving you … I'll be right back. I've got to go out in the driveway to try and send a signal that you are here." The sleeping woman didn't appear to register actually hearing his message, but Ed trusted she knew.

He felt his way through the kitchen which was now dimly illuminated by the radiance of snow piling up outside the windows. He could walk anywhere in this house blindfolded, but the total dark of the cellar was another matter. There was a flashlight out in the garage on the shelf at the top of the stairway. He reached for it, reassured when its beam exploded in the dark. Ed's optimism surged, and down the cellar stairs he went.

Walking behind this light, Ed opened a small drawer in the workbench. He found what he was looking for: batteries, piles of them.

The powerful beacon that made this plan work had been stashed on the trunk beside the workbench a year or so ago. An old faithful geyser of light if ever there was one, this was it. Ed knew, with batteries, it could work.

Sweeping the flashlight around again, he found the bin containing the essential apparatus: his now-antique Morse code transmitter. Lifting the cover for the second time today, Ed pointed the beam inside and saw it. He lifted it out with an exclamation of pleasure. When it was on the workbench, he pushed the shutter up, praying it would move easily enough and slice a clean slab of light. But it hardly moved at all. Ed swept the beam of his flashlight over the contents of the shelf above the workbench. His trusty bottle of Mystery Marvel Oil was still where he had placed it last fall. He administered a three-drop blessing on each of the hinges. The shutter reacted to his gift immediately, opening and closing with ease.

Up the stairs then, back into the garage, across to the car, he opened the door, stepped up and into the driver's seat, and turned the key in the ignition. The cab lights illuminated, allowing him two hands to load the batteries into the beacon. It was cold out here; his bare hands began to move slower, clumsy within seconds. At a final push, the clip settled, and with a few deft moves, the beacon spouted light like a whale's blow. The garage lit brilliantly. With a few more minutes of tinkering, and the beacon's light streamed through the manual coder. Before Ed engaged the switch, he said a prayer to Saint Joseph, his personal favorite. When he said, "Amen," he flipped the switch, engaged the coder, and watched the *dits* and *dots* flash across the ceiling. Ed crowed with success and then spoke his thoughts aloud: "Okay now, let's get this out there. Jimmy, to say it in your way—you better be *goddamned* nearby." As he passed the bench, he grabbed a handful of bungee cords and paused to clean the years of accumulated dust off the signal light transmitter lens. Ed believed in bungee cords for everything, always had them around. He stuffed them into his pocket. They would be needed to secure the apparatus in this wind.

Ed went out the side door. Everything disappeared behind him within in a few steps. He stopped, suddenly afraid he would get lost. It took a minute to reconfigure where the street was and to locate the all-important cottage, which showed up only as a mound of white. He trudged cautiously, boots slipping on the icy driveway. A fall with this precious equipment could ruin all chances of rescue.

Wiping snow out of his eyes several times, he got the device set up and secured. He decided that the mailbox on the right of the driveway was the place to anchor the light. First, he cleared an area of snow big enough for the beacon. The old sailor positioned the beacon so its beam would shoot straight up into the sky. He secured it with bungee cords, and then switched it on. The intense heat of the bulb quickly melted all the snow in a small circle around the beacon, as well as the flakes that were falling near its heat. Ed jimmied the shutter in sequence a few times, practicing his SOS. Then he got serious. The familiar message shot up into the dark, lighting the thick fall in its beam. Ed chuckled to himself when he saw the old words of light spinning above him. He tapped the symbols deftly: *dot dot dot—dit dit dit—dot dot dot; SOS—SOS—SOS.* Over and over and over again in thirty-second loops, he kept at it for what seemed like a very, very long time until the stealthy invasion of cold began to seriously slow him down. Even then, he tried to keep going for as long as he could. He hoped someone would see the light, and whether or not they knew code, they would at least know it was a call for help. If Jimmy saw the light, he would know and come for sure.

The ferocious winds were studded with sharp snow crystals stinging Ed's face. He raised and lowered the shutter for a few more minutes. Slowing down with numbness, he couldn't stand the conditions any longer. He was dangerously cold; warmth was leaching into the wind through the exposed skin of his face and hands. When he could take it no longer, Ed left the torch lit, bungee-corded to the mailbox at the driveway's entrance. The now-steady stream of light sliced up into the sky in a tall fountain. Ed judged that the batteries might last an hour or so more, but that hour might just coincide with someone, somewhere in the area spotting the signal.

When Ed stepped into the quiet of his garage, he took off his coat and boots, glad to be relieved of their cold weight. He shook the snow off his hat and gloves, and left them all on a hook by the kitchen door. Entering the house, he rested against the kitchen counter; warmth embracing him, it allowed him to relax.

But once in the living room, he found Pamela Iverson sitting up on the sofa, looking straight at him. On her face was an expression of fear so deep that it spiked his pulse and stopped him from moving toward her. It would be up to him to help this woman deal with what had happened; help her discover how she had come to be in this desperate state. The real rescue was about to begin. Ed steeled himself. He had to trust he was up to the job. There was no one else available.

CHAPTER 19

SOS

Drakes Island
Christmas Eve, 1999

There was no light, no motion, and no sound in the car—nothing. Relief flooded Jimmy as he saw it was empty. All he could make out was the usual car interior, cold and dark. Then he saw a purse on the passenger seat, and a burst of hope made him reach for it. This would at least tell him what he needed to know. The person leaving the car had left in a hurry, not thinking of anything being stolen. It would offer sure proof as to the driver of this car.

He slammed the door closed and waded to the idling truck. As he pulled himself out of the water and into the cab, the expression on his friend's face demanded a quick answer. Jimmy shook his head and put a thumb-up to signify that he hadn't found what they both feared.

Before Taddy engaged the gears, he waited for Jimmy to open the purse. Searching the contents quickly, he found the picture of a woman on a Maine driver's license. Beside the picture was a name: Pamela Iverson. With that, he looked over to Taddy and shouted over the wind and the idling motor, "It's her!" Continuing to rifle the contents, he took out a prayer card, one with a picture of Jesus Christ, one hand up in greeting. The men looked at each other grimly. Jimmy spoke up. "I hope this means something good. We know where the woman *is not*. Now, where the hell *is* she?" Jimmy put the license and card back into the purse, hoping he would be able to return it to Pamela Iverson soon.

"Okay, Taddy boy, there's nothing more for us here—the car is empty. We know this is our girl, and she's down here somewhere. Here in some dark, freezing place—either dead or tryin' to stay alive. Christ, what do we do now?" Again, his frustration got the better of him, and he became the judge. "She must have the brains of a cat to be out on the island in the first place. Either that or she didn't expect this storm. We'll have to drive the island, drive slow and steady, look everywhere for signs: light, broken windows, anything that looks out of place." Taddy nodded, engaged the gears, and lit another cigarette.

The big truck backed out of the lot, then inched along down the hill and out onto Drakes Island; a lit ship on a dark sea. The possibility of death so near had affected them both.

The hulking truck wove tracks as it descended the hill, moving out of the parking lot; snow obscured the headlights. They had become prisoners in the cab. Taddy accelerated gently as they traveled down the narrow road parallel to an unrecognizable sea. The men were quiet, awed by wind's screaming crescendo, a force field just outside thin panes of window. Once they were level on the road, Taddy engaged the plow handle with a clank and a grind; the iron spade lowered. A loud thud banged when it met the road. Waves of snow parted on either side of the truck, cresting like waves on the beach beside them. The metallic racket filled the small heated space, overwhelming any conversation. Neither man felt like talking anyway.

Jimmy's feet had warmed up a bit, but the freezing tide had gone deep. He was shivering in spite of the superheated air spilling from the heater.

Taddy opened a new pack of cigarettes as he drove, keeping his eyes into the storm. Jimmy noticed that the ashtray on the dash was suspiciously empty. He looked at his friend questioningly. "Did you empty that ashtray in the parking lot, you dummy?" Taddy heard him and ginned sheepishly. Shaking his head in the affirmative, he hollered across the seat, "Jesus, Jimmy, those butts will be all the way out to Jamaica 'fore morning, and nobody will give a damn," adding sarcastically, "I thought it was the tree-hugger thing to do." At that, both men laughed uproariously, shredding the darkness around them with their private brand of humor.

Soon, though, the laughter died as they both wrestled with what their next move should be. She could be in any of the snowy humps of cottages they were passing. And then there was the other less optimistic possibility: she might not have made it to safety, might be in the ocean or in this sea of snow somewhere as the plow lumbered past her.

Jimmy spoke for them both: "I'm goddamned stymied, Taddy. How the hell are we gonna find someone in one of these cottages with nothing to tip us off about which one she might be in? There's no electricity in most of 'em anyway, and if there was, it wouldn't be on because the lines are down."

The frustration in his voice was an unusual thing. Taddy looked over at him with concern. The death of someone, of this woman, would be a great sadness in the ocean community. The fishing village had existed for many generations. The sea and storms like this had a long tradition of taking life. Jimmy was the man driving the rescue. He was responsible, and he knew it. Taddy felt for his friend.

Jimmy had resumed the searchlight, focusing on the snow-covered cottages they passed. He aimed close, looking for the smallest evidence of a break-in—a ripped screen, broken glass, tracks in snow—anything to indicate where she might have gone. But in this snow-thick atmosphere, his surveillance yielded nothing. He sat back, releasing his grip on the light, needing relief from the blinding, freezing snow. In frustration, he took one of Taddy's cigarettes and lit it, hoping to provide inspiration or insight or even just to calm down. He needed help. Taddy smiled as Jimmy held the lit butt, but stayed silent. He couldn't relinquish his powerful hold on the wheel for even a second.

After a few minutes of quiet, making slow progress in the whiteout, Jimmy sat up suddenly. He threw his butt out the window and turned to Taddy with something approaching excitement. "You know, Taddy. Ed LaCasse lives down here. Maybe he'd have an idea about where she might be. I know it's a long shot, but let's head down by his place and see if we can raise him. I saw him up at the diner earlier this evening. There's no place else he could be but home. Take a left down there at Winnow's Edge; head over to Blueberry Lane. His cottage is at the end of that street next to the marsh."

Taddy nodded in agreement, with his twelfth cigarette in his mouth, smoke rising straight up into his tense face. As Jimmy looked at Taddy, he realized that with the deep wrinkles his outdoor life had earned him, he could've played Humphrey Bogart while sitting behind the wheel tonight. Jimmy laughed at the thought in spite of himself and shared his impression with him: "Christ, this is good enough to be a Hollywood movie. You'd be the hero, my man, Humphrey Bogart or better. 'Here's lookin' at you, kid'!" he roared.

Taddy, unimpressed, began a slow left-hand turn, pumping the brakes, feeling out the angle and speed, the chances of a spin out being ninety to ten. Mid-turn, and for no apparent reason, Taddy took the cigarette out of his mouth and threw it out the open window, stopping the truck dead in the road. He reached over to punch Jimmy on the arm. Startled, Jimmy swept his light over the landscape on the driver's side, looking for what had spooked his friend. "What the hell's the trouble, Taddy?" Jimmy said as he tried to find what had caught Taddy's attention, but there was nothing but snow.

Taddy threw the door of the cab open and stood on the runner board, hollering with an uncharacteristic zeal. Ducking back into the cab, he grabbed Jimmy's arm and shouted, "Jimmy, look over in the direction of LaCasse's place. Look up over the trees in the sky. What the hell's that? Can you see it?" He straightened up as he went back to see the light.

Jimmy jumped out of the truck on his side and looked to see a geyser of light spout up in spite of the heavy snow. "Jesus, that is one spooky-looking thing, Jimmy. It practically shouts, 'Here I am!'"

Jimmy kept looking through the curtain of snow at the light. He watched it bounce up off the snow into the air in a sequence: "· · · − − − · · ." And again: "· · · − − − · · ." The light repeated. Suddenly, Jimmy howled and began jumping up and down.

"Taddy, my boy, do you know what that is? That's a goddamned SOS. That's what it is! A goddamned message, and if I know anything about anything, it's got to be comin' from Ed's place. He's Coast Guard, you know. That's Morse code … and by Jesus, he knows that I know the code too. That's what this is about. He's calling me in; he's got the woman. That just has to be it. Drive the hell over there, Taddy. This night is getting weirder and weirder as the minutes tick by. I got to hope he's got her at his cottage and that she is all right. I got to hope, my boy, goddamned hope!"

Taddy took his seat behind the wheel of the truck to begin the delicate job of shifting the direction of the snowplow on narrow island lanes. As they began their drive down to Blueberry Lane, they sailed for Ed's light as if this snowfield was the sea and that light was a refuge from the storm.

CHAPTER 20

A CLOSE QUIET

Blueberry Lane
Christmas Eve, 1999

Pamela awoke from a sudden rustle of shifting logs on the hearth. Eyes flickering open, she was in a warm, dim room she didn't recognize in the small space lit by firelight. She was on a couch, covered with a blanket, alright, comfortable but still on the edge of some fear she couldn't quite grasp.

She sat up quickly, anxiously, but sharp pain rocketed around in her head, and she was forced back onto the pillows. It was quiet here, wherever here was, but just outside, wild winds were buffeting windows. She closed her eyes again, hoping and willing herself to disappear into sleep. They wound around her though—the thoughts. She began to remember: the previous day, so ill spent, came back disheartening her. The flight from Chick's Crossing this morning, abandoning the car, and then almost getting lost in the freezing terror of a blizzard—it all replayed, each image sharper and harder to endure than the last.

Outside this warm room wind told her the storm still raged. Within her, guilt and remorse became monsters. Monsters wearing her face.... She had caused the people she loved to suffer, had almost lost her life, and now, she was literally lost. Remorse clamped over her, remorse that allowed for no hope, no forgiveness, and no light save that from the small fire that burned on this hearth.

Hearing a sound to her right, Pamela pulled herself up to a sitting position once more to face whatever would come next. A man stood in the doorway of the room looking at her, a man she remembered somehow. Her vulnerability was complete, and so real it hurt. A cry broke from her lips. She closed her eyes and allowed herself to lean back against the sofa, the fear of regret rolling within.

Suddenly there was the soft touch of hands on her shoulder and a voice she had heard before, a voice that offered gentleness with no rebuke or anger ... only calm presence. "Pamela," the voice said, soothing, like cool water. "Whatever this is, we can talk it out. Right now, right here, you are safe. This storm makes everything seem worse, but we are lucky to be back in this cottage tonight. After the ordeal you've gone through," the soothing voice went on, "you need to give yourself time to understand, to see what could have happened, and what did; to get over whatever it is you've been through. I'll get you some water, make you some hot chocolate, something to eat ... you need water and food by now, I imagine. I know a little bit about you but I want to know more."

With those kind words, Pamela dared open her eyes; the man was kneeling beside the sofa, dimly visible in soft firelight. She focused her gaze on him holding his words close, words like balm to her heart.

Ed took his time, stayed where he was, smiled, and let her adjust and calm down. "I know enough to say that what troubles you can be released. You got through this terrible night, and probably other nights like it too. That proves you have the strength. We could have lost you, Pamela. I am so happy that you are here now and not a headline in tomorrow's news." He realized as he said it that he truly was. "My name is Ed, Ed LaCasse. There is nothing to fear here. You can trust me," he said as he reached over to hold her clenched hands.

Ed felt himself stretch trying to help her. As he spoke, he wondered where the words were coming from. He wasn't used to expressing this depth of feeling. He smiled at her taut, worried face, and then rose to get her some water.

Pamela watched him walk away. She believed him, and knew that because of him, she had shelter and refuge for a while. She dared a direct look into his eyes as he came back to her with the water. He was a gentleman, one whose face displayed age handsomely, with kindness. His patience and concern were focused on her. She felt better, felt herself calm down just within this brief encounter. When Pamela took the water he offered, she realized how much she needed it with the first sip and she drank it gratefully.

Ed retrieved the empty glass and went back into the kitchen. The beam of his flashlight ignited the dark room; she heard the rustle of opening cabinets and the clink of cups. She missed his presence already.

Outside, snowdrifts were piling up, everything transforming under the stunning depth of snow. As it often did on the beach plane, snow now turned to ice and pinged strongly on Ed's windows. Light from the sputtering fire cast shadows that took on shapes that didn't seem menacing. She was comforted. Raising her hands to the ache in her forehead, she closed her eyes. His kindness embarrassed her. What must he think of her?

Within a few minutes, he was back again, holding cups of steaming hot chocolate and offering cookies on a plate. He put the cocoa down on the hearth to cool.

Pamela dared to speak, hoping she could muster a voice in her state. "How did you do this?" she asked, referring to the welcome hot chocolate.

He replied, looking at her steadily, "Gas stove, thank God." In his reply, his words sounded so normal, relaxing them both on this uncharted night. His calm words were almost funny enough to chuckle about.

After a few minutes of deep silence, Ed handed Pamela the cup. She held it in her hands; it warmed them as she inhaled the drink's fragrance. When she allowed herself a sip, nothing had ever tasted so good in her life. Ed watched, sipping from the cup he'd made for himself. The intimacy of this precious, simple moment was disturbed by the return of regret for her actions today. How could she ever make this up to her family, to this man? Pamela realized she had invaded his privacy. She'd destroyed his Christmas as well and put him at great personal risk.

"Ed," she said so softly he had to lean forward to hear her, "I would like to say how sorry I am for causing all this trouble. I interfered with your holiday. I am so very sorry. Will you, can you, forgive me?" And then she came to tears again.

Ed regarded her for a minute. When he spoke, he phrased the truth simply, hoping to lighten her obvious suffering. "Pamela, I had nowhere to go tonight except to church, and I really have no one to account to but myself. I was going to be alone. Tell you the truth, I'm glad of the company."

Another wave of pain started in her head. She put her hand to the bandage and took a few moments to regain her voice. Then she asked incredulously, "You're glad of my company?"

Ed continued, "I am glad—glad that I caught the reflection of your car lights down at Jetty Beach. Because of Jimmy Casey's announcement at the diner—he's the town cop most likely out looking for you right now—I already knew someone was out there and in trouble. Looks like the Almighty had special plans for me tonight, though I had none for myself."

That said, they both sipped the chocolate for a while. Ed noticed with approval when Pamela reached to the plate for one of the cookies. She sat back, eating the wafers, and he continued. "Soon's the power's on and they do some plowing down here—which could be a while yet as this island's usually last on their list—we'll get in touch with the police and notify your family. Til then, you've got time to rest. There is nothing you need do or say now."

Pamela dared another look at him and nodded; the quiet of the moment undercut by the wind's roar. Ed felt it right to let things be. He occupied himself with small tasks that needed doing. He stood and went to the fire to put on a few logs and rustle up the flame, and then he lit his flashlight and went back to the kitchen for more cookies, as the plate had been emptied.

When he sat down again, he had gathered enough courage to broach the weighty subject of why all this had come to be. "Maybe you could tell me how this happened to you," he began cautiously. "I've been told I'm a good listener." He smiled again, his gaze soft.

Pamela sopped up his concern like warm milk. She focused on his face and the possibility of understanding. Even in this dim room, she could see a downturn of shoulders. When he spoke, his sympathetic tone suggested he had experience with grief. Not a young man, Ed was thin, tall, and, she thought, handsome. But the furnishings of this room, visible within the small circle of firelight, had clearly been chosen by a woman—that was certain. A plate collection, looking from where she lay like a landscape series, hung over the fireplace, and there were figurines on the mantle.

She could see too, in the fresh burst of fire from the hearth, that this room hadn't been tended to for quite a while. Books and papers were piled on the floor in stacks, and cups and plates littered one of the side tables. As her gaze returned to Ed, he sat waiting for her answer. His precious sincerity broke over her like a wave. He was listening to her, openly and honestly, with no judgments already formed. This caring wasn't a thing to waste.

Pamela put her cup on the floor beside the sofa and then put her feet on the floor and pulled herself up as best she could. Taking a minute to collect the energy she had left, she set herself to respond to what he had asked, trying not to be sidetracked by her fear. And still, the winds outside careened, shaking windows and doors, threatening everything with wild power.

She began speaking while looking at her hands. "My husband died … over a year ago now. That's at the heart of it, Ed. I was lost—am lost—after that. So lost that I went into hiding myself; stepped out, and turned away from the life I didn't want to own. I am the master of denial. I closed my eyes against what happened and the pain, hid it away in some part of me, then moved fast, created another person, another life because mine died when he did. I discovered I was most comfortable where no one knew me at all. My go-to places were where people came and went, but few people took notice of anyone else. I liked it best when no one recognized me or talked to me. I didn't want to be alone, but I didn't have the courage needed to live a real life, so I just got good at pretending. It ended up that I felt all right when I was in supermarkets. So I began going every day; it became the world to me, the real world, a world that I could be part of in this secret way.

"I took up a pretend residence in these places, if you can understand that. I began feeling at home, started rearranging things, putting things where I would have them exclusively for my use: magazines, creams, perfumes, a package of cookies here and there. I ate all my meals at the café and bakery, went home only to rush back each morning. It was like *I* worked there. I sometimes rearranged shelves, did comparisons of products and sales, and kept myself totally busy. The market I liked the best was the Eastside in Providence, Rhode Island. It's organic and elegant, full of exotic things. I lived in a fantasy of owning the place. Sounds silly now, but at the time, it allowed me to go on."

She stopped her story, looking to Ed for his reaction. He was still looking intently at her. He saw she needed his encouragement, and he smiled it for her. "And ...? Don't stop there. How does that connect with tonight?"

"Sounds crazy, but it was all so real to me. The Eastside was the only place I could be in without that emptiness filling me. I admit it, Ed. I can be a coward, I know." Pamela stopped to lean against the sofa back for a minute, closing her eyes. Ed fixed his attention on her face, still looking for signs of trauma. What he saw was evidence of deep emotion. He waited for what would come next.

Soon enough, she sat up to resume her story. "But the management at the Eastside Market had been watching. They saw my 'intrusion,' as they called it, as a criminal act. Everything came down around me one Sunday over a year ago now, when I destroyed the floral display. It's hard to explain why and how I did it, but I'll try. It happened on my birthday. I so desperately needed something to change in my life. I was disappearing, even to myself. Suffice it to say, a little accident happened, sort of innocently. I pulled a few plants out of the display, and the whole thing crashed into the aisle. Cracked pots spilled dirt and flowers all over the vestibule floor. There's another part of that story where monarch butterflies put in an appearance, but I need to know you better to tell you about that. It would be too much information for tonight...."

At the mention of the monarchs, Ed's pulse shot up several beats.

Pamela continued, "Long story short, I was barred from the Eastside that day, told never to come back, or I would be arrested. Not the greatest reputation for a woman my age—kicked out of a supermarket as a probable thief." At the upshot of this surprising confession, Ed had trouble stifling his laugh. The woman bore no resemblance to a thief, none at all. So as to let her know that he was still interested in her story, he leaned over to put his hand on her arm and asked her to go on.

"Someone—I don't know who—called my daughter. Of course she was concerned that her mother was going crazy and she came to rescue me, brought me to live with her for a while. That's how I got to be here in Wells. That's it, Ed. Today, I just couldn't stand the pain, so I ran again. And it felt good … until it turned bad."

Breathing a sigh, she let him know she had finished the tale. She looked to him and let her eyes meet his. He recognized the courage her confession had taken. He looked directly back at her, sitting in his seat, holding her hand, reaching inside for what he could say. The monarchs— the glowing creatures that had circled in front of his windshield. This collision of her words and his experience teased him with the thought that it had all been planned somehow. But he would keep that to himself for now.

In the dim light, she started speaking again. "This morning, I couldn't bear going along with Christmas. It was too painful. I don't know how to make you understand, but pretending to be happy and looking forward to the evening—and tomorrow—took faith, hope, and strength I didn't have." Pamela drew a few breaths in the quiet. He followed her gaze and saw that only glowing coals graced the hearth now.

"Hold up. I need to get some wood from the garage and get this fire back up to blazing. I hadn't noticed it was low. Take a rest. I'll be right back." He put his hand on her shoulder before he left, adding, "And thank you for trusting me."

Pamela listened as Ed bustled around with his chore, as if this night were just like any other. Cold air from the garage swirled into the warmed air of the living room; the delicious smell of wood smoke wafted on currents. She heard the door close, shut her eyes, and heard the logs land on the hearth; feeling the burst of warmth on her skin when the fire sprang back to life. When she opened her eyes again, a rosy glow filled the room, and Ed was back beside her.

"Ed, I haven't got the strength to tell you all of it. I just want to say thank you for tonight and thank you for being the good person you are. I am … I feel better just being here. You can understand my fear for my family and what I have put them through, can't you? Oh my God, if I only could undo what I've done."

Ed felt her trust and wanted her to feel it wasn't misplaced. He would respond with his own experience. "Pamela, I know about loss. My wife, Sarah, died a few years ago, and I suppose I have been hiding out here some too, though I never thought of it that way, but *I get it.* I get what it feels like to not want to live your life anymore. Trying to *just* get along is a very familiar routine to me. I've held on to what was and hoped I'd find my way or it would find me. Seeing your struggle is like watching myself. We are free to hide out as long as we want or free to accept what has happened and move along. The death of a loved one brings chaos and loneliness … and fear that the place of comfort and joy of that life is gone forever and that all that will be left is emptiness and dullness. And that feels true, but only for as long as you want it to be. Pain like that leaves no room for anything new to enter. The love of your family, the love of those around you, enjoying being alive—all of those things get crowded out. We—and I include myself here—have to accept it, see it, feel it, and let it go if we want a new life to begin."

The steadily growing firelight spread into the room. After the tumble of emotions and the events of the night, Ed felt exhaustion rising and feared he might not quite be up to this conversation. Since Sarah, the world of feelings was a foreign territory; he was getting lost here.

Pamela fought the urge to tell him how what he had said touched her. She was still more comfortable hiding her feelings.

"So how did you come to be at the beach when the storm blew in? Didn't you hear about it on TV or the radio? Not very good planning for a girl clever enough to stay alive out in the elements tonight…." His face crinkled into a smile.

Pamela answered, "I didn't think—I just reacted. I used to live around here years ago. You wouldn't have recognized the place then. Drakes Island was my retreat, my favorite place in the world. I spent many, many summer afternoons on Jetty Beach. When I needed to get out of the house this morning, it was the only place I could think of going. The feeling of coming home swept in when I turned off Route 1 and saw the ocean. It didn't register that it was under storm skies. The waves were almost black. I should have known they meant trouble. I didn't hear any weather reports, or they didn't register."

Ed countered her. "I knew Drakes Island back then. I choose to see it that way still, in spite of the way it's changed. So your being there was really accidental? People were saying a lot of things about you, including that you might want to kill yourself." He realized that when he had said this, released it into the room, he might have made a mistake. "I don't see any signs of that, Pamela."

She looked troubled at his statement, "Oh no. Not that. I have already caused terrible hurt around me; I am not proud of it, but if my daughter has heard suicide, it will break her heart."

Ed again shared his plain wisdom. "Most hurts can be mended if people will trust each other. I'm sure your family can and will understand what you have shared with me. It's been a rocky road, Pamela, but it's your road all the same; you have had to walk it. There is no shame there, only hope that a new path can be found now. You may need help walking it, and there are people to help. You and I, all of us, can't go back. Living in the past is not really living at all." Ed stopped. He believed these words; he just didn't know where they came from exactly and why he hadn't thought them before now.

Ed's genuine caring warmed Pamela. *How lucky*, she thought. *How lucky to have been saved out of this storm by this man.* As she let this thought sink in, there was a tapping at the wall she had built around her, the wall that kept her prisoner. A single, hesitant smile rose into her eyes, and, this time, she didn't stop it.

The two shared a close quiet, one to the other, until grinding and scraping sounds above the howling outside compromised the moment. They looked at the windows to see a large, black shape float up out front, lights flashing a red that colored everything around the same hue. Pamela and Ed looked at each other, then toward the window. Rescue was at hand, but the two new friends were reluctant to let go of this precious moment.

CHAPTER 21

AMONG THE LIVING

Blueberry Lane
Christmas Eve, 1999

The plow truck rode hills and valleys of snow down to Blueberry Lane. The plume of light was still shooting straight up into air, anchored in Ed LaCasse's driveway, calling them in like a beacon on a landing field. The plow's heavy weight made quick work of the storm's accumulation, flattening anything in its way.

Jimmy was out the door before the truck stopped. He bent doubled over to fight through the wind toward the beacon still miraculously bungeed to the mailbox. Looking up into the torch's powerful output, he muttered, "Ingenious." Heat from the light had melted a twelve-inch circle in the snow around it. By the time he turned to look for him, Taddy stumbled up behind him inspecting the apparatus for himself. "Got to hand it to LaCasse," Taddy shouted into the roar.

"Goddamned ingenious," Jimmy howled, then laughed aloud.

After the inspection, the two men turned their attention toward the house, shielding their faces from stinging icy wind. Both men recognized this stage in the storm's progress; snow turning to ice announced that the following edge of the storm might be somewhere near. Morning might just dawn clear; no telling what time it was now. There was no light in Ed's cottage; power was obviously out down here like up in town.

The men slogged up the driveway, bearing right, moving blindly toward the garage. As they neared the side door, Ed flung it open, flashlight in hand. Jimmy called out loud and clear, "LaCasse, you bugger, I am mighty goddamn glad to see you standin' there. Taddy and I stopped by for tea and crumpets!" His roar of a laugh leavened the seriousness of the night. Ed knew the boys, judging by their high spirits, had already guessed she was here.

Lifting his free hand in response to the greeting, he said, "I'm damned glad to see you myself, boys. Come on in. Someone I want you to meet, so don't stand on ceremony. I've even got a fire to warm yourselves by." As he finished his invitation, gusts of wind propelled Ed backward into the garage and hurried the two visitors inside. He slammed the door shut quickly, shook off the icy cold, and turned to his visitors. "You know, that blast felt like hurricane-force wind. This is one for the books. I even heard thunder a few hours ago."

Once in the secure space, Taddy and Jimmy stamped snow from their boots and brushed their clothes, all the while fixing Ed with searching stares that begged the big question of the night. "So, Ed," Jimmy began, "What's the SOS all about? I read it, buddy, loud and clear, but don't know what it's about. You got the woman here or what? Is she alive or dead? Equal chance at either ... we found her car over at Jetty Beach—empty, thank God. ... I was some nervous about openin' that door, I can tell you. What's the situation? I read from your lighthouse out there that a rescue might have happened, and I pray it did. Give it up, Ed."

Ed responded quickly, happy to relieve their fears. "She's here, Jimmy, and she's okay. That's the long and short of it; she's right in there on the couch, resting to get over what she's been through. My Jeep spun out in the road down by Jetty Beach while coming home from the diner. Headlights sparked on her car. I knew nobody in their right mind would be out at the jetty tonight, not even Massachusetts wave watchers, so I put two and two together and figured it had to be the woman."

Jimmy exhaled visibly with relief. "Jesus, Ed, just think if I hadn't run into you at the diner, you might not have known about the woman and her car. Details make all the difference all the time."

Ed smiled and continued, "Like you, I mustered the courage up to open the door and saw an empty car. I was relieved and scared at the same time. Where she could have gone is what I needed to know. It came to me that if I drove up and down the streets, laying on my horn, she might just hear me and come out of wherever she had got to. So I did, *and it worked.* She was in one of the cottages on Ocean Drive. I was travelin' real slow, blasting my horn, when I heard a pounding on the back of the Jeep. I didn't think fast enough; jumped the brakes, and the Jeep stopped quick. Pamela slammed her head on the rear window. Then, with the shock of it, she collapsed into the street. I got her in the car and back here just before the power blew. She's inside now. I bandaged her head up as best I could and have kept her warm. She is pretty upset about the trouble she's caused; heartsick about the family up on Chick's Crossing. Now I'll bring you guys in to talk with her, but no rough stuff. No joking, Jimmy. She's had all she can take for one day."

As Ed turned to lead the boys into the house, Taddy and Jimmy exchanged knowing looks. Ed had revealed protective feelings for the woman that neither of them had ever seen in him. Jimmy knew better than to make any jokes, but the boys smiled to each other at the same time, Taddy sharing Jimmy's drift without words.

The smell of a wood fire beckoned them through the dark kitchen and into the living room, which was glowing with firelight and warmth. Ed stood beside the sofa where Pamela Iverson rested, her eyes closed, with a bandage visible on her forehead. At last, the elusive woman had taken on substance and form in front of them.

When Pamela sensed that they were watching her, her eyes fluttered open. With obvious effort, she sat up, her anxious gaze on them.

Ed took over the introduction. "Jimmy, Taddy, I'd like to introduce you to Pamela Iverson." After those words, he sat beside her on the sofa, taking her hand. "Pamela's had a *wicked bad* day and night." He used the great Maine imperative to give a warning to the boys not to misjudge the "missing person." "She needs everyone to understand that her disappearance wasn't anything she planned; it just happened. She had to have some space and chose the wrong time and place to look for it. She fell asleep in the car with the storm coming in; battery died … end of story. The rest of it, you already know."

Allowing a few moments to tick by, to let this all sink in, Pamela spoke, voice faint and raspy, affirming what she had been through. "Thank you for being out in this storm for me. I am so ashamed of what I did. The possibility of this storm, the danger I put myself and you in … none of it was part of my planning this morning. When I went to the island this morning …." Here she stopped and looked up to Ed. "It's still the same day, Ed, isn't it? Feels like this day's a month long."

Her hand reached involuntarily to the bandage as if to confirm that this all was too real, and then closed her eyes for a moment, resting before resuming. "Ed has been telling me about you, Jimmy, and he assures me that you are a brave, smart cop. Only special people take on such risk for someone they don't even know. Thank you a million times, and if you have any energy left, I have one request to ask of you. I've got to get word to my family that I'm all right."

Surprised and touched by Pamela's words of concern for them in the thick of all her troubles, Jimmy felt compelled to speak first. "Lady, we're some damn glad to see you safe and out of danger. We've been lookin' all over creation for you. I'm sure there's a story about how you came to be where you were, but we'll get word back up to your family that you're all right. Can't imagine what's goin' through their minds by now. We got a radio out in the truck, so you tell us what you want us to say, and we'll do our best to get the message up there. But now that we know you're safe and in Ed's hands, we got to get back out on the road like it was yesterday. There are roads to plow and more people to rescue. Storm like this always brings out troubles of many kinds."

"Officer Casey, that's the whole message … tell my family that I'm safe, that it was a mistake on my part … nothing else. I just fell asleep in the car. Oh God, that would make a world of difference if they knew that."

Taddy nodded, and then spoke. "My truck'll get us up there, or we'll radio ahead and have someone up plowin' the area drop by. You rest here, Pamela. We'll take care of it." He stood to get back on the road, offering her the blessing of a smile reserved only for "townies."

She, for the first time, dared a look directly at the men. "You mean ... it's that easy? You have a radio? You can get a message to my family now?" She collapsed back down again as quiet tears began, tears which so unstrung all three of the men looking on that they actually shuffled their feet in embarrassment.

Ed asked the two friends to stay long enough for the hot chocolate he was making. A bit reluctantly, Taddy sat down again, getting very uncomfortable in this warm room with all his gear on. Pamela remained still, and Jimmy took the opportunity to ask her a few questions. "Pamela, the folks up on the Crossing may want to know why you did it. Is there anything we can tell them to make it easier for them to understand?" he asked as gently as he knew how.

"I needed to think about some things. With Christmas on the threshold, I felt confused about being a person back in a town where she *used to live.* I felt lost and wanted to figure out how to go forward," Pamela answered. "When I parked at Jetty Beach, I had no idea this storm was so near or so fierce. I fell asleep. When I woke, it was on me, waves rolling like mountains down the jetty, and wind ratcheting up to crazy force. I had to abandon the car; the battery was dead. I knew I wouldn't make it through the night if I stayed where I was."

Merely talking about it filled her features with visible alarm. Then she remembered more horror. "And, oh God, how could I forget? I broke into a cottage down on Ocean Drive. I'm confessing it to you, Officer Casey; it was me, but I had no choice. Ed's the hero in all this. If he hadn't done what he did, I don't know what would have happened. I was having a dream at the cottage, or something like a dream, and these butterflies ... monarchs ... woke me up. I was probably delirious; I saw a glow from outside the kitchen window. Thinking it was the butterflies, I fought my way out of my blankets to find the light. The light was coming from Ed's Jeep as he drove by. Then I heard the car horn and knew he must be looking for me. I ran after him until I crashed into his car." Exhausted from the tale, she closed her eyes again, letting her head fall back.

Jimmy's attention flipped at the mention of the butterflies. He asked Ed quietly, "Butterflies? Did she say something about monarchs?" Ed nodded. He wanted to hear more about their appearance in her story since it had been only a few hours since their appearance in his own life. And hadn't Ed said something about them as well? What the hell was going on here? Showing up, even in the form of a dream, amazed him. He wanted to sit the two people down who were in front of him and do an interrogation, but there was no time for that. Even the mention of them—just after Darnice's hand had been in his—made him blush with the pleasure of the thought.

Taddy spoke in his understated way. "You won't be prosecuted for the break-in, Pamela. It's a matter of survival, might have to clean up and pay for the damage, though. People with cottages on the beach are fussy, but you'd have a lot of people go to bat for you there."

"Hey, Ed," Jimmy shouted, "Where's that hot chocolate? Taddy and me got to get back out to the truck and radio this in. Chief will have my ass if I … oh, sorry, Pamela. Chief will be none too pleased if I don't get this information to him."

Ed came from the kitchen with two mugs of hot chocolate. Jimmy and Taddy took them, blew ferociously to cool them, and downed them as fast as they could manage. The warm beverages were appreciated and needed after the energy the guys had put out.

"What's your phone number down here, Ed? They'll want that up at the station. You don't know which of the houses on Ocean Drive you broke into, do you Pamela? They'll want to know that too." He smiled at the thought of the complaints they would most likely get about the break-in. "Don't worry about it any. I'll take care of it."

Ed got the house number and address for her daughter from Pamela and wrote it down. Handing it to Jimmy, he added his own phone number to give to the worried family.

"I just don't have words to thank you both—and Ed—my rescuer," Pamela offered. I don't know which one of the cottages it was by name or number, but it's in the first two or three off the parking lot. Please, get up there to Chick's Crossing. That's where the damage still is now."

She stopped them again before they left the room, her voice a whisper as if she had used all the energy she had left. "Tell my family I'm sorry …

so, so sorry ... and I'll be on the phone with them as soon as the lines are up. Ed will take me home when the roads open. Tell them I love them all and that this will never happen again. I've learned an awful lesson. Tell little Robbie that Nana is coming home soon. Please tell them."

"That's a lot to remember," Taddy said, "but we got the gist of it. By the way, folks, it's past midnight. Merry Christmas to all of us and thank God we are all still among the living! Morning ought to bring some clearing. G'night, Ed, Pamela."

With that, they took one more look at the no-longer-missing woman, donned their caps, and went through the kitchen and out to the garage. They climbed back into the truck, and with a great grinding of gears and a long pull on the horn, they started out on their mission to Chick's crossing, red taillights disappearing into the still-falling snow.

CHAPTER 22

TRAVELING MERCIES

Wells, Maine
After Midnight, Christmas, 1999

With the truck still running and the heater going full blast during the visit, the cab was sweltering. The two traversed the freezing air and jumped in. Going back to guesswork navigation, Jimmy and Taddy rumbled off toward the island access road. The hot, stagnant, atmosphere of the cab soon overwhelmed them. "Turn that damn thing off, Taddy," Jimmy shouted. "Jesus, we been using gas the whole time we were in there? How long do you suppose that visit was?"

"It couldn't have been more than fifteen minutes, Jimmy. Don't get squirrely on me just 'cause I left the heater on. We found our girl! What they don't know about gas down at the DOT won't hurt them; let's keep it that way." Rules had to be bent at times for survival and other purposes. Anyone who worked these jobs knew that.

Taddy picked up the speaker to call in to DOT. "Tad Stevens down on Drakes Island, callin' in. Anyone listenin' down there ... R-35 here ... anyone on Dispatch ... copy?" He released the switch and waited for a response. It didn't take long for a dispatcher's answer to crackle over the airways to him.

"DOT headquarters, Wells, Maine ... Taddy, holy crap; we've had everyone lookin' for you and Jimmy. Where the hell you two been? Your route's waitin' on your spade. Fill us in, boy … copy." The familiar voice of Vince Coughlin sounded a million miles away as the lit cab sailed through the night.

"R-35 … Vince, while you been paintin' your toenails, Jimmy and me been out lookin' for the missing person, and we found her. Get your ass over to the PD and tell the chief Pamela Iverson is no longer missing. She's down on Blueberry Lane in Ed LaCasse's cottage. For the most part, she's okay. She got a whack on the head from Ed's Jeep but nothin' that can't wait for treatment. Next step is someone's got to go up to Chick's Crossing and tell her family she's been rescued … copy that!"

There was a pause at the other end, then a shout of relief. "DOT Wells. Great work, guys! I guess we can overlook your neglected roads. Problem is, no police vehicle is gonna make it out to the Crossing. Taddy, your *new* route—and don't wander off this one—is out to Chick's Crossing. Boston just checked in to tell us the storm's end is approaching its city limits within a few hours. Wells should have relief by morning … s'posed to blow itself out around sunrise. I sure as hell hope so."

Taddy responded in the affirmative, hung up the receiver, and returned to smoking and driving intently at the same time. They were moving, albeit slowly, through a gyrating landscape on icy veins of roads.

The pressure off for the moment, Jimmy let his head fall back against the seat, and closed his eyes to let his energy refill. He was drained from the tension of the last few hours. Cursing always seemed to ease things, and since he knew he couldn't insult Taddy, he turned to his companion and began. "I'll be goddamned if she didn't manage to make me feel sorry for her. The hell she put everyone through … it's almost over, I hope. Guess it could happen to anyone. Well, no, it wouldn't happen to me or you. We got too much native smarts for that, but maybe it wasn't as friggin' brainless a thing as I first thought. Women have their way of bein' in the world; looks wicked strange to men—to me—anyhow." As Jimmy finished brandishing this opinion, Darnice's sweet face flashed in his mind. He'd better be careful what he said from now on; he wouldn't want that girl to hear him say what he just had.

"I liked the girl," Taddy spoke up. "I think Ed liked the girl too. What she did was unwise but not crazy. Did you see the look on Ed's face?

He was being mighty protective of his guest. I don't remember him ever behavin' like that before. I don't remember him ever talking as much as he did either. He used to be a solitary guy. Change over!" Taddy said with a laugh that kindled its echo in Jimmy.

As they lumbered slowly on, the smiling vision of Darnice resumed its assault on Jimmy's mind, making him feel unsettled. He hadn't missed the mention of those butterflies in Pamela's telling of her rescue. They were showing up everywhere. Jimmy, knowing there was a lot of time to kill before they got to Chick's Crossing, decided to take advantage of his friendship with Taddy to see what he might think about the romantic episode at the diner earlier.

Jimmy was direct mostly, went to the heart of things, but he decided to soft-pedal on this particular subject. "Taddy," he began, "you're married, right? I've seen you around town with your wife. Any children?" In saying this, Jimmy realized how little the men of this team really knew about each other, though they worked together all through the year, winter and summer.

After a few drags on his cigarette, Taddy put it down and looked over to Jimmy. "Yep, been married to Martha for twenty-two years; kids raised and gone. One of 'em came back last year. Still with us but savin' to get out of the house again. Martha's a great wife: good cook, don't complain when I work these long storm hours … fun sometimes … sometimes not. All in all, I'm a lucky man. What's up, my man? We been together many days and nights. You never asked about Martha 'n' me before." The wild noise around the truck's cab, the smoke filling the chamber, the success of their mission in finding Pamela Iverson—all this between them made the time seem right for Jimmy to come out from behind his bravado and ask for help. Taddy heard, and had taken note of, a new tone in his friend's voice. He was still looking over at Jimmy, now with a suppressed grin. He was ahead of him.

"Well …." He breathed out in preparation, moving carefully on this new territory. "Something happened that was pretty unusual. You know I dated a little after Melissa left, but nothing came of it; left me cold. Never found anybody I was interested in. Down at the diner, something happened. I can't get my mind around it, and it's got me all upset."

Taddy was taken aback when he heard Jimmy mention Melissa; he never talked about those days. Folks felt bad for him at the time, but like a good Mainer, nobody snooped in Jimmy's business. They wouldn't bring up what was happening or even mention her name. Jimmy, who was the ultimate Mainer, kept his personal life—which there was precious little of—locked up tight.

"But," Jimmy continued, "at the diner I was walkin' over to sit with Ed LaCasse. We were talking about the Iverson woman when Darnice came over … you know her … ? Darnice Littlefield … ? And Jesus, something went on or off. Something unusual happened for sure. We both tensed right up. She got nervous; I got nervous. We just sat there, looking at each other for what seemed like a month. Then, when she went to pour my coffee, she almost missed my cup, and truth be told, I was feelin' just as dizzy. Tell you the truth, Taddy; I'm still under the spell of it. What do you think? What's goin' on? You see this stuff happen on TV but don't figure it's real." Jimmy stopped speaking, embarrassed, but stayed quiet, hoping for some understanding and direction from his friend.

For his part, Taddy understood and honored the earnestness in his friend's question. For once he put kidding aside and took his time to think about how to answer. After a few deep drags on his cigarette, he spoke. "I don't know, Jimmy, but it can't be a bad thing. She's a nice girl—nice lookin'—not one to date around a lot. Doesn't she have two kids? Come to think of it, you two went through the same kind of trouble with your marriages, right? You both been alone a long time. Maybe it's the season, all that friggin' mistletoe." And here he just laughed at his own joke. "So what's your plan, buddy? You gotta have a plan." He let go of the wheel long enough to punch Jimmy on the arm playfully.

As the truck progressed under Taddy's steady hand across the dangerous flooded road up to Route 1, they came out of the protective shield of trees to cross the open marsh. Suddenly, the truck was a toy in the wind as a gust caught it broadside, blowing it off course and into the now-frozen soup of tidal wash. Taddy shouted in surprise, redoubling his hold on the wheel. "These winds got to be wicked to catch us out like this! No car could be out here." He didn't speak again until they had backed the truck out of the dangerous flooded marsh, narrowly missing going into bottom-less tidal inlets. He fought to regain the road and pass into the protection of trees out of the wind's force, and up the ascent to the main road.

The dark signal light on Route 1 came into the headlight's field of view in still-falling snow; the butterflies were circling here again, only memory now, one Jimmy would never live down. He knew better than to mention it to Taddy. The tender moment with Darnice was one thing, but monarchs in the blizzard were another. He would keep the image to himself, but it convinced him of just how different—not to say magical—this night was. As unusual as any night he could ever remember. Maybe being snagged in the prison of his empty life and the dream of flying above his sad, empty house had led him to wish hard for something more; something so different that it had taken on this shape. Jimmy was so absorbed in these thoughts that he didn't hear Taddy trying to get his attention.

"Jimmy, wake up, man! You can't be asleep. I've been thinking. We go right by Stephen Eaton Lane on our way up to Chick's Crossing, right? After we deliver the good news to the Iverson woman's family, you want to give *someone* an early Christmas present? If you promise not to tell no one, we could do a little private plowin' gratis for a 'friend' as we go along home. I bet Darnice would love wakin' up to a plowed driveway. Do you know her address?"

"Hell, no. I know it's up that way … but you just wait a minute. I know how to find out."

Jimmy took the transmitter off the hook and called in his request to the PD. "I need an ID over here. This is Jimmy Casey. I need to get the address of Darnice Littlefield up on Stephen Eaton ASAP!"

The dispatch officer on the other end took the request with the perfect seriousness appropriate on a night like this. "I'll have it in a minute, Jimmy. You out with Taddy? Good for you. Get right back to you." Jimmy released the connection while the two men laughed in collusion with the devilishness of their plan. "It's too easy to have fun," Taddy said, although Jimmy was having a little more trouble with the deception.

"You guys really do this kind of stuff? Hope no one finds out," he said.

"Jimmy, we do this *stuff* all the time. It's harmless and keeps us awake; besides, we're doin' double duty. Hang tight, buddy. We'll plow her out after we go up to the Crossing. No one we don't want to know ever will." Taddy was obviously enjoying the little deception.

The receiver buzzed, signaling the address was at hand. Jimmy picked it up. "Got that address?" The crackle of the call erupted in Jimmy's hands. "Yep, got it Jimmy: 279 Stephen Eaton Lane."

"Thanks, my man. We are on our way up to Chick's Crossing. Be back to the station soon as that mission is done." Before cutting the connection, he had another question for the dispatcher. "Hey, do you know if Congdon's is opening for storm crews this morning? I'll pick doughnuts up for all of us if it is."

"That's affirmative. They just called in and offered, even though it's Christmas Day. Make mine blueberry filled, Jimmy, and watch they don't over-cream the coffee like they usually do."

"Roger and out," Jimmy said, then looked at Taddy, raised his eyebrows, and said, "Okay, bud, what a great Christmas this is turnin' into." Taddy smiled broadly as he engaged the plow, and the truck pushed the deep layers of snow aside in white waves.

Part Five

CHAPTER 23

SPREADING JOY

Chick's Crossing
Before Dawn, Christmas, 1999

Taddy aimed—more than drove—the truck up to the main road, plowing all the way. Although a truck had already been through once during the night, the going was slow; treacherous really. Taddy put on his blinker for the left-hand dip off Route 1, over a railroad crossing, then down onto Coles Hill Road. Jimmy laughed at his caution: he felt like laughing about everything. Inside, he was practically giddy. The back wheels of the plow slurred right and left on the pure ice under snow; then the chains bit in for the steep assent of Merryfield Hill.

As they ascended, Taddy lifted the plow to allow the truck to climb. They saw that the tree cover had kept snow accumulations on the roadway down, a small blessing. This steep hill was bad enough to drive dry. The two men willed the big rig up and up and up again, holding on—one to his seat, the other to the steering wheel. At last, the road leveled, and the snow-covered houses of Chick's Crossing rose into the headlights on the right, like hay mounds in a field. The men slowed their progress. They were crawling down the road, looking left and right until they came to the driveway that matched Pamela's description. Jimmy aimed the searchlight toward the structure, skimming over the snow banks until a number showed up on the house. Destination confirmed, Taddy braked but couldn't attempt the driveway. They looked at each other hesitantly. What would this message delivery look like to the family inside? Not good, they agreed with a nod.

Jimmy took responsibility quickly. He was representing the police, and this was an official visit. "At least, I got good news," he quipped. "It could have been some worse."

Taddy put on the brakes and the truck idled at the driveway at 64 Chick's Crossing. Jimmy swung down into snow that was over his knees. Taddy lost sight of him as he advanced toward the house. Power was out up here as well; darkness stretched around him, darkness full of snow.

Jimmy pushed against powerful winds as he approached the outline of the darkened structure. Up here, on the Crossing, meadows stretched in three directions; wind could get rolling pretty powerfully with nothing to stop it. It took Jimmy awhile to etch a path to the door. As he approached, he took off his gloves to rap loudly, but he needn't have. The door swung open at his approach. Someone was watching for them. He put the gloves on quickly, his fingers feeling a bite of cold. He had no idea what kind of greeting he would get, but whatever the situation, Jimmy had lots of practice in giving news … good and bad. His approach would be direct and firm. Tonight's message was a piece of cake.

The door framed a man and woman standing, candlelight behind them. They were young, and Jimmy could see even in this light … very tense … appearing to hold each other up, waiting for a life-or-death announcement. When he saw the worry and tiredness in their faces, he felt the elation of being a good angel.

He wasted no time. "My name is Officer James Casey with the Wells Police Department," he said. "I am here to tell you that Pamela Iverson has been found alive and well. She is resting in the home of the man who found her car in the Jetty Beach parking lot down on Drakes Island hours ago now. His name is Ed LaCasse. Couldn't be a better man anywhere. No need to worry about Pamela. I have just come from there and saw her myself. She will be all right."

As Jimmy finished his message, the woman broke into loud sobs, her knees buckling under her. Her husband took her in his arms and moved into the interior of the house, guiding her to a love seat in the foyer, comforting her with soft words.

Jimmy stepped across the threshold, shutting the door against the maelstrom blowing. He stood respectfully a few feet from the couple, waiting for the woman to calm down.

The husband looked at the officer over his wife's head and addressed him. "Officer Casey, I'm Paul Collins, and this is my wife, Leslie. My God, if you knew what we have been through. This is wonderful, wonderful news, but it is still terrible. That she is alive seems like a miracle to us. We are eternally grateful to you and whoever saved her. Have you talked with her? My wife has done everything to help her mother get settled, find some peace. We just don't understand how something like this could happen."

"Officer Casey, thank you—thank you." Now it was the woman who spoke through her tears. "I am Leslie Iverson Collins, Pamela's daughter. I thought she was dead! I am so grateful to you for finding her or whoever did find her. Do you know why she left us like that? I need to know what we did. We have been crazy all day, wondering what we did."

Jimmy answered from a deep well of common sense he'd gained over the years. "From what Pamela told us, she needed a place to think, had some heavy things on her mind. I guess you would know more about that than me. She fell asleep in her car, and the storm came in … caught her. She actually was very brave, getting out of the car and walking through snow and wind to one of the cottages. That bold act saved her life. She broke into one of the cottages and wrapped herself in blankets she found there until Ed came by in his Jeep. She heard him somewhere out there; he was driving around slow, blowing his horn. She woke up, heard him, and ran out of the cottage just in the nick of time. She's got a nasty cut on her forehead from colliding with Ed's Jeep when he heard her and stopped short, but she's going to be all right. Soon's the power's back on, she'll call you, and Ed will take her home when the roads clear. Every part of this story's lucky. No worries now; you can relax. Ed is the best kind of human being; she is safe, and he'll bring her home. I have his phone number here so you can call when the lines are up." He handed the paper with the number to Leslie. "Pamela wanted a special message delivered to the little boy who lives here. She said, 'Nana will be home real soon.' I think that's all of it."

The couple held each other for a moment, and then rose to thank Jimmy again, making him promise to drop in for a Christmas toast when he got off duty. Jimmy said he would do his best, but there were many more situations he would probably have to deal with in the wake of the storm. They shook his hand again and saw him back out into the night. Closing the door behind them, they returned to a more hopeful Christmas Eve.

Taddy was catnapping when Jimmy lifted himself back into the truck. He tapped him softly on the arm and waited for his friend to come around. As this location and mission returned to him, he looked drowsily at Jimmy and asked how it had gone.

"Good ... real good. Being the bearer of good news is much easier than bad. They don't care what Pamela has done; they want her home and safe. I told them Ed LaCasse was the first-class hero. They'll be all right until the phone lines are live and they can get to see Pamela Iverson in person."

Taddy sat tall, revved the engine, yawned, and engaged the gears. The vehicle turned around in the road, its mass skating down the hill more easily than it had gone up; the two Magi inside moving on to the third gift of the night.

As they turned onto Stephen Eaton Lane, an anxious Jimmy flicked the searchlight on looking for something to identify Darnice's home. There was no power here either.

"Hey, this isn't going to be as easy as I thought. I can't see anything on the side of the road. Got any idea where number 279 might be?"

"We must be in the two hundreds by now, Jimmy."

"Slow down Taddy, I do know there's a bunch of driveways around here. We're coming up on them now." Taddy skimmed in closer toward the mounds of snow Jimmy was referring to and then came to a slow stop.

Jimmy opened the door, jumped down, and brushed snow off the mailbox in the snow bank by the driveway. He signaled an okay to Taddy. "We've got it. This is the place." Once Jimmy was back in the cab, Taddy wheeled the truck sideways into the empty road, expertly positioning the plow for the first pass. The heavy metal spade banged down again, and into the driveway they swung, both of them laughing like fools.

Jimmy let his imagination fly forward into the house, seeing into the morning when Darnice discovered a neatly plowed driveway. He wondered whether she would connect him to the unexpected gift. He was aware that this favor carried implications; at least, he hoped it did. Just to think of her face warmed him up. He would continue on in this mysterious state until December 26 when he could at last go back to the diner for breakfast. Until then, speculation would have to do.

"Hey, Taddy." Jimmy punched his friend in the arm to get his attention from plowing. Taddy let up a little and squinted over at Jimmy, the ever-present plume of smoke in his eyes.

"Yeah," the driver asked.

"You pickin' up doughnuts at Congdon's this mornin'?" Jimmy asked.

Taddy nodded in response. It was the guys at the DOT that Congdon's opened for especially; they never missed an opportunity to thank the DOT crews. The doughnuts were famous in Wells and in most of the New England states. They had been voted "number one" in a Boston radio poll.

"Big, big, big, favor ... pick up a bag for Darnice. Drive them out here? Come on. I know it's off your route ... but please, my man, please? Say they are from me. Now that I know your secrets, I could blackmail you."

Taddy looked at Jimmy now with an unrestrained grin. He took the cigarette from his lips to laugh a little. "Buddy, I just can't figure you out. Somethin' mighty special must be goin' on in that mind of yours ... or is it your heart, Jimmy? Jesus, I didn't know you had one," he teased. "Okay, pal ... I'll deliver, and in your name. Any special kind of doughnut, your majesty?" he asked, still teasing.

Jimmy was ready with an answer. "Yep, they have the chocolate frosted peppermint raised on special for the season. How about four or five of those and some blueberry filled ... half a dozen at least. I'll owe you."

"You bet you'll owe me! I'll make it hurt, too. Doughnuts for Darnice? Who woulda thought it? Jimmy's gone soft!" With that, the truck roared back out on the roads, laughter leaking out the cab windows.

CHAPTER 24

CHRISTMAS ON STEPHEN EATON

Stephen Eaton Lane
Sunrise, Christmas, 1999

Amanda Hurley was up early making little stacks of presents for her daughter and grandchildren under the tree. Even though Darnice, Amy, and Danny lived their own lives—often to the exclusion of their mother and grandmother—Amanda was happy to be this close, ready to lend a hand or listen. She so wanted this to be a good Christmas; she knew things would change. She had tried to make it up to Darnice and the children after he'd left; they had to go on—without a husband, without a father. Her presence as the elder of this family offered only total understanding and love.

Her cache of gifts was stowed all over the small cape; in closets, under beds—all around. Operating on a tight budget, Amanda bought presents all through the year, when and wherever she could. The School Around Us craft fair offered unique work by local artists: jewelry, art, homemade sweaters, and pottery—at prices she could afford. She attended all the November and December sales put on for Christmas. She made the rounds of the more reasonable local gift shops during sale events.

This year, she had found hand-knit sweaters and scarves for Darnice and Amy; these were most welcome when January's freeze was on everything. She'd bought earrings for the girls made with recycled paper molded and painted into lovely replicas of birds: a pair of barn owls for Darnice, and red cardinals for Amy to dangle at her ears against the white, snowy winter days ahead. Winter was so long here; people needed things to lift the gloom. Danny's gifts had been more challenging: a scarf and gloves with leather palms, as well as a local artist's painting of the marsh from down on Mile Road—one showing the sun setting in pastel colors of lilac and pink that reflected in small pools among the grasses. She thought he would like this memento of Maine. He would probably not stay in this area once he graduated from college.

Finally finished with her display of gifts, the seventy-year-old woman poured a cup of coffee and sat down to enjoy her own preparations. Memories of years past came to her reflection: pleasant thoughts of birthdays, Christmas Eves, Darnice's wedding. Then she thought of that terrible Christmas Eve when Darnice arrived on her doorstep with the children, all of them crying with the loss of Kyle.

Her daughter experienced sadness way too early in life. Though Amanda had objected to the marriage as strongly as she could when she sensed real problems in the boy, Darnice was headstrong, wouldn't listen. Kyle had used her from the start; he couldn't keep a job, had fathered two children he never seemed to care about, had spent zero time getting to know them—and then abandoned them when real responsibilities and bills began to appear. Although Darnice had suffered, Amanda had been secretly relieved when Kyle finally left. There was nothing anyone could do to change the boy's sense of values, and those had never included his caring for his wife or children. When he left town, Darnice, now with a family of her own, returned to this, her childhood home. Things had slowly improved.

Amanda put her coffee down to go after one more gift she remembered stashing in the bread maker in the pantry. The Christmas storm had kept everyone home last night. They were all asleep now. Secret Santa work had to be done before they woke up; it was the last minute. She sat back on her heels, listening to the quiet of snow outside insulating everything in its white, feathery piles. She could feel that the whole town was sleeping. She reveled in the wonderfully whole feeling of family here, close, well loved.

She offered a prayer of thanks as she straightened up the living room a little, took glasses and plates from last night's late supper to the kitchen, and made more coffee. She had a turkey to stuff and vegetables to prepare, but there was time for that after breakfast.

Her thoughts ticked along, letting her create the orderly, pleasant world she wished for and seemingly had. All was well: Amy would graduate from high school this year and wanted to go up to Orono to the University of Maine. Her grades were good, and she had applied for financial help and would likely get some. Danny was working in Kennebunk and doing very well at York County Community College. Maine didn't offer much to keep its young people here; jobs were hard to find, and taxes were high. She didn't think the kids would stay in the state. This truth caused her to sigh. Change came at you fast; what you complained about one year became what you missed the next.

She set the oven to "warm" to heat a quiche for breakfast. With coffee burbling into the carafe, Amanda went back to the living room and plugged in the lights on the tree. Lit, they shimmered around the room, bright colors glossing everything, giving new warmth and cheer indiscriminately.

Darnice's dad had passed on years ago now, long enough that Amanda had outlived the daily imprint of who he'd been in her life. She never had to live alone. Darnice had moved in with her, bringing the babies into the house just before he died. They became a new family very quickly. Amanda had been needed by her daughter, so needed that her own life was suppressed when she became the nanny to the children so Darnice could go to work. Those grandkids were like her own children.

Amanda could see sunrise in her living room windows. There were houses blocking her sight, so she didn't have a "view," as they called it, but she loved being able to see the same sunrise each morning that the people at the beach saw. She walked across the living room to open the drapes, even though the sun wouldn't be up yet. With the storm, morning might not be clear enough for a Christmas sunrise anyway. She hoped the storm had finished up, guessed it had since she couldn't hear the winds howling anymore.

As she approached the windows, Amanda heard the unmistakable sound of a truck rumbling outside. When she opened the curtains for a look, it took her a few moments to understand what she was seeing. The driveway had been plowed clean. Snow was still falling but had tapered off some. And yes, a rumbling DOT truck was parked outside. How was that possible? Plowing for this development wasn't a town job. They had Kenny Shields do their driveways. As she stood watching, a voice behind her said, "Merry Christmas, Mamma." She turned to see Darnice was up.

"Good Morning, Darnice. Merry Christmas to you. What are you doing up so early?" She went to give her girl a hug, after which she said, "Something weird's going on out there. A town plow truck is outside the door. What in blazes can they want? We've been plowed out. I can't remember that ever happening before. Why would the town trucks plow us out?"

Both women stood at the window and watched a man get out of the truck and come to their front door, carrying something.

"I think that's Taddy Stevens," Darnice said. "He works for DOT. I know him from the diner. What in jolly hell is he doing here?" The doorbell rang in the middle of her wondering aloud. When she opened the door, Taddy himself stood there—tired, shabby, and disheveled—but smiling. "Taddy, is that you? Merry Christmas! But what the hell are you doing here?" Her language exposed her surprise.

Taddy held out a white paper bag to Darnice and began his prepared speech. "Special delivery from Jimmy Casey. He ordered these up for you, and I'm the delivery boy. Got them at Congdon's. They opened special for the town crew. You have a nice Christmas, Darnice. Hope we got the driveway the way you like it. Don't tell anyone you saw me here … okay? I'll see you at the diner." And with what looked like a wink, he turned to go, only to turn back for a few more words. "By the way, thanks for all you do for us town guys. We really appreciate having the diner. Well, I got things to do still. See you." And Taddy retraced his steps to the truck, leaving behind an astonished Darnice holding a bag of warm doughnuts, the scent of frying fat and spices spreading cheerfully.

When she had closed the door and returned to her mother, Darnice was smiling so broadly, her face could hardly hold it. Obviously pleased as she came into the living room, she said, "Mamma, is the coffee on? I've got a story to tell you that you won't believe."

Amanda noticed something in her daughter's eyes ... something bright, something lively and new. The two women went to the familiar old kitchen with the doughnuts and sat at the table by the back windows, looking into the marshes decorated with as much white snow as any Christmas they had lived here. Darnice put the doughnuts on a plate. They spilled out of the bag with appetizing appeal: chocolate chips piled on dark chocolate frosting, blueberry filling seeping out of sugar-covered pillows of fried dough, peppermint-frosted raised doughnuts, and apple-studded fritters. "Can you believe it? Doughnut delivery to your door on Christmas morning."

But they didn't talk about doughnuts for long. Jimmy's stop at the diner last night along with the parallel tale of the missing woman out in the storm was what riveted Amanda. Darnice related how Jimmy had put everyone on notice that they were part of the rescue in conditions like last night's and that there seemed to be a ... she didn't know what to call it ... a connection between her and the cop. A warm, friendly something that kept them both tongue tied. She knew they had both felt it.

Amanda sipped her coffee, thinking about this *thing* that was happening that she didn't trust completely. "Darnice, honey, are you sure you're not dreaming some of this up? I've never known Officer Casey to behave like that. What would possess the two of you?"

Darnice trusted her mother with the whole story. She knew, in some way, that the parts of this story were pieces of a whole: Jimmy, the butterflies, and this happy little doughnut delivery today. It had to be for good.

"Mom," Darnice began, "I have to tell someone about what happened on the way home last night. I'd like to tell you, but you have to listen and believe me. Can you promise me you will try?" She waited for her mother's sober tone to register the moment.

"Why, Darnice, I always take you seriously. What's this about? Nothing too awful, I hope."

"Last night, after we closed the diner, I headed for home as usual. The roads were terrible. I was going along real slow, thinking back to what had happened between me and Jimmy, probably overwhelmed by it, I admit. Everything was going all right. No one else was on the road, so I had it all to myself. Well, when I got to the police station and was ready to turn up to Stephen Eaton, I felt the winds come rushing up, like they wanted to knock me off the road. The blast was so powerful, it stopped me from accelerating, and … I saw something … something bright swirling around in my headlights. I took my foot off the gas to look closer."

Here, Darnice paused, signaling with a look to her mother that this was something big. "Now, Mamma, I know how this is going to sound, but the things flying around in that light—they were butterflies. Monarch butterflies. I'd know them anywhere, but to see them in the middle of a Maine blizzard—well, it was almost unbelievable. They swarmed and flew up in a tight cone, all wings on the outside. When I got just right under the streetlight, I looked straight up at them. That's when they started flying faster, around and around, and next thing I knew, they flew off down Route 1. And within seconds, they disappeared into the snow. I felt like they wanted me to follow them … but I just didn't dare, roads being what they were. I had to come home. Weather was fixing to get worse."

Amanda put her coffee cup down and sat looking at her daughter with concern. "Darnice, did you have anything to drink before you left the diner? I know you think you saw what you saw, but it's pretty hard to believe there would be monarch butterflies in the middle of a blizzard on Christmas Eve."

"No, Mamma, I didn't have anything to drink. You know me better than that. There was some kind of spell out there last night. I don't know what to think, but it was some interesting." Sounds coming from the back of the house told them Amy and Danny were up, and it was time for gifts, breakfast, and the start of a new day.

"Enough for now, Mamma," Darnice said as she hugged Amanda. "Don't tell the kids! They'll think I've lost it. Maybe I have!"

CHAPTER 25

MORNING LIGHT

Blueberry Lane
Christmas Morning, 1999

The glare filled the room. Pamela closed her eyes against the sharp, bright light, taking her waking slow. She knew where she was now, recognized the room; that small thing assured her. After a few moments, her vision adjusted and the living room came into focus; a room seen only in shadows up to this moment. The fire was dead out, and Ed, wonderful Ed—the man who had saved her life last night—was sleeping in the chair opposite the sofa. As she looked at him, she said to herself: "He saved my life."

The feelings that came from that truth overwhelmed her. She could only speculate about what would have happened if she were still in that cold kitchen; she doubted she would still be alive. Pamela took this unobserved opportunity to send this man all the gratitude she had on hand, and still he slept on. Yes, it had come to that. Someone had had to save her life. Tears began to course down her face. Where had she been all this time? What had she been thinking? Shielding her eyes from the brilliant post-storm sun streaming in the front windows of the cottage, she sat up firmly, ready for whatever this day would bring; the morning delivering a stark clarity.

The rustle of her movements woke Ed; he, too, had to cover his eyes in the light. When he recovered sight, he saw that Pamela was also awake, looking at him; uncertainty in her soft features mixed with a smile. He leaned across the small space between them, patted her hand, and smiled reassuringly. "No worries now. The best things that could have happened already have. You're safe and sound, and you found a new friend. I'm on your side, Pamela."

And smiling still, Ed stood and stretched from the long night. He walked to the window in light just broken through yesterday's dark skies; everything around him was glowing in tones of pink and yellow. The view he witnessed declared that the storm was officially over. Snowdrifts reached to the middle of his windows, magnifying light from outside. In this glare, Ed saw that his home appeared dusty and ill kept. He let this fact register on him silently, promising himself he would do something about it straightaway.

Turning to Pamela, who hadn't taken her eyes off him, he came back and sat beside her on the sofa, and looked at her. Ed chose his next words carefully, meaning to put the worst of the night behind them. After a few moments, he squeezed her hands saying, "We outlived the monster and can still take nourishment. Come over to the window with me, Pamela. I want you to see something rare, very rare."

Ed helped her to stand, supporting her as she started out, though she walked steadily enough after a few steps. Out of the windows, down on the beach, great luminous waves were rising into a clear blue sky, then crashing and mounding on the sand in great curls only to smash into brilliant shards of aquamarine and pearl. Seagulls hovered in chains on the strong gales that swept in after the storm; wing tip to wing tip, they rippled over the watery hills.

The two stood shoulder to shoulder, transfixed with the scene until a loud jangling erupted from somewhere, canceling the quiet mood. The phone was ringing. Ed and Pamela looked at each other in startled confusion; another intrusion. They hesitated, both unwilling to let the precious moment be invaded. This meant that power lines had been restored, and her time for a reckoning was at hand.

Ed crossed the room to the nearest light switch and flipped it on; the lamp beside him lit. The routines of life could resume, invited or not.

Suspecting that the call would be from Leslie, Pamela recoiled visibly, angry at herself for the worry and fear she had brought to those she loved. The momentary comfort of being with Ed was overtaken by her intense feelings of remorse. "How could all this have happened in one day?" she asked herself.

Ed nodded, eyes direct, letting her know he understood what she was feeling before he walked to the phone to answer. "Hello." His voice sounded steady. "This is Ed LaCasse speaking."

The voice on the other line was talking fast and loud; Pamela could almost understand what was being said from where she stood. She knew it was Leslie; cadence in her words made it clear she was emotional. The thought of speaking with her daughter stung her with regret and roiled her inside. She was so ashamed. She just couldn't face her actions now.

"I do know the whereabouts of Pamela Iverson," Ed said, smiling a quick reassurance to Pamela, his voice transferring the call to her. "She's standing right here in my living room. She suffered a head wound, which has been seen to; it will need more attention. Your mother came through the ordeal well, has had some sleep, and is probably ready for something to eat. I'll let her tell you the whole story. I won't keep you waiting."

Ed held the phone out to Pamela, but in that final moment of facing her daughter, she backed away, not daring to take hold. Ed saw the panic in her eyes and decided he had to take the risk of intruding in this family's business.

After a small gesture of understanding, he spoke into the phone again. "Pamela is a little confused right now. She is unable to talk about what happened. She needs coffee, food, and time to regain herself. Could she please call you in a few minutes? I guarantee she is in good condition physically. It has been a terrible night, as I suspect you can guess, but she really is okay." Pamela heard her daughter's voice on the other end of the line, agreeing to the delay.

"Thank you," Ed said and hung up.

Pamela went back to the sofa and covered her face with her hands. Any sense of relief or beauty she had found in the bursting dawn had vanished. "I don't know what to say to her. There can be no forgiveness for what I did. I was selfish and stupid. I wouldn't be surprised if they never want to see me again. This isn't the first time either. I've been a disappointment to her ever since ...." She didn't finish the thought aloud. The words leaked out between her hands like tears.

Ed sat beside her and took her hands, waiting until she gave him her full attention. "Pamela, not one thing you just said is true. We all have the right to see and to change what we have done, and what we don't like; we can leave it behind for good, like it never existed. That's what it's all about anyway: change. That blizzard wasn't your doing. Your daughter is anxious to talk with you. She is waiting for you to call her. She will not—cannot—be all right until she hears your voice. I personally guaranteed that you would call her.

Ed continued, hoping he wasn't presuming too much for this new friendship. "You know, forgetting at times who you are and what's important in your life isn't so uncommon a thing. It happens to most people. Your going to Jetty Beach yesterday was an innocent attempt to find a place to deal with emotions you couldn't face. Emotions from a past that needs to be accepted and then lived beyond. I hope to convince you that your inner struggles are a sign of growth, improvement. Your friends and family are there to support you in your struggles, and you will be needed to support them at times. You can't do this alone. I envy you. You're courageous, strong. I'm way too willing for everything to stay just the same; I guard against change, not move toward it. Not you—you're on the road to a new way of being. It was only a mishap; you would have been back home in plenty of time if you hadn't fallen asleep. You have a chance to live your life in a new way because of the serious wakeup call of the events of last night. Don't waste what you learned on anything but have gratitude for what you still have: a family that loves and needs you plus the chance for a new future. And, don't forget, you have a new friend, Pamela. We are friends now, right?"

His smile was almost too close for her, too warm. She had to turn away from him, afraid to show him how much his words meant.

Ed, sensing the vulnerability of the moment, became quiet—stayed quiet—but didn't move even an inch away from her. Even though he had firsthand experience of what he had said to her, he had never seen it quite this way until today. He wasn't talking only about her. There were many mornings, afternoons, evenings, whole days when he lived here trapped in his own sadness. Those days were doors on a past life that he had to close. Ed knew ... well, he *felt* that the time for him to move ahead might have arrived with this blizzard and with Pamela. What was it he had said just before he left home yesterday? *I want to be good for something again.* Here was his chance.

His entreaty was spoken again. "Just for now, call Leslie. Listen to the happiness in her voice when she hears from you. I'll get you home as soon as the roads are clear and you have something to eat. Sooner or later, the memory of all this will fade, and good things will flood into the places pain has gouged. You're a courageous woman; you proved that. If you like, I'll walk alongside of you; that would help me in turn." Ed's blue eyes were bright in spite of his lack of sleep and his part in the ordeal. Pamela held onto his words. They would keep her standing; she just might get through that call. She reached for his hand, pressed it firmly, and nodded an assent to him.

After he brought her a cup of coffee, Ed offered her the phone and watched as she dialed the number. He waited until the call was connected, then stood at her side, his hand tight on her shoulder for the first few moments. After the hello and the strength of Pamela's voice evened out, he went into the kitchen to give her privacy.

Though he tried not to listen, it was impossible not to overhear the conversation from the living room. Her tears and laughter told him the family was together again.

"I don't know why, It had nothing to do with you. Please believe that," she was saying. "I only needed to get away, go for a drive. The storm, falling asleep, being in that cottage—it was all accidental. I'll share it all with you when I get home. I don't know how the roads are, but I will get home as soon as they open. Tell Robbie I can't wait to see him and play with all his new toys. Leslie, we still have time for a good Christmas dinner together, but you have to let me invite Ed." Saying that, Pamela realized how badly she wanted him to come. "I'll be home as soon as I can get there. Merry Christmas to my wonderful family!" Then there was quiet in the house.

Ed had gotten busy assembling things for breakfast. While he worked, his mind connected the dots backward to Pamela's parking at the beach. She did something anyone might have done; she'd gone to the beach to think things over. He had done that himself, right at Jetty Beach. If the storm hadn't blocked her way home, she would have returned there by dinner. He could see that, in a way, the storm had played into both Pamela's and his rescue. But she couldn't have gone on with this life of despair for much longer. And neither could he. Ed recognized these events could put a stop to his own self-pity. He *had* been useful to someone. That little detail, the red spark of a car's lights, and everything changed.

Pamela replaced the receiver and sat quietly by the window for a while. Ed, knowing this moment was necessary for her to reconcile her feelings, waited, looking out the kitchen window at the pines behind his house. These were the oldest trees on the island; they rose in an awkward circle, planted by someone from generations ago. The powerful sea winds that were perpetually blowing had chiseled and angled them away from the sea. The deer took refuge here, on Ed's land; the state had designated Drakes Island as a wildlife preserve. Gardeners didn't like the deer ravaging edible crops, but their beauty and gentleness were a calming sight.

Peering in under the trees, Ed could just see the trusting herd now. He thought of them as neighbors of his. They knew him as the bearer of apples and carrots, which was probably why they took refuge in this particular stand of trees when deep snow made grazing on island paths impossible. On days like these, they could be prey to packs of dogs. At least Ed could do something about their hunger. He would bring food for them; perhaps Pamela would come with him.

At that idea, memories of he and Sarah flooded him; often they had gone to feed the deer. Ed had continued this errand of mercy. Today he felt encouraged rather than sad about the prospect. He wasn't alone. He could see that something new had begun weaving itself into his life, along with something old—never one or the other, always both.

New Year's Eve was only a few days away. He and Sarah had celebrated most of the new years since they lived on the island by bringing food at dusk to the deer, then returning home for a home-cooked feast for themselves. They would go in search of the deer until they found the herd's gathering spot; then would approach—putting down plump apples and bright carrots—and back away giving the graceful creatures space to enjoy the food. Some years they found the deer on the beach; that was the rarest sight of all. As a New Year's moon rose over the waves, the deer would come close and feed from their hands.

Ed turned away from the window to find Pamela, still in quiet thought, here in his living room. It seemed important that Pamela was here. Maybe on New Year's Eve, he would invite her out with him for the tradition. He hadn't gone out for the deer since Sarah died. When Pamela stood to come into the kitchen, he was ready with the invitation.

CHAPTER 26

THE VIEW FROM HERE

Wells PD
Christmas Day, 1999

Wells was a picture postcard in the early morning light. Seasonal decorations, so carefully placed in early December, stood out against last night's snowfall, shining and blowing in the blustery winds that swept the storm north. Traffic lights—green, yellow, then red—flashed in syncopation up and down Route 1 as far as the eye could see. The scenery didn't interest the exhausted boys driving trucks though. Worn out from their night fighting the elements, they wanted to go home, though they were far from finished with their responsibilities.

After the long night, DOT crews climbed out of their salt-crusted plow trucks and into their own vehicles. Many had contracts to clear parking lots and driveways of churches, businesses, and private homes. As this was one of the few days of the year everyone trotted out to attend services at local churches, church parking lots were of the first order. Hannaford Plaza could wait since the stores didn't open until noon. Cumberland Farms and other convenience stores needed to be plowed out yesterday as everyone needed something after the storm.

The turnpike was open, made passable by state and town collaboration; speed was down to forty-five miles an hour. Being the quickest route to the hospitals (north to Biddeford or south to Portsmouth), it was crucial to keep the 'pike open for emergency travel. Abandoned cars along the sides of streets, now snow-covered lumps of steel and glass, prevented a clean sweep by the plows. Two mothers had gone into labor during the worst of the storm, ambulances getting them to the hospital just in time.

In the PD, Dispatch was still shuffling a small staff around to attend to the still-growing problems of bad weather plus the holidays. The hope was that local roads would open soon and that power, on now in most places but still out in the fringes of town over by Ogunquit and up to Kennebunk, would operate in the entire area.

The missing person's alert had been canceled; most of those who knew about it already knew Ed LaCasse had rescued the Iverson woman down on Drakes Island. News traveled faster by word of mouth here than by wire. People already knew the woman had been in the storm for hours, victim to the elements, and knew she was hurt but that she had made it through, thanks to Ed. They were happy about that. Now that the phones were back on, the news of the rescue got passed through a network of neighbors.

The PD called DOT next door and asked them to get an update on the Subaru at Jetty Beach. The next shift was reporting in, getting in their trucks to go out to the island.

Taddy Stevens, tired to the nth degree, held on tight to the wheel as his truck eased off Route 1 into the recently plowed parking lot at the PD. He had one hand at the ready to protect the steaming coffee cups and bags of still warm doughnuts beside him. He angled the truck diagonally in front of the door in the back of the building and left it running while he went around collecting the Congdon's treasure. His hands full and the eternal cigarette in his mouth, he banged with his boot on the door to the PD and stood waiting for someone to open it.

When someone finally complied, he wished them a merry Christmas—butt bobbing, ashes falling around him—and walked to the lounge, repeating the greeting to everyone he met. It *was* Christmas Day, after all. Turning by rote down the dark hallway, he entered the small, messy staff room, couches on three walls and a table overflowing with ashtrays and empty food containers in the center. Not that the room was ever neat; this morning it was a disaster.

The person Taddy was looking for was sound asleep on one of the couches. Jimmy had come back to the PD to operate Dispatch for the remaining hours of his watch after he and Taddy had secretly plowed up on Stephen Eaton Lane. After being relieved by Farrell, who had returned to help out early this morning, he'd crashed on the couch and was presently dead to the world.

Taddy put the bags of doughnuts and coffee on the table, stubbed his cigarette out, and prepared to torture his accomplice. "Jimmy, get your carcass up and get operatin'. The sun's up, buddy; the roads are cleared." In a teasing, singsong voice, he bent near the cop's ear and continued. "I made that delivery up on Stephen Eaton like you asked me; you got some things to attend to. Get movin', me boy." With the last jibe, he chuckled, and softening his voice, continued in Jimmy's ear, "Man, I could blackmail you but good. If the chief knew you made me plow out your girlfriend and deliver her doughnuts, he'd have your badge."

At this, Jimmy squirmed into consciousness and sat up. Scanning the lounge to see who else might have heard Taddy's indiscretion, he replied, "I drop off for a few minutes of sleep, and you get to be my nightmare? You're the one who came up with the plan. That makes *you* the bad guy." Jimmy rubbed the totally inadequate sleep from his eyes and stretched from his confinement, finally smiling in collusion with his friend, now laughing aloud.

Taddy put down the coffees and ripped open the bags; the coveted pastries spilled out onto the table in an array of golden-brown and frosted glory. "Get over here. We got blueberry filled, chocolate sugared, apple fritters … it's a Christmas feast, my friend. All sent to us gratis from Congdon's." Taddy sang the invitation out loudly enough for the men on duty to hear.

"So, how'd it go over on Stephen Eaton?" Jimmy asked, all attention now. "Did you see Darnice?"

"Yep, and I got to see how flummoxed she was by the whole plowin' escapade. I told her the 'favors' were per your direction, and that girl smiled something wonderful. Judging by her reaction, I don't think you're imaginin' this, buddy. Anyway, today's a new day and anything's possible.

Especially after last night's win." With that, Taddy bit into a lemon-filled doughnut the size of a small squash.

Jimmy, encouraged by Taddy's optimistic report, grinned back and approached the table, picked up a coffee, and sipped it while considering which doughnut he would eat first. He chose an apple fritter and bit into it, the deliciousness of the fritter and the sweet memories of the night breaking over him. "Taddy, this has been the most interesting twenty-four hours of my life so far. I can't wait to see what happens next!" With that, he consumed the doughnut in a few bites. "But, 'til then, I better get down to the island and take a look at that Subaru if it's still there. I expect Ed might need help getting the Iverson woman back up to her home on the Crossing too."

"Want me to go with you?" Taddy asked.

"No, you've done your duty and more," Jimmy said conspiratorially, winking at Taddy, who was already moving toward the door at this dismissal. "I expect you are done in. Good job, Mr. Stevens." And here he slapped his buddy on the back as he passed by. "You go home and sleep the storm off now. Missus will be lookin' for you anyway. Bring along some doughnuts for her. I'll keep you posted with events when I see you after Christmas," he said with a wink.

Taddy, exhilarated by exhaustion and by the unusual events of the past forty-eight hours, chose a few doughnuts for his wife and got out of the PD while he could. Once in his truck, he tooted a goodbye to Jimmy navigating his truck back to the yard where he parked, and walked to his car at last. Winter had begun; he would see a lot of his truck before the rains of April came. It was only December, after all.

After an hour or so of briefing the new crew just arriving for their shift, Officer Casey was back in the patrol car. The high, white banks on the sides of the roads made extreme caution necessary. For the second time in less than twelve hours, Jimmy took a slow right off Route 1 toward the island, phantom butterflies repeating, but this time from a sunlit, post-storm sky. Jimmy mumbled aloud to himself, "Maybe life isn't what we think. Christ, I don't know anymore."

The cold front that swept in behind the storm had hardened the salted slush into icy ruts. Jimmy sighed, accepting the fact that the winter driving season was also here. The rules of the road now were to reduce speed, turn carefully on surfaces, and be aware of how to drive in the often-dangerous conditions.

He drove Seaward Lane down to Jetty Beach, looking out for small herds of deer that were sure to be out for food. As he turned the corner onto the perimeter of the island, he realized the ocean had eddied around the beach and over the marsh to come up behind the parking lot, forming a sort of lagoon. The tide was as high as he had ever seen it, filling the marsh up to and over the roads.

Jimmy drove carefully through the ponding puddles. He stopped for a few minutes to absorb how beautiful the view was; snow-packed grasses flattened by the wind's winch stretched out to the rough blue texture of the sea. He inched up the small incline into the parking lot of Jetty Beach, stopping when he saw the car. The front wheels were no more than a foot from the granite ledge of the jetty itself. It looked like the car had been picked up by the tide and carried toward sea. Another hour of that storm at full intensity, and the car would have been swimming in the channel. There was seaweed on the hood, and dings visible from rocks slung by waves. Jimmy realized at this moment how close they had all come to a tragedy last night. He knew, too, that he had to get that car moved before the next high storm tide threatened to come in at surge height.

Walking to the Subaru, he opened the door as he had last night. The replay gave him goose bumps when he realized this story could have had a very different ending. Voluntary or accidental, the death of Pamela Iverson could easily have been headlines in the papers this morning. He had to hand it to Ed LaCasse … the right guy in the right place at the right time. It was more than lucky, and counting in the butterflies, it really was miraculous.

Jimmy was still standing by the car door when Ed's Jeep chugged into the parking lot. He waved to him, his friend's appearance buoying Jimmy's mood even more.

Ed's Jeep navigated the ridged surface slowly, bouncing over the ice. Pulling up beside Jimmy, he opened the door and invited him into the warmed cab. The friendship between the two men had deepened through the charged events of the past twenty-four hours. Ed was smiling when Jimmy stepped up and sat.

"I've got to hand it to you, LaCasse. You came out last night in a big way. The *County Coast Star* reporter called the station this morning about rumors concerning a rescue. You're goin' to be famous." At this, he looked around the car. "Where's the woman in question? Did you get her home already?"

"Yep, the ride up to the Crossing was just about doable. It seemed best for her that I drive her home as fast as I could get her there. I knew my Jeep was up to the job, and the ride gave us a little more time to talk. The circumstances of our meeting couldn't have been any more anxious, but when I got to know her, I saw she's a real nice person in the middle of tough times, Jimmy. Woman gone 'nutty,' she isn't!" Ed looked to Jimmy as he parroted the descriptor Jimmy had used within the last twenty-four hours.

Jimmy, nodding, got his drift. "She's carrying around some scars. I guess you and I can understand how that feels, huh?" He let a few minutes tick by as the suggestion that they were experienced in the "scars" department settled between them. Jimmy kept his eyes steady on Ed, thinking that this was more talk than he had ever heard from Ed at one time.

Ed eased the gearshift into park and settled back. "The *Coast Star* must need news bad. I didn't do anything anybody wouldn't have in the same situation. The mystery is the timing of it all. A few minutes later, and I don't want to think what could have been the outcome." The deep gusts of wind coming off the ocean rocked the Jeep, accentuating the heft of Ed's speculation and revisiting both men with the image of Pamela out in that storm.

After a pause and a nervous glance at Jimmy, Ed decided to share the one thing he just couldn't reckon with in the whole experience. "Jimmy, something pretty wild happened last night. I have to say I'm happy to have played the part of the hero in this story, but that's not the half of it."

Here, he reached over and put his hand on Jimmy's arm to accentuate what was coming next. "Now, I know you and you know me, but … well … I'm going to trust you with something I wouldn't tell anyone else. Last night, you heard Pamela mention butterflies … right? So did I. I almost choked when she did. I wouldn't tell you this if she hadn't brought it up, but … well … makes me think something bigger than simply you or me was going on during that storm."

Jimmy's attention tightened in on what Ed was saying. He suspected he already knew what was coming next, but he didn't let on.

"After I fought my way into this parking lot and found Pamela's car here last night, I sat dead in the road, trying to figure out which way she might have gone. I was some scared. Well … okay now … just listen, Jimmy." Ed took a deep breath and looked his friend squarely in the eyes. "These … ahh …." He stopped again, unable to say the words. Jimmy sat in silence, already ahead of Ed. "These butterflies—monarchs I think they were—they showed up, swirling around in the headlights at first, then right in front of the windshield. It was all I could do to make myself sit there and not take off for fear at the sight. Whoever heard of such a thing? They headed off down the road, disappearing into the snow, then circled back until I got it that they were trying to lead me down Ocean Drive. When I understood that, I followed them. It was then that I thought about blowing the horn … and wouldn't you know it? Everything came together just as I got to the cottage Pamela had broken into. Once I got just in front of where she was, they took off."

Ed stopped and looked at Jimmy, shaking his head and lifting his eyebrows in disbelief. "I'm telling you, Jimmy, I wasn't drinking, and I know what I saw." Ed finished, not knowing what else to say. "It was the butterflies that led me to her. I don't care how weird that sounds. That's the truth!"

A smile slowly spread across Jimmy's face. Then he laughed and kept laughing long and hard, with Ed looking at him in confusion. Reaching across the cab, Jimmy put his hand on Ed's shoulder. Ed, afraid to think his trust in Jimmy had been misplaced, relaxed when his friend finally spoke. "Okay, mister, since we're coming clean with each other, let me tell you about *my* miracle…."

Jimmy's description of his encounter with the spectral monarchs on Route 1 on Christmas Eve didn't sound as strange now as it had when he revisited it over and over in his own mind. He knew Ed was a believer, and though they tried to figure it out as they talked, neither of them could bridge the gap between a miracle and a reality that had opened up and swallowed them both.

After a few attempts at trying to explain how it might be conceivable, Jimmy remembered a quote he had heard somewhere. "Albert Einstein said, 'Either everything is a miracle or nothing is.' Something like that. This whole night's one damn miracle if you ask me. And here's another one: I don't know if you were paying attention to Darnice and me at the diner or not but, man … did that really happen? I was getting the feeling that the girl warmed up to me … huh … did you catch any of it?"

Ed affirmed his friend's assessment of the night's events. He knew from his own burgeoning feelings for Pamela how important corroboration was for Jimmy.

"I saw it all right, and it was a stunner. I've been there at the counter many times before with you both; nothing like that ever happened. But last night, you were two people I've never seen before. It looked all right, though. I even envied you; you blushed, you know. So did Darnice. So … what's next?"

Jimmy was so grateful for Ed's confirmation of what he hoped had happened; he felt himself soften up. So it was a real thing and not just his poor delusion. This meant everything. Jimmy spoke softly. "I don't know my way around this territory very well, but I've taken a few steps on the path. Taddy Stevens and I plowed the driveway at Darnice's house middle of the night last night. I had him bring her doughnuts from Congdon's this morning so she knew who to thank. Maybe it's too much too soon … but I don't want this trail to go cold."

Ed looked to Jimmy and smiled broadly at the picture of Jimmy and Taddy on a romantic mission: Taddy's Sancho to Jimmy's Quixote. "I'd have given anything to see you two plowing in the middle of the night. I take it that was after you showed up at my place? For two old second-hand bachelors, we were both in interesting situations last night."

"Thanks, Ed. What with the butterflies and all, I've got to think there's something going on here that's favoring me … and—by the way—favoring you too!"

"Yep, I'm going to dinner tonight up on the Crossing. I'm on my way home to 'pretty' myself up some. Pamela's daughter insisted I come for Christmas dinner. I hope the CVS is open. I want to get a gift for the little boy and some wine for dinner … and some cologne." The men laughed over the cologne until they remembered the car they had both come here to inspect. "Have you looked at the Subaru? What kind of damage did you find?"

"I'll call for a tow and get her car up to Brownie's. He won't open until tomorrow, but it doesn't look like too much damage to fix—none inside anyway. Not totaled by a long shot. Tell her not to worry. A few days, that car will be on the road again."

"Thanks Jimmy … I better get along to my errands. I'm due for dinner around four this afternoon."

Jimmy opened the door of the Jeep and stepped out into the powerful wind. Looking back up at Ed, he smiled slyly and nodded his head. "Friggin' butterflies in a Nor'easter. Do you believe it? We better stay quiet about this, my man. I'm trusting you!"

With that, Jimmy pointed in warning at Ed, winked, and shut the door, still laughing to himself. He was in a new mood; one he didn't know how to control. But he liked the view from here. The mighty Atlantic continued to roll on up the jetty. Jimmy stood on the edge of the waterway watching Ed bounce out of the icy parking lot … and just felt good.

CHAPTER 27

THE DAY AFTER

Chick's Crossing
December 26, 1999

Pamela woke. She was home, on Chick's Crossing; it was the day after Christmas. The windows opposite her bed glowed in frosty spirals as the first rays of early light touched them. The familiar blue wallpaper looked like blue sky. Her sweater and black slacks, placed on the chair across the room, centered her in time; reminding her of last night and Christmas dinner and Ed.

Today was a very different day, and there was relief in this. Still, she sensed an anxious feeling within. Had she overslept ... missed something that needed to be done? Her waking seemed always to be to a warning.

Downstairs, she heard a door close and a car start in the driveway. Vague thoughts sharpened quickly. Paul was leaving for work. Wonderful, forgiving Paul ... who had welcomed her back yesterday as though she hadn't laid waste to almost all their Christmas celebration with her bad judgment and equally bad timing. Well, at least last night's dinner had been bright with family and her new friend at Leslie's Christmas table.

Today was December 26, the day after. Memories of her situation just a day ago—the rescue, the cold, the fear—took shape again, holding her in terror. But then, there was relief in how it had all turned out. *Oh my God, did all of that really happen?* she wondered. Was it possible that so much could happen in one day? When she put a hand up to her forehead to search the source of a dull ache, the bandage she found still in place confirmed the answer. But, if all that misery could happen in one day, then the reverse was possible. The law of opposites—and Ed himself—promised that. This day could be as different from that one as night was from day.

Pamela found it hard to choose what to think about first; all the events tried to crowd into her mind at once. To have had so much happen, to be in as much danger as she was, unnerved her.

Images spun behind her eyes: the dark car on Jetty Beach, waves crashing around it showering the car in heavy, debris laden freezing water; the wind howling, pawing her, enclosing her within the small prison of vision as she walked. Again, she heard the dull click of the key in the ignition, then, the stark silence in that car. Now she was walking, crawling, over the endless space between here and somewhere she could find safety— to get out of the sharp edge of a freezing wind. Down the hill she trudged with her head buried behind her arms; her slight body blowing along the deserted road, trying to block the terrible wind and snow. The smashed glass … the cold kitchen … finding blankets, then sleep, and the dream: the lovely monarchs coming—the saving monarchs of her dream in the kitchen, lifting her up and pushing her out; out into the dark night. She saw the light as Ed passed by.

It all started with the monarchs. They were with her now in memory: symbols, guides, companions … She didn't know what they were. This was what they were known for, wasn't it? Messengers of transformation … emerging from the crucible of the chrysalis as new beings; very different beings. And this is what Pamela had now become: a new being. It began with them, on the beach on that Sunday when they announced their presence. And then just yesterday … on that same beach she had walked within the blizzard.

Feeling safe now, Pamela rolled over in bed. Unobserved, she mourned all she might have done and might have said. Again, she walked the aisles lost in the labyrinth of the Eastside that morning, the morning of her birthday. Again, she came around the corner to find the trembling wings of the monarchs waiting for her: harbingers of this day—this hopeful day. She saw herself there on her knees surrounded by people wanting to understand, wanting to help. She was unable to see the whole story until this minute—*here*—*now*. She had been led all along, following the monarchs into this day of promise.

And now there was Ed: his kind words, his light, his friendship. Her 'today' dawned clear ... this precious day. *Today*. She could—and would—*live* today. Now she understood it; now it was confirmed.

Pamela stretched out in the warm comfort of her discovery. In her dream on the island, the monarchs traveled in the light of Ed's Jeep, igniting the frozen windows of her prison. She might have missed that light—might have slept right through it—and misconstrued it all as a dream or coincidence. It was neither. She had faith that she was worthy of the mystery of these inexplicable moments of grace that had come from some hidden, loving place. In this morning's clarity, she knew Ed was the agent of this joy-filled mercy. She remembered him at the dinner table as he had been last night: warm eyes on her, smiling, tie for the occasion—a new friend—one who saw her for whom she was. It was *her* first gift of Christmas.

Ed had showed no signs of anything but delight. Dinner was sumptuous; Leslie's cooking made "delicious" a common adjective at her table. The whole feast—seafood chowder, roast beef with béarnaise sauce, vegetables, mashed Maine potatoes, pecan pie, and coffee and brandy to toast to the holiday—was a work of art. When they finally pushed back from the table against offers of more, everybody was glowing.

Robbie nodded off to sleep early after the excitement of the day and the relief of having his nana back; mounds of toys received were piled under the tree. But best of all, he had made a new friend too: Ed was a guy who knew a lot about how things went together and loved playing with him. When Robbie began to nod off, eyes closing, his father scooped him up and after another round of thanks, took him up to bed.

Leslie sat beside Ed, sharing the discussion of commonalities of living in Wells. He answered questions about himself humbly, but his many talents and his pleasant nature bought quick respect and the appreciation of those present, especially Pamela. It encouraged her to see he was glad to be there, his interest in all of them genuine. She knew things about his life after being in his home on Christmas Eve. She knew he was alone, much as she was; and she knew he was enjoying having a family to be with tonight.

Still time traveling, Pamela arrived at the most pleasant of all the evening's memories. Ed had finally excused himself, exhausted from the rescue and celebration. She showed him to the door, retrieving his coat from the hall closet. Just as he was ready to leave, he'd held his hat in his hand, shuffled with the door a little, and then asked whether she would spend this New Year's Eve with him. He promised champagne at his cottage, a home-cooked meal in front of the very fire she had revived beside on Christmas Eve, as well as an excursion to find the island's deer and bring them carrots and apples.

Was it possible things could change this fast? Could a person walk out of one life and into another as quickly as she seemed to have done? It all made Pamela's head spin.

As much as she wanted to stay within these pleasant anticipations, in the privacy of her room, she felt the growing need for one more visit; this one would take all of her courage. Many were the times that the doorway between Andy's world and her own had opened without invitation, keeping her running from the tidal wave of sadness it always brought. This morning, Pamela would go bravely to that doorway on her own, would open it from her side. She knew it was within her power.

She prepared herself, sitting up closing her eyes; asking for an audience with her beloved. Then she waited. She was always aware that the option of communing with him in some energetic form was possible, but she hadn't been able to withstand the surge of despair that meeting would cause. Today, she sat still, breathing deeply and asked Andy to approach. And he came. She found herself engulfed by a cloud of tenderness and regard, heard her name being called. Her pulse raced as she felt his presence; it was as if he had never gone.

Speaking soft, "Andy, thank you for everything. Every last thing we ever shared is enshrined in my heart, never to be forgotten. I have needed to say that for so long."

He didn't come closer but stayed somewhere in the perimeter. He spoke no words but nodded an acceptance, offering love to her with the placing of his hands on his heart.

Pamela, knowing this dream or trance—or whatever it was—couldn't last for long, hovered on the edge of joy and sadness so deep, she had finally to turn away. His thoughts, in his own dear voice, sounded in her heart. "Live for yourself ... now, you must live for yourself. We'll all be together again, just not now." With his beautiful smile bridging the distance between them, he faded; turning to her once more to smile into her heart. Then, he was gone.

Pamela let tears fall as the door between them closed gently. When she opened her eyes, it was to the plain room in her daughter's home, here, in the life she had left to live.

Quick on the heels of the tender encounter, the bedroom door burst open, and Robbie swept in. He hopped on Pamela's bed and bounced a few times before settling beside her. He sat looking at his Nana for a minute. When he saw the tears on his Nana's face, he wiped a few away; trusting things could be fixed that easily. Then his face broke into a grin. "Nana," he said in his sweet voice, "I just had to make sure you were here. I was afraid when you got lost yesterday and couldn't find your way home. But you're here! I love you, Nana." With that, the little boy threw himself into her arms.

Her grandson's loving words grounded Pamela, sweeping away the sorrow of the visit. There was so much here for her—beginning right now and here with this grandchild.

"Robbie, how about you and I go downstairs and make blueberry pancakes for Mommy," she offered. Leslie, most likely sick of the kitchen and exhausted from the rescue ordeal, would sleep a while longer. Pamela saw an opportunity to make up some of the unhappiness of the last few days and pamper her daughter.

"Okay, Nana, let's go. I want to make a funny face with the blueberries in mine ... okay?"

"Robbie, we'll make funny faces for Mommy and for Nana and for you too... and we can bring Mommy breakfast in bed. *Shhh!* We have to be very quiet so as not to wake her up if we want to surprise her."

The two crept downstairs, the little boy ecstatic with the secret plan and his grandmother back at home.

CHAPTER 28

9:13 EXACTLY

Maine Diner
December 26, 1999

The diner clock hour hand took a slow march around the digits: December 26, nine o'clock in the morning. The scent of blueberry muffins just pulled from the ovens graced the warm air along with sweet, earthy coffee tones and, as always, rich bacon accents. Just breathing the air was heaven. Darnice had opened this morning and would be here through noon.

The day after Christmas was rarely busy. Although the weather had started out with thick overcast and cold temperatures, it had recovered some, and the sun was out. During most Maine winters, storms lined up like pearls on a string—gray pearls—lining up one after another, leaving little time to get complacent with fair weather. Today was to be savored. On a day like this with no wind and a clear-blue sky overhead, temperatures would crest from the middle to high twenties ... not really cold by Maine standards. The expectant waitress busied herself with taking orders, delivering plates of steaming food, and clearing things away, always with an eye out every time the door with its bell tinkled opened.

The splurge at Varano's had been a sumptuous four-course dinner. It was their custom on Christmas day. It meant more to her each year as Danny and Amy appreciated being together with their mom and grand mom, showing greater tolerance than they had when they were younger.

Darnice was thinking about this as she worked. The dinner had started with minestrone for the table, then salad, scallop lasagna in pesto cream served family style, finished off with cannoli and coffee. Who cared about the tab? Not on this one day anyway.

Darnice felt a little guilty as she realized she was distracted for some of it, looking forward—forward to today. The minutes of yesterday had ticked slowly by as well, toward December 26; she had been anxious to get back to work if you could imagine such a thing. That clock was ticking now. She wanted the number-one Wells police officer, Jimmy Casey, to come through that door and put the Christmas Eve miracle to the test.

Counter talk this morning was all about Pamela Iverson and the now-famous rescue by Ed LaCasse. For all the world, Darnice couldn't reconcile the quiet, solitary guy who often sat in her section—with the hero she had read about in the *County Coast Star*. Darnice knew Jimmy must have had something to do with it. The pulse of what went on in Wells was often taken right in this little establishment, the Maine Diner. And after all, he had announced that they were looking for a missing person right here on Christmas Eve.

"Darnice, dear, could you give me a refill?" The request came from Florence Bath, a unique personality in this town, one of many. Florence ran the Lobster Claw, down the road to Wells Harbor, out behind the PD, just off Route 1. She did a great business in the summer, featuring lobster rolls, steamed lobsters and clams, ice cream desserts—all the tourist fare. She closed up in early fall, right after Labor Day, with a long sigh at the simplification of her life. That was the day Wells, Maine, emptied out of tourists. I-95 heading south on that day was something to behold. Most Mainers were glad to get some space back. One year, Florence had introduced lobster ice cream; it hadn't done too well. Today she was dressed in red-and-green Christmas plaid: wool shirt and a knit beret angled on her pure white curls. Her eyes, the same sharp blue of much of the population around here, were snapping with curiosity this morning. She had been watching Darnice's attention to the door and her frequent glances at the clock. Not much got by Florence. Her request for coffee was an opening to find out what was going on.

"Sure, that's half decaf and half regular, right? Cream on the side, dear?" Darnice knew this order as well as her own name. In a place like this, the regulars' likes and dislikes were soon committed to memory.

"Yep." Florence smiled her appreciation. "Nobody makes coffee like you do, Darnice." She gave the compliment though they both knew the coffee was the same all the time, no matter who made it. Darnice brought the two pots over, mixing the sustaining liquids as she poured.

Florence was knitting as she lingered over the remains of her breakfast. Blueberry pancakes, a house specialty, along with two eggs over medium and bacon had once graced the plate still in front of her.

"So, I hear there were big doings goin' on over Christmas Eve down t' island. Word is, a woman got herself stuck in that storm with a dead battery; no one knew where she was. All happened at Jetty Beach, but she got rescued by Ed LaCasse. I wouldn't a thought he had it in him." Her voice went up an octave, suggesting something. "That's a hard one to figure. How the dickens did he know where she was? Butter usually wouldn't melt in his mouth, and here he is a hero. Humph! They say she broke into one of the beachfront cottages—no light, no heat. Someone's goin' to have to pay for that," she added, the lilt returning, lifting the sentence to a warning. "Summer people don't take with bein' *that* neighborly. Sounds mighty odd to me. You waitin' on Jimmy Casey for the news, Darnice?" Florence asked, an interrogatory light in her eyes.

"What're you knitting, Florence?" Darnice replied, cutting Florence off at the pass with talk about her favorite hobby. "Getting a head start on next year's Christmas gifts?"

"Well, yes, dear, I am. Scarves and socks—those are my specialties—and it takes a whole year to get all the knittin' I need to do done. Everyone loved what I made for them this year, and with the storm, it was just in time too. But Darnice dear, what's the scoop about the woman? I 'spect you know?" Florence said this with a serious air. She wanted to be let in on the gossip.

Florence was still waiting for her answer when the tinkling bell diverted Darnice's attention again. Whatever Florence had asked was forgotten on the spot. Jimmy had arrived! Darnice glanced up at the clock: 9:13 a.m. exactly.

The man in question stopped for a heartbeat while he closed the door behind him. He sent a glance up the aisle to where Darnice stood, removed his gloves and hat to prepare for what he'd been anticipating ever since the last glance between them. The hope that Christmas Eve hadn't been just a passing moment kept his heart fluttering. This was as tough an assignment as facing any criminal. No—it was tougher … there was no rule book for the encounter just ahead of Jimmy. He was on his own here.

When he looked at Darnice, Jimmy had a sudden fear that he hadn't prepared himself well enough, though he had taken more time with his ablutions this morning than usual. His hair, crew cut as always, was brushed today, with a clean shave that wasn't always the case. He had pressed his uniform before dressing and added a few of his many medals to the ensemble. He had hoped to be acceptable in this new world in which nothing was the same. Still standing by Florence, Darnice smiled at him holding two coffeepots. In the light of that smile, Jimmy forgot about everything else. In quick response, his face broke into an unguarded grin that showed his feelings exactly. All the complicity and intimacy of the gifts of illicit plowing and doughnuts—as well as the previous evening's hand-holding—took on new life and bloomed between them.

Jimmy walked straight to Darnice as if a string stretched from one heart to the other. He tried to not allow any hesitancy or confusion to show. Strong energy between them kept him moving true.

Florence, seeing Darnice's face break into a broad smile, stopped talking and turned to see what had taken Darnice's interest so completely. When she saw Jimmy coming toward them, she guessed what was happening and softly suggested to Darnice that she put the coffeepots down before she dropped them. Without taking her eyes off Jimmy, Darnice did so.

She, too, had taken care of her appearance. Although she wore the mandatory uniform of the diner—a T-shirt—this one was in a shade of blue that complemented her eyes and dark hair. It bore one of the logos of the Maine Diner: the image of a lobster flipping pancakes. In her hope to be ready for this encounter, she had braided her hair, wrapping the braids with sprigs of holly. The style was a little juvenile, but it grew up on her mature good looks. It allowed her, though, to look more confident than she felt.

Jimmy sat down at the counter beside Florence without a word of greeting for her. His eyes were on Darnice. He was taking great pleasure in finally being able to look into the face that had been floating before him in his mind for two days. No one spoke for a long while; a noticeable quiet filled the space between the two smiling people.

In the extended pause, Florence got flustered, this state of affairs not being usual. She looked from one to the other, waiting for someone to speak to her. She wasn't happy about being so thoroughly ignored.

Jimmy, heart pounding, skipped any small talk and took the direct route Ed had suggested. "Darnice, what've you got planned for New Year's Eve? I'd like to take you out," he said, swallowing hard after the words were said.

The question landed with a smack on the counter between the three, taking Darnice by surprise and annoying Florence. Darnice had been ready for small talk, maybe about Taddy's favor to her, the doughnuts, or the weather, but she wasn't ready for this. Bowled over by Jimmy's forthright question, it took a few seconds for it to register that she had just been asked out on a date. The world she lived in wasn't the world she was in this morning. While she let the pleasure of his request settle, she reached for a cup, leaned toward him, and poured black coffee into his cup making the act seem intimate.

Florence finally broke into the silence, inserting herself. "Well, what's your answer, girl? I haven't got all day, and I want to talk to Jimmy about what happened out on the island. Come on, tell us."

Darnice laughed at the unlikely collusion of these two, which allowed Jimmy and Florence to relax. "I sure hope you're not laughin' at *me*, Darnice," Jimmy said, midway through the cascade of chuckles.

"No, no, Jimmy. I'd be happy to spend New Year's Eve with you, though it will be the first date for the big night in many years. You have anything special in mind?"

"I heard somewhere you like Varano's down at Mile Road. I'll make reservations for seven; we can go over to Ogunquit after if you want. Lot's goin' on there. I can't say I know what specifically, other than the trouble that gets stirred up for police to have to deal with, but we can risk it for one night."

"Or maybe just go back up to Stephen Eaton and watch for the big moment at my place." Darnice voiced the idea to see Jimmy's reaction.

He replied quickly, "That'd be fine, Darnice. I should be on your family's good side after my Christmas gifts." With that cloaked reference, Darnice grinned, and then began to laugh aloud.

Florence was *tsk-tsking* loudly now. "My God, how old are you both? It's dangerous bein' out on New Year's Eve … people drinkin' and drivin' reckless. And you, Jimmy—who's going to be on duty if you're not?"

"Florence," Jimmy responded, finally looking fully at her, "every dog has his day. We are going to celebrate this New Year's to make up for all the ones we haven't, the ones we have been serving the public. You'll just have to excuse us this year."

"So, what time you want me ready?" Darnice said, as much to countermand Florence's disapproval as anything.

"Let's say six-thirty?" Jimmy's eyebrows went up with her quick acceptance. Still unsure that this was really happening, he ventured, "I'll get reservations and call you." Here he paused, and making it a ceremonious request, said, "Would you give me your phone number, Darnice?" There was no fear she would refuse, but the words still came hard.

Darnice wrote her number on a check and handed it to him. Florence sat shocked at the exchange. When Jimmy stowed the number in his shirt pocket, Darnice asked, "So, Officer Casey, what's for breakfast today? Specials are on the board." She broke her attention from him long enough to glance at the list above the kitchen window. When she looked back to him, he hadn't taken his eyes off her. Darnice warmed visibly under the intensity of his stare. She pointed to the specials, insisting he pay attention, but Jimmy held her off with his gaze for a moment more before obeying her unspoken command.

Still part of the threesome at the counter, Florence finally got uncomfortable enough to pack up and leave, sputtering about displays in public and people who ought to act their age.

"See you, Florence. Happy New Year!" Jimmy called loudly after her retreating figure. Then to Darnice, he said, "I'm celebrating today. How about the lobster benedict, home fries, a corn muffin, and more coffee? By the way ... now that Florence is out of here ... did you enjoy the doughnuts?"

"That was one of the best Christmas presents ever," Darnice returned. "Doughnuts warm from Congdon's. I'll never forget it. Thanks!" Her obvious pleasure got to him.

"We'll make a tradition of it; it was only the first annual doughnut drop," Jimmy said, feeling the promise of the words. "Same place, same time next year? Course, we'll have to have a blizzard for them to open," he said as he laughed at his own joke.

The intimacy of this banter pushed them both into a comfortable silence. Once she served his breakfast and moved back to her other duties, they kept finding each other. Jimmy ate a breakfast fit for a king. Darnice stopped for a word or two with the town cop when she could, with Ed as the main topic.

Out on the island, Ed's coffeemaker had snapped into action at seven o'clock, the burbling sound making a comfortable alarm clock. Ed rose, stretched, and had his first cup, letting his mind replay the past and looking forward to this day—December 26. How different it felt from recent mornings on Blueberry Lane.

As he dressed, he looked out at the trees on the edge of the marsh, but it was the wonderful evening with Pamela and her family he was seeing. The teddy bear he'd brought to Robbie had done the trick of transforming a stranger into a friend. He was comfortable with Leslie and Paul—comfortable in their interest in him—and loved it that they thought him a hero. In his own mind, he knew it was probably Pamela who had rescued *him*, but that would be his secret.

Suddenly hungry, Ed decided to go to the diner for breakfast. The idea of the place was inviting in a very new way after the events of Christmas Eve. Actually, the whole world was a little bigger than it had been yesterday. He wished Pamela could be beside him with her trust and interest. She had changed the luck of his life already. But there were chores to do because of yesterday's storm, and preparations for the next one, which was undoubtedly forming up somewhere south of here now as he sat in memories and dreams.

After the short drive up the road, he swung into the diner, the Christmas bells announcing him. Just as he sat, Darnice emerged from the kitchen with three plates of eggs of one sort or another balanced on her arms. Seeing Ed, she smiled and promised with a wink that she would be right back to take his order.

While he waited, he looked around the plain room, wondering just what had been going on Christmas Eve. The transformations of that night with its butterflies and romance were real; he knew that because he was part of it, but that didn't make it any less mystical.

True to her word, a few minutes later, Darnice landed a coffee in front of Ed and looked him over carefully. "I haven't ever seen a hero this close up," she teased while telling herself quietly that he did, indeed, look different. Ed's whole face was lighter.

He broke into a laugh at her kindly observation, shook his head against the honor, and answered, "Darnice, you wouldn't believe what Santa had in store for me when I left here the other night! Order me up some blueberry pancakes, fill my coffee up again, and I'll tell you all about it."

There was nothing Darnice liked better than a story. She filled a cup for herself, folded her elbows on the counter, and prepared to listen while Ed told his tale. *All this and Jimmy too? Life is just too good right now, she thought.* When he got to the part about the monarchs guiding him, she straightened up and crowed in surprise. Her experience of the monarchs' appearance was only part of the story. When she told him about her sighting, the two sat looking at each other in wonder. What could they say in the face of such potent magic that had touched so many lives?

CHAPTER 29

NEW YEAR'S MOON

Blueberry Lane
New Year's Eve 1999

Ed knelt by the hearth, gently blowing on responding small spurts of flame and igniting the kindling. The spreading glow gave Ed ... encouragement. The small, bright tongues of fire climbed into the air until the blaze was ready for a small log or two on top. He was daydreaming, looking ahead to the evening. In his thoughts, the word *encourage* repeated. At its root was the word, *Coeur: coeur*—meaning "heart." His native language, French, made much of this word: '*coeur*: heart; to have heart; to have hope; to give hope; *to hearten.*' He was heartened. Thanks to the *York County Coast's* newspaper story, the rescue of Pamela Iverson was now historic, and their budding friendship was an "item." In a small town, small news was big news. It *heartened* him.

Ed saw now that he was—had been—held down in his holding to the worn paths of a previous life. Even though the life was one he'd loved, it wasn't possible to go on in that way anymore. His current reality had been knit from the whole cloth of loneliness, sewn together with memories. Tonight would mark a change, a new pattern; one that could free him from a past that was over and open him up to the possibility of the present. His enthusiasm for this new life frightened him with its optimism; frightened him and called him out at the same time.

As he fussed over the fire, a certain quiet entered the room and settled. Sensing it, Ed stood and turned slowly. He looked deep into the dimly lit corners of the room. He had felt a sense of Sarah's presence before, had come to believe she could be—*was*—here in some subtle but real way. He felt her breath on his skin, the pressure of her touch, the sense of *her*, known so intimately after their years together. This presence surrounded him now, making itself known.

"Sarah." As he spoke her name, it fell softly in firelight; this had been her favorite place on earth. She loved living close to the sea. Years ago, on an idle summer ride, they had taken the fateful right turn off Route 1 to Drakes Island Road, and Sarah had never looked anywhere else for home. The first time they drove these streets and saw the blue ocean rise to meet them, so close and innocent; they knew they were home for good.

Ed's memories returned from the past and into the present. "Sarah," he spoke, again scanning the room to prove her presence. All looked the usual, but he trusted she heard. He needed to say this.

"Sarah, you are here," he asserted. The snapping of wood from the fire answered him. "My life with you was heaven, always. I feel your absence every day and remember every precious thing we shared. Tonight, I must take one step away and invite someone to share my life. What I know about where you are tells me you are all right, are good … and you want me to go on until I have lived this life out fully. Forgive me. I will love you forever. You are the best part of me. I only hope to find some of what we had in this new friendship. Happy New Year, darling. Happy New Year to us both."

He stopped speaking, waiting for something, though he didn't know what; something to anchor this feeling of her presence. Her Christmas tree was still in the front window, her plate collection mounted above the hearth. But this was a room she no longer needed. His need for change was so palpable on this night, it overwhelmed him. When he turned back to the hearth, the fire was crackling nicely, the clock read 4:30; and dusk had fallen. New Year's Eve was coming in and the day had disappeared. Pamela was due soon.

Feeling Sarah still, Ed crossed the room to the little tree in the bay window, snapped the lights on, and watched the lively color reaching into the corners. For just a second, he could see her smile at him within the tree's soft lights. This cheered him, encouraged him as well, and he smiled back as the chimera of her face dissolved. He turned his thoughts and intentions back to this night, although not without a hesitation; a sadness.

Ed had spent the morning cleaning. At last, there was a reason to prepare the house for guests. He had shopped down at Hannaford's for ingredients to make the seafood chowder, and then made a special trip up Rt 1 to Herb's Seafood in Kennebunk for the scallops and haddock. Herb had sold seafood for twenty years or more and recognized Ed when he walked in, even though he hadn't been up here for a while. Sarah was the one who had shopped here. As Herb wrapped the seafood, he chatted with Ed in the lingo of a Maine fisherman, recounting local gossip and reviewing the storm of a week ago now. When Ed left, he felt he had a friend. Maybe he would drive up to shop here more often. He was smiling while going south on the way home.

The stew simmered on the stove all afternoon: potatoes, onions, fish stock infused with spices. When it was ready, Ed added the seafood, letting it cook just barely through before pouring in cream and sherry, a sprinkle of coarse pepper and sea salt. Stirring once, twice, three times, he turned the heat off to let it rest and develop 'character.' That's what the recipe said anyway... you had to believe that food held onto the feelings added by the cook and not *just* the ingredients. Ed had filled this stew up to the top with hope ... and ... well ... the word still embarrassed him: love. He came from a generation of men who had rarely spoken of love; he guessed he had better learn how.

The flame was licking through the wood now; he could trust it to burn for a while. The stack of apple logs waiting by the side of the hearth was from Laudholm Farm up the road; trees that had fallen years ago were ripe picking for those with the time. Now bone dry, they were ready to give up their heat. No one else cared about the fallen trees strewn in the old orchard, but Ed did. It had taken him a few mornings last fall to gather and stack the old apple boughs in his garage, where they had been waiting for tonight. He liked thinking he had been preparing for Pamela, even though he hadn't known it. Flame burst from the heart of the wood, releasing a smoky perfume, a scent like cider or clove, something deep and sweet.

He had shared this precious wood with Pamela on Christmas Eve, though the tension of events had overshadowed the enjoyment. Tonight she was coming here again, coming for a walk on the island, coming to feed the deer and savor the beginning of a new year. Ed knew Pamela had some idea that her being with him tonight meant the world to him, and he hoped, to her as well.

He had wanted to drive up to Chick's Crossing to get Pamela, but she was adamant that she would drive herself; said she needed to prove she could go it alone after that night. The roads were clear with no storms forecast, moonrise would be early, so there was no need to worry about her, he guessed. Somehow, after the rescue and what he had learned about this woman, she still appeared vulnerable to him. He kept telling himself that he had to relax about her independence, an odd mix of capability and need; he needed to support her, but mainly he knew he had to help her regain courage. There was that word again: *courage* … full of heart; that was its real meaning. She was that, no doubt about it.

As he stood by the fire, musing, the Subaru turned into his driveway, headlights signaling her arrival in the deepening dark. Her car had been cleaned up and pounded out, with a brand-new battery installed. There was still bodywork to do, but that could wait.

CHAPTER 30

ON THE BEACH

Drakes Island Beach
New Year's Eve, 1999

The Christmas tree in the window offered Pamela the marker she needed as she searched Blueberry Lane for Ed's house. She hadn't been back since the night of the storm, and Ed knew she might have a little trouble finding the cottage. Driving past the cottage, he had left the garage door open, an obvious welcome.

Her approach caused him gentle panic. A sense that things were getting out of control flooded him and he began to pace in front of the fireplace. What was he doing? A man of his age beginning a relationship now, after so many years of this predictable life he'd made for himself? And he had to admit now that he was beginning something. His racing pulse told him that.

Her knock at the kitchen door put an end to his angst. He put away his doubts and went to open it. "Pamela, I was worried about the roads, but I guess they are all right. Drive okay?"

She entered the kitchen, smiling warmly, but not responding to his questions. She unbuttoned her coat, put it on a kitchen chair and walked into the living room, the same room that had been so welcoming on the night of the storm. She finally turned to Ed and spoke. "The roads were fine, Ed. A little slippery here and there, but I know how to drive Maine

roads." Then she approached him, took his hands, and looked steadily into
his eyes, saying, "Oh, Ed! Coming through this door brings it all back …
what you offered me that night—my life back really. Thank you. Thank
you again and again and again." And she embraced him, holding him
tight, close, and long, scaring him almost to death.

Taken off guard Ed backed away when he was released, but smiling,
keeping his hands in hers. "Okay now Pamela, your part in this is just as
important as mine. I haven't had anyone to celebrate this night with for
many years. I guess I could be as grateful to you. Matter of fact—I am.
Thank you too." And they stood, the pas de deux of gratitude gathering
depth until it got uncomfortable.

Her careful preparations for their evening hadn't gone unnoticed. She
had a wonderfully blue sweater on with earrings of the same color. Instead
of the white, distraught face of a few nights ago, her cheeks were pink, and
her eyes glowed in the firelight. He was a little dazzled by how lovely she
looked and wanted to tell her so but didn't quite know how. He decided
to try anyway.

"You sure do clean up well," he stuttered. When she broke into a
soft laugh, he was embarrassed, but he trusted her laughter to be kind.
Ed led her toward the now-robust fire, offering her a seat on the sofa she
remembered well from her ordeal. When she was comfortably seated, he
announced, "I have champagne on ice. How about a glass to start us on our
adventure?" His eyes were sparkling in response to hers in the soft light.

Pamela nodded enthusiastically, which sent Ed on a mission to the
kitchen for the champagne waiting in the refrigerator. She rose from
the sofa and went to the little Christmas tree. Spending this night with
someone so delightful close at hand had such a wonderful feel to it; she
felt it encompassed her. It was almost overwhelming to be so—dare she
say it?—happy. Turning, she looked into the blaze on the hearth. "Ed," she
called, "what is the wonderful smell in here? It's so sweet!"

Her host appeared in the kitchen doorway, towel wrapped around the
neck of a bottle, prying gently at the cork to avoid the inevitable plume.
"That's apple wood … I picked it off Laudholm Farm's fields. Better to
use it like this than to let it rot with no one to warm by it. Lovely, huh?"

"It's indescribable. It makes me think of perfume. All this and champagne too!" Her obvious pleasure connected.

He was back with two flutes and the bottle of ice-cold bubbly wine. "I didn't think to ask if you liked champagne. Do you?"

"I love it! Though I haven't been doing much celebrating in the last years, this is absolutely a moment to savor ... I am grateful again. Cheers!"

Ed offered the glass and sat beside her, holding his up for the sound of good luck as their flutes clinked, then the first sip. They relaxed into small talk about events since they had last seen each other. Pamela made sure Ed knew how much her family liked him, especially Robbie who wanted a return visit as soon as Ed could make it. He had plans for the man who knew how to play.

Ed took great pleasure in describing what was for dinner in great detail, outlining the process of putting together a real Maine seafood chowder, as if Pamela didn't know how to do it. She, as guest, stayed quiet about all the chowders she had made in her lifetime, letting Ed take the glory for this evening's supper. He deserved it for this and for much more. As she sat listening to his earnest chatter, she realized that the happiness of the moment wouldn't have been possible without the integrity and unselfishness that powered the heart of this remarkable man. Her smiling attention to what he was saying hid the thoughts of how fortunate she was to just be in this room with him.

After a glass for Pamela and two for Ed, they shrugged into winter coats and hats for their journey out to the deer. Because of familiarity with the island, Ed drove. His Jeep brought the scene of Pamela's rescue into sharp focus. As she sat beside him, anxiety began to rise in the pit of her stomach, spiraling up until her breath was affected, coming in short bursts against the ingrained synapse of fear that had lodged so deeply, she wasn't aware of its existence. Jetty Beach had just appeared in the windshield when she reached out and put her hand on his arm, asking him to stop. Her voice, tight in her throat, told him the tension in her grasp was for real.

"Ed, I don't know if I can do this. Even driving in this direction, even with you here, just seeing the place where I left the car. I see only the blinding snow, hear only screaming winds. It's bringing it all back, the feeling of utter abandonment, of being alone in the dark is taking over."

Ed eased the car off the road, thrust the gear into park, and turned to Pamela; there was no one here to push them on, no traffic, nobody who would be inconvenienced by their stop. He took her hands, which were visibly shaking, and lifted her head which was down in the beginning of tears. He spoke in a clear, strong, soft voice. "You're with me, Pamela. It's New Year's Eve, 1999. We have a job to do together. We must feed the deer."

When she lifted her head, he was looking directly into her eyes. "I have a lantern to light our way and a feast for the deer stowed in the back. It's a different day, Pamela, a different time, a different world, my friend. I know you have been disappointed in your life before. Have faith in me, faith that we will get there safely, as we planned, meet our friends the deer, and get home just fine for a *wicked good* dinner. The first of many, many I hope." His Maine phraseology lightened the moment and made her smile. His gaze was gentleness itself. He had her hand, gloved though it was, in his. He smiled the question. "Permission granted to move ahead, Ms. Iverson?"

Pamela wiped away a tear and nodded. Looking into Ed's eyes had done the trick. She turned in her seat to allow the drive to the end of the road; the road that passed by the cottage she had broken into on that terrible night. As they drove up the small rise into the parking lot of Jetty Beach, the trauma that had etched every detail of this landscape deep within her sounded again. She had to use every inch of her courage to face them down. With Ed, she knew she could.

When they had parked the Jeep, Ed reached into the back for the basket of apples and carrots collected at the house and the lantern. He looked over at Pamela, waiting for her to signal she was ready. In front of them, the shallow waves of a peaceful ocean surged comfortably at low tide, like blue silk rustling, they rolled in under the rising moon.

Ed could see his companion had tears in her eyes, tears that meant something sweet and deep to him. Going around to her door, he offered his hand, and she took it, stepping down onto the still-slick surface of the lot. She and Ed held onto the car as they walked around it. He lit the wick of the lantern, the light of the flame seeping into the now-deep dusk. The two walked the wooden ramp to the beach in the soft light, each step mixing the past with the future.

The moon was a ladle of silver with Jupiter and Venus just below, a straight arrow up to the North Star. Since the night wasn't really cold, a mist was rising from the snow-covered dunes, hovering in small clouds here and there.

Stepping off the wooden ramp, they let hands fall in the balancing act of walking on shifting sand. The ocean repeated on the shore in quiet ruffles of white. Off to the side, away from the jetty, six or seven deer were to be seen, heads down, eating dune grass. Ed and Pamela stood still on the long, empty beach, watching, waiting. The deer soon discovered them, lifting their noses to the wind, gathering the scent of house and fire from their clothes. They sensed safety as well and then moved cautiously in the direction of the two who were waiting.

Pamela, enchanted by the silvery beach washed in celestial light, couldn't take in enough of this beauty. The deer moved ever so quietly toward them; toward the man with his basket of apples, his lantern, and his smile. There was no wind, no snow, and nothing to fear. Before long, the two were talking softly to the gentle guests, offering them the sweetness of food in deep communion with their wide-eyed innocence.

Pamela straightened to survey the charmed world she was standing in. The landscape of the past just dissolved in this light. And she was here, now, in this perfect place. She sensed there would be other days like this … days in all seasons. The New Year was about to begin, and it had come just in time.

EPILOGUE

Wells, Maine
April, 2000

Pamela pulled out of the parking lot of the Maine Diner. The first blush of spring was just rising in the trees lining Route 1, a blushing tide seeping up gray trunks and out onto branches that had withstood the cold, snowy winter just past. Now, in early April, her Subaru hummed along, heater overtaking the chill of the car; the same car she had almost lost during the great blizzard of '99.

As she thought back on the conversation shared with Ed and Darnice this morning over breakfast (as had become their habit), a sense of contentment filled her. Who would believe she could feel so comfortable in the common course of days after the years of isolation and confusion she had lived?

Darnice had been entertaining them with a story about Jimmy Casey, someone Pamela now held as a friend. The story was, he had been sent out to an address to find the chief and give him some information requested. Not realizing the chief was deep in a stakeout, Jimmy had driven straight into the police area, gotten out of the police cruiser, called the chief's name aloud, and thus blown his cover and ended the stakeout.

The chief, out of sight behind a mound of discarded cars on the property in question, tried to hustle Jimmy out of sight, cursing as he went, but the jig was up. The police cruiser in the yard alerted the subjects to the surveillance, and that was that. Pamela would like to have seen that. She knew Jimmy was a champion curser … but was the chief?

Traffic had picked up on Route 1. Folks were coming back for weekends now to open summer property; restaurants and shops were under way with the yearly painting and planting for the waves of warm weather ahead. The sun had made an appearance today, but the deck of clouds was thickening. It would probably rain by afternoon. Had to expect that in Maine; rain was the price for the gorgeous canopy of green overhead and carpet underfoot all summer. By July 1st most years, the sun broke through for good and rewarded everyone with the ultimate in summer weather: blue skies, warm days, cool nights, and dry, clean air. Perfection.

This was Pamela's last day of freedom. Funny word for it: *freedom*. She was glad to give it up. She would be going to work, beginning a job tomorrow at Hannaford's Supermarket down the way on Route 1 by a few miles. Taking the job had been Ed's idea. As she had shared more of her story with him, he had suggested she might be happy working in that kind of environment. She liked the idea immediately. Why it had never occurred to her to try it before was a mystery.

On automatic pilot, Pamela was thinking about her orientation yesterday and the jitters she felt when confronted with lots of things she didn't know and would have to speed up to learn. Being out of the work force for as long as she had, she felt a little vulnerable about her skills. But she knew how to fake it. What was that saying? "Fake it until you make it." She could do that blindfolded, had just come out of a life devoted to it. She knew she would be all right. She trusted the little glow of interest she felt when she pictured herself in the market. Ed had been right; it was the perfect place for her.

Up ahead, the Drakes Island light blinked in the middle of the road. Seeing it now sparked dark memories of December 24 and the rescue. She felt herself slow down automatically. Suddenly, the sound of a siren shocked Pamela out of her comfortable drive. Looking in the rearview mirror, she saw the flashing blue lights of a police car urge her off the road. Anxiety sparked quickly as she eased the Subaru off to the roadside. When she saw Jimmy Casey get out of the cruiser, however, her fear faded. He walked toward her, a big smile on his face. Pamela would never get over how the Wells town crew could be so casual in their duties. She knew the whole story about the doughnuts and the plowing for Darnice. Jimmy probably just wanted to say hello. She rolled down her window and prepared a response to the official manner he would undoubtedly adopt.

"Excuse me, lady, but did you know you were going ninety when you passed me down the road?" His words were tough, but his eyes softened the effect considerably.

"Officer, I was distracted. I was thinking about this cop who ruined a stakeout and blew Chief Littlefield's cover a few days ago. It's a funny story. Want to hear it?"

Jimmy threw his head back and laughed along with Pamela. When he came back to himself, he said, "I don't have to ask where you heard that; must've been up to the diner. Is Darnice responsible for spreading this one? Don't answer … I know she is. Can't tell that woman anything you don't want in the news."

"Don't worry, Jimmy. She makes you look good. I think the girl likes you," Pamela said, a flip in her voice.

Jimmy flushed a little at this, his smile widening. "I'm glad to see you out and about. I hear you're going to work down at Hannaford's. You'll be one of the regulars then, no more bein' from away."

"Jimmy Casey, I was born in Maine. I can't be from away. Wish me luck in my new job?"

"I do … all the luck possible. Ed still up to the diner?"

Pamela nodded. "He'd like seeing you." She put her hand on Jimmy's and smiled. "Okay, officer, I have to get along."

"Thanks for the warning." Jimmy waved and turned to walk back to his cruiser. Pamela rolled up the window, grateful for friends.

Back on the road, as she passed the turn off for the beach, she decided on impulse to take it. Snapping on her blinker, she turned and headed toward Jetty Beach. Though goose bumps rose on her forearms, she just kept driving. It wasn't that she hadn't been back here. She had been here with Ed on New Year's Eve, on the beach under the moon. It was that she hadn't been here *alone*.

The sea came into view as she drove up and into the parking lot. Today the Atlantic was slate blue, high on winds, waves crashing over the seaward end of the jetty, shattering to white foam on the rocks.

Pamela pulled her spring jacket closer, put gloves on, and then stepped out of the car. She walked against the strong gusts down the boardwalk to the beach. There she stopped, looking up and down the familiar expanse. A few walkers, far down the beach, were pushing energetically against the gale.

Pamela turned slowly, looking full circle around her. Dune grasses, bleached by winter, were giving up to green shoots rising from roots sewn deep. Birds, rolling and darting overhead, were kites of color, connected to strings no one could see. Her heart and mind supplied the monarchs, their satin wings fluttering in her memory, rising in this wind was spring and change, beauty and mystery.

Pamela lived here now. She had come home.

AFTERWORD

This edition of *Dusk on Route 1* is the culmination of over twelve years of dedicated writing and revision. The original idea for the book first came to me in 2007 over a cup of coffee at the Maine Diner in Wells. I recall looking at the brightly lit florescent tubes of the wall clock and hearing, "The neon rim of the diner clock spun color into the dim, warm dining room; tints of red, blue and green pooled on plates like gravy." From that moment, my writing life was consumed by plot and character development for what would become this book. The character of Pamela Iverson came to me first, followed by Ed LaCasse. Both lived within an already existing story arc; I was their scribe. It was the most exciting and enjoyable part of my life for all those years. I miss the process immensely.

Why a new edition? The opportunity to publish a revision of the book with Androscoggin Press was too much to resist. Taking up the delightful task of going through the whole story again with an eye to tighter and more compelling writing and improvements to cover design, I rewrote *Dusk on Route 1* over a year's time; missing pages from the first draft even mysteriously appeared from some hiding place and were included.

With this new revised edition, I have done my very best for my characters, my readers and myself. I hope you've enjoyed sharing Pamela's journey as much as I've enjoyed telling her story.

—Cynthia Fraser Graves
West Kennebunk, Maine, 2019

Made in the USA
Lexington, KY
04 November 2019

56527445R00136